T0385202

ONE CAME BACK

Also by Rose McDonagh

The Dog Husband

ONE CAME BACK

Rose McDonagh

To my husband, Ross Galloway,
with love always

First published in Great Britain in 2025 by Trapeze,
an imprint of The Orion Publishing Group Ltd
Carmelite House, 50 Victoria Embankment,
London EC4Y 0DZ

An Hachette UK company

The authorised representative in the EEA is Hachette Ireland,
8 Castlecourt Centre, Dublin 15, D15 XTP3, Ireland (email: info@hbgi.ie)

1 3 5 7 9 10 8 6 4 2

A CIP catalogue record for this book is
available from the British Library.

ISBN (Hardback) 9 781 3987 1767 1
ISBN (Export Trade Paperback) 9 781 3987 1768 8
ISBN (eBook) 9 781 3987 1770 1
ISBN (Audio) 9 781 3987 1771 8

Typeset by Input Data Services Ltd, Bridgwater, Somerset

Printed in Great Britain by Clays Ltd, Elcograf, S.p.A.

MIX
Paper | Supporting
responsible forestry
FSC® C104740

www.orionbooks.co.uk

'The undiscover'd country; from whose bourn
No traveler returns . . .'

William Shakespeare, *Hamlet*

'He heard the creaking of the bolt as it came slowly back, and at the same moment he found the monkey's paw, and frantically breathed his third and last wish.

The knocking ceased suddenly, although the echoes of it were still in the house.'

W.W. Jacobs, *The Monkey's Paw*

Two boys set out from the village and one came back. They left in the evening so that they could camp in the foothills and begin their climb early the next morning. The boys were not supposed to go rock climbing without an adult, especially at this time of year when the remains of winter were still clinging to the mountain, and so they lied about where they were going. The younger boy told his parents he was staying at the older boy's house. The older boy said he was heading to his friend's farm for the night. They expected to get caught, but only after the plan was completed.

The older boy packed the climbing gear: the coiled ropes, the harnesses, the nut tools and the belay devices. The younger boy took the camping equipment from under his bed and divided it into two rucksacks. A family-sized tent, winter-thickness sleeping bags, roll mats and cooking supplies. When they met at the wooden cattle bridge, the older boy took up one of the rucksacks and shook it and said, 'Hope you didn't bring any teddies,' and the younger boy pretended to punch him.

The boys were thirteen and sixteen. The older was tall and dark-haired, the younger had the red hair that ran on his father's side, the pale skin which caused him to flush easily. They walked along the coffin route instead of the road on the way out so that no one from the village would see them and stop to offer them a lift. Late winter blurred with early spring; the sun shone though there was still snow lying in thick strips on the peaks. It would nestle there for some weeks yet.

The two reached the low ground where they intended to camp, a wide grassy flat near a copse of Scots pines. The space was not visible from any road or house, and this hiddenness was what they wanted. They pitched the tent first, a small battle to see who could bang the pegs in fastest – not a real contest, the younger boy was always going to be slowest – then they set about cooking, really only heating a can of mini sausages and beans over a struggling fire.

The light eased out of the sky. After they had eaten they sat around the flames and talked about the route for tomorrow and then about girls, about sex. The older boy had a girlfriend, she was seventeen, and he was the only one in their group of friends who was no longer a virgin. 'She'll move on once she meets a real man,' the younger boy said.

'Fuck you,' the older boy said, grinning, knowing he didn't need to assert himself more than that. Soon enough he switched the talk to something else, going on about shinty, about the team's chances in the autumn. Then about a planned trip to Glasgow in the Easter break, would they still go? They would, and they'd drink vodka on the train from a plastic water bottle.

Soon the sky was dark and the stars were hard and they were too cold to pretend they were not cold so they got into their winter sleeping bags inside the large tent, wearing all of their clothes. Strange to fall asleep in an outdoor coat, so that you felt like you were both drifting in bed and still out walking through the heather somehow.

They each woke at separate moments in the night. Different things stirred them; the sound of the wind against the canvas, a line of roe deer passing through the ferns. Maybe they were also wakened by some instinct in the body to check on unfamiliar surroundings, like animals in a new den. They rose with the sunrise, they didn't need to get dressed, they just shook stiff limbs, rubbed their faces with dew. It was odd not to put on fresh clothes in the morning, as if the night had never been.

For breakfast they ate cornflakes from small plastic boxes with packets of UHT milk. They'd learned about climbing from the PE teacher at their school who gave lessons and ran trips in his spare time on Saturday mornings. Other kids had come to the lessons but it was the two of them who'd stuck with it and become good at it. They expected him to be both annoyed and secretly pleased that they had taken the initiative to go out alone. They tidied everything away before moving on, as he had taught them.

The hike up the east side of the mountain was rapid, following the winding path through the bracken. Their rucksacks seemed heavy but they were experienced enough to know that the sensation of weight would eventually fade.

When they met with the face of rock they planned to climb, it was the younger boy who took the lead, the oldest boy who stayed back to belay, acting as a balance in case the first boy fell. It had been like that each time they set out with their teacher so they didn't pause to discuss the order.

They moved slowly putting the gear on, following and double checking each step as they'd been taught. Once the younger boy was off and climbing, both boys had a separate cluster of seconds where they considered that maybe they shouldn't be doing this, maybe they shouldn't have set out on their own. The thoughts passed like clouds and then they were back to focusing on each careful movement.

The younger boy paused halfway up and looked round. The oldest boy was grinning, thumbs up, then two fingers. 'Fuck you,' he shouted cheerfully. The younger boy carried on, seeking out the best handholds. There was always a point where he became dizzy when he climbed but he could push it away by focusing. Hands then feet, hands then feet.

He was about four metres from the lip of the cliff when a piece of rock crumbled away from the ball of his foot. His leg dropped, his hands lost their grip, and his body swung away from the rock. There was the jolt of falling, his heart cinching.

The oldest boy took a solid leap from his position on the ground almost without thinking. The rope attached to him snapped taut and the younger boy jerked to a halt and thumped into the cliff face. White flash, bone into rock. He cried out. He would have hit the rock harder if the other hadn't taken his balancing jump, as they'd been taught to do. The oldest boy planted his feet firmly and shouted encouragement until the younger boy had gripped the rock surface again, found places for his fingers and the toes of his old boots.

When he was steady, when the shaking had slowed, the younger boy resumed his climb. There was a buzzing in his head, a rushing in his ears, but he didn't allow in any thoughts other than where to place his hands and feet next. The oldest boy kept speaking to him as he made the rest of the distance. Short statements; *You're doing it. Come on. Nearly there.* When he finally reached the overhang of the cliff and climbed onto flat ground, the older boy was laughing, clapping, stamping his feet.

With his hands trembling uncontrollably, the younger boy began to change the equipment so that he could belay from the top. 'Take your time, don't get me killed,' the older boy yelled from the ground. When everything was in place and checked and rechecked, the younger boy gave him the thumbs up. He did not say anything; he did not trust his voice. The ground at the top was flat and a gentle slope led away on up from the cliff edge. They had planned to walk back the long way, no more climbing. The dangerous part was over for the younger boy; knowing that was like gulping cool water on a hot afternoon.

The older boy began to climb. Feet then hands, feet then hands. Soon he was halfway there. The younger boy leant back and gazed at the sky. The thought of looking right down over the cliff edge made him feel slightly sick now. He began watching a buzzard circling above them so that he was surprised when he heard the older boy's voice just below. 'Make way you little shite, I'm coming up.' Within minutes, his hands appeared and he was hauling himself over the top.

The older boy scrambled clear of the edge. The younger boy found his eyes were burning with tears and he willed his eyelids to suck them back in but they wouldn't go. His face flamed. He waited for the older boy to say something damning but he said nothing; maybe he hadn't seen. They both walked a distance from the cliff edge and flopped onto the spring mountain grass and rolled onto their backs. The younger boy slapped out an arm, patted the older boy on the chest. Just for a split second his hand was over his heart, it seemed he could feel his heartbeat.

Once they were divested of their harnesses they began walking again. The younger boy found that the pain in his knee started up properly as he stepped out, a hot needle of sensation. The leg worked fine, though. He'd only have a bruise like a badge of honour. They had done it. The view now like a reward stretched on down into the valley, over the white speckles of the village houses and across the sea loch and out to the open water that reached to the islands. The sight of it came with a floating sensation. Both in their own way, they felt like demigods striding through the sky far above the world of humans below.

They picked a place to eat. They made another fire and boiled the water to make tea; though they didn't really like tea it was what they had done with their teacher. They ate another can of sausages and beans, joked about who would fart the loudest. They dropped little pieces of tinfoil into the flames to watch them become drifting fire bugs.

When they stood up to go again, the older boy made a play of pushing the younger into the fire, grabbing him and dragging his feet towards the edge of it. The younger boy managed to elbow him in the stomach and make him fall back so that they landed in a tangle. They shouted, swore, screeched, voices echoing over the valley. When the younger boy was no longer laughing, without a sign from either of them, they rolled apart, got up and dusted themselves off. The two of them packed the stove things away. In the distance they could see some other hillwalkers in their green and blue jackets. Three people with grey hair taking a different route. The boys hoped they wouldn't come near. They wanted the isolation. The younger boy was half playing a fantasy in his mind that he and his friend were fugitives, that their lives depended on not being caught or seen. The older boy said, 'Any luck we'll be back before rain breaks.' They kicked over the ashes of the fire and peed on it to be sure it was out.

They began the hike down the west side. The rain fell in sheets at the far end of the valley but didn't reach them. It was a kind of magic, watching this far curtain of rain while being untouched by it.

In hardly any time, they were back on the road to the village, the afternoon still fresh. Walking on the flat tarmacked surface made the triumph of the day ring clear. The sky had darkened above them again but the rain had still not caught up. Their limbs sprang fresh as if they had just set out, though the younger boy occasionally grimaced at the twinge in his knee, exaggerating the hurt. 'Fucking hell piglet, you nearly died there,' said the older boy, feigning a blow at the other boy's arm.

'Shut up. I fell about five centimetres.' He waited for the older boy to say something about him crying but he did not. The rain reached them now, the tiniest sparks of drops. It gathered pace, making pattering noises in the ferns. Sweet scents rose from the foliage at either side of the road. They were at the point where the tarmac twisted sharply round the loch and they fell into peaceable silence, each drifting into his own thoughts. A little gap opened up between them, the oldest boy at the front, the younger boy at the back. The rain switched to heavy, fat drops, falling so rapidly it was hard to keep their eyes open. The older boy looked back and grinned as if he had made it rain so heavily to give them one last challenge before getting home.

It was at this time that the chemistry teacher, who'd been drinking since the late morning, set out from his remote house onto the back road that led into the village. He had the idea that he would catch the shop before it shut. He usually went for social-seeming drinks, bottles of red wine that looked as if they might be shared. He knew people knew, but he couldn't do without the pantomime of buying crates of red with an unwanted loaf and party-sized packets of crisps, and biscuits that would end up in the bin. To just rush in and out with booze was too exposing. The back road was quiet and he knew how to drive with a drink in him. He only had to be more watchful. Hold his hands tighter on the wheel. Open his eyes wider. Keep bringing his mind back to the road like bringing a dog to heel.

The rain drumming down, he had the radio up. It was on a talk station and next they were going to debate whether diets really work and the voice of whoever they'd chosen to interview was irritating. Pious and patronising and slow. He knew the voice, but couldn't name the speaker and he wanted the voice gone. He fiddled with the dial to change the station and lost the signal altogether. There was that heavy gunning white noise that

7

got inside his teeth. He glanced up at the road, the pine trees either side leaning close. The rain hammered the car, making circles within circles on the windscreen. He looked down again, tried to find a new station. Blips and dabs of sound and voices. But he couldn't persuade the radio to stay on one thing. When he looked up again from the dial a boy was in front of him. The grey back of his jacket a different grey from the branches of the pines in the low light. He swerved to miss the figure. Electricity ran through his chest. The car seemed to speed up. And then another boy in a black jacket was right there inches from him at the edge of the road. There was no time to swerve again though he turned the wheel anyway. On impact the boy seemed to fold down and disappear as if maybe he hadn't been there in the first place and the car turned across the road and dipped down the verge on the other side and crumpled its bonnet into the trunk of a pine.

The older boy, the one who had been struck, rolled down the bank on the right and was gone. The younger boy heard a splashing sound, or recalled that he did later.

He was frozen for a moment, his body not following commands, and then he was scrambling towards the bank. Jagged plants scratching at his hands. He could see the older boy face down, the water around him in the shade of the pines was black like melted tar. The younger boy slid the rest of the way until he was in the loch up to his shins. He lifted the older boy, dragged his head and shoulders up. He was absurdly heavy, like his body was made of rock. The water cut with cold.

The younger boy's throat opened. 'Help me,' he screamed without any sense of who he was screaming to. He dragged the other boy's body by the armpits, up onto the bank. The body so heavy it seemed something in the water was trying to drag them back.

He fumbled for a pulse on the warm skin of the neck. He felt nothing and didn't know if that was because he was doing it wrong or because there was no pulse. He stood up and looked around. He didn't let his eyes focus on the car where the teacher was slumped forward behind a spiderweb of glass. He thought of CPR like they had seen in a video at school but he couldn't recall the images in a sensible order. A horror of the body came over him. In a second he decided; he turned and ran for the nearest house, the old smithy, the McLellans' place, at the start of the village. It was eleven minutes before he got there, before he was through the door without knocking and shouting for the phone. It was a further twenty-three minutes before an ambulance arrived, coming from the station point at the next village.

The younger boy would often think back to the empty moments that followed, sitting in the McLellans' house, watching the ambulance pass on the way to the hospital. He'd gazed out from the kitchen window; a blanket had been put on his shoulders, a cup of diluting juice pressed into his hand by then. The ambulance engine revved as it passed the house; he knew the driver, a familiar doughy face through the windscreen, the tyres splashing up water. There was no siren so the flashing blue lights seemed to flicker to an inaudible beat.

This is how I imagine it happened. I wasn't there. Some of the details were told to me, some I have guessed at. On the day of the climb, I was at home in bed with flu, watching the sunlight change shape on my bedroom curtains. The day had been long and boring. I remember lying on my back, walking my fuzzy, blue-slippered feet up the wall. My nose was red and stinging. I had period pain on top of the flu, a tight fist just below my belly button. Neither was the reason I wasn't on the climbing trip; I had not been invited. Aged thirteen at the time, I had never been climbing and did not generally spend time with the boys outside of school. It is tempting to try to pinpoint what I would have been doing at the exact moment the accident happened but that would be a further fabrication. To me, the day blurred even as it was happening, a mash of sleep and waking, reading and staring out the window, tissues and hot baths and sickly throat remedies. I did not hear about Nicky's death until the following day.

(You might think I was leading you on, going on about the climbing and the mountain when the accident happened on the road. But to my mind, he had set out for the mountain and not come back, and that thought – of the mountain having taken him – stayed with me.)

I remember my mum coming into my room the next morning, before I'd gotten up for breakfast, when I was still under the duvet and half asleep. She stood in the doorway and said, 'There's terribly sad news about wee Nicky Harper,' and stopped there.

And I remember sitting up, and saying, 'You have to tell me, I need to know, you have to tell me.'

And she covered her mouth with a tissue, my mum who wasn't the weepy type at all, and said, 'It's awful sad news I'm afraid pet.'

I said again, 'Tell me, tell me, I need to know.' Though I knew, of course; why else would she have said it like that?

The bridge was a way of escaping into the company of other people. It was New Year's Eve and I'd been sitting in my flat with a person I'd known for four weeks. We were at the tail-end of a not-quite relationship. The windows were covered with frost, the Christmas fairy lights still strung over the bookcase. I'd realised a few hours before, during a long meal, that I didn't want to be with this man, but it wasn't the time to break up with someone so we'd ended up having sex almost out of politeness. Afterwards I'd smiled and put my head on his shoulder and thought about when and how it would be least hurtful to him to end our almost-relationship. It wasn't about the sex, just that the whole thing began to feel like an effort. I had been hit by a fundamental gap between our outlooks that I had been trying to pretend wasn't there. After we were dressed again, and I'd put glitter in my hair in an attempt to be jokey, midnight was approaching and I couldn't think what else to do. We were awkward in each other's company like two barges manoeuvring round each other, and I found myself saying, 'Why don't we go to the bridge?' So, as if we were a couple in love, we wrapped ourselves in scarves and gloves and padded winter coats and ran out into the cold holding hands, to go to the nearest canal bridge to watch the fireworks rise and burst above the castle.

We arrived ten minutes before midnight, stars standing out above the bridge like small flecks of ice. I'd wanted to find some of my friends, wherever they'd got to in the city, but there wasn't time. The cold bit into me; it was almost pleasing to withstand it. As we waited side by side, I realised we had forgotten to bring our bottle of fizzy wine but it was too late to go back for it. A few other people gathered, shady figures in the light of the nearest street lamp, laughing, hugging, swigging from plastic cups. There was no traffic. Everything became quiet in the last minutes of waiting, then someone started up a radio. Classical music began to play in a tinny, faraway fashion. I had been linking arms with my not-quite boyfriend but when I took my hand away to put on my gloves, I didn't give it back.

Finally the countdown began; I only realised and joined in at eight, seven, six. I fixed a smile on my face. I wasn't unhappy, just flattened. I tried to think a good thought as the time came. I focused on my resolution to try learning Gaelic again, or at least go to a few lessons. The small group on the bridge began shouting. The fireworks started after a breath of a pause, a beat behind midnight. They were more complicated than I remembered, with triple sets of colours circled inside each other. Couples began kissing and so we kissed too, briefly, and then stepped away from each other, unlinked. We murmured meaningless comments, *Pretty. That's a good one! Is there more? Oh, there's more.* I thought about how I probably wouldn't see him again, the man I was with, not deliberately, though I would likely run into him in the city streets sometimes. I wasn't sad or pleased about the relationship ending; it only bobbed up as a thought and floated away again.

People on the bridge began to turn to strangers, to look at the unknown figures gathered near them. The closest couple came up and hugged the two of us. Others shook hands, kissed unfamiliar faces. A group of girls in stiletto boots passed me their bottle of pink wine. I wiped the top with my coat sleeve and took a gulp then passed it on to another woman to my right.

The fireworks kept spluttering on against the Edinburgh skyline. The cold was becoming uncomfortable. I turned to check if people were starting to go. It was then that I saw him.

Sliding past the group of girls with the pink bottle, he was wearing a dark puffer jacket in the style of another decade, following a woman with sequins on her face and devil horns on her head. He hurried after her, reaching for and missing her hand, smiling in the dopey, drunken way everyone was smiling. He was more than familiar. As I stood on that frosty pavement, I had the sure sensation that he was someone I absolutely knew. He was someone he couldn't be. He was Nicky Harper. The boy I'd known in school, who died. Here he was, grown up and celebrating the rolling over of a new year, just as I was.

I'm not usually very good at recognising people. Sometimes I meet a client from work in a different context and though I may have had an hour's conversation with them only a week before, I still stare at them blankly in the supermarket as they smile in recognition. I find it even harder to recognise people if they've dyed or shorn their hair, or if the years have passed. But in that stretched minute, watching that man go by, I knew it was Nicky in the way I knew that my feet were my own. I didn't think, *There is someone who looks like Nicky Harper, isn't that weird?* I was sure it was him, even as I understood it could not be.

I watched the man hurry down the street, following the woman with the red horns. They weaved along the middle of the road then stepped back onto the pavement as a lone car came trundling past. Pink and green streamers from a party popper trailed off his shoulder. He and the woman bounded on, dodged a couple of drunk partygoers, and turned left at the shuttered newsagent. That was it, I could not see him any more.

I stared at the space where he'd vanished until the man I was with said, 'What's wrong?'

'Nothing, just thought I saw somebody I knew.' He pulled me closer by the shoulder, kissed me on the lips, breathing beer on me, then turned away to kiss a woman who was reaching for him drunkenly.

I looked down at my phone. The screen had a short string of messages wishing me a Happy New Year. I tapped on the one from Leti, my closest friend, who I'd known since primary school days. I typed, *HAPPY NEW YEAR! Btw I just saw Nicky Harper*, and didn't press send.

I looked at the words for a few seconds.

'Do you want to go back inside?' my non-boyfriend said.

'Just a minute.'

I deleted what I'd typed as the last of the fireworks popped above us, little silver jumping balls leaving comet trails behind them. The smell of gunpowder reached us on the wind. My head was padded with drink. I wrote the text out again and sent it.

We returned to my flat, walking over broken glass and trampled streamers. The man I was with followed me politely, a step behind. I was tempted to ask him to go home but there was no kind way to do that. I opened the front door and we headed in. We perched on the couch and drank the bottle of fizzy wine we'd forgotten to take outside. A text came in from Leti, which just said, *What have you been drinking??* I put my phone away.

I offered to make hot chocolate. 'Sure, thanks,' my non-boyfriend said, so I heated up two large mugs of milk in the microwave. We smiled at each other over our cups and his smile seemed slightly strained and I could feel how mine must look the same to him. He didn't want to be with me any more than I wanted to be with him. The image of that other face flashing by in the dark kept playing on a short a loop in my mind. Already, my sense of the event had shifted so I thought of the person on the bridge now as someone who looked like Nicky only. Because that's what the explanation had to be. The dead don't come back. A premonition of embarrassment, a sense of how awkward it would be to explain my text to Leti, drifted into my head and was soothed away again by the fog of the wine.

'I'm knackered, shall we get to sleep?' I said. And so we slept together under my winter duvet. He lay diagonally across the bed – I ended up curled in a foetal position with my knees against the wall and couldn't get comfortable. Outside, footsteps tramped past, voices rising every so often. Unseen passers-by made their way home long into the night so that I woke and drifted, slept and stirred, and was roused time and again by unfamiliar voices.

On New Year's Day I drove out to the country for a walk with Leti. The familiar path wound by a church and an old graveyard, then ducked down to a river and along a narrow track through woodland. It was a place we often visited for walks. Though the woods couldn't have been very large, we never seemed to get to the other side of them.

After we'd been walking a while, chatting about the holidays, Leti asked, 'What did you mean, about seeing Nicky Harper?'

'Just what I said, I saw him. He's back from the dead.'

We both giggled awkwardly, then caught each other's eyes and stopped.

'No, but really what did you mean?'

I felt a heave of embarrassment but pressed on through it. 'I don't know what I meant. I thought I saw someone who looked a bit like him. I must have been going kind of nuts. New year crazy.' The trickling sound of water surrounded us, the river and the dripping from the dark spokes of tree branches, both calming and gloomy. We always seemed to go to this place on damp days.

'Poor Nicky,' Leti said. 'You know, I haven't thought of him in a while.'

'Aye. Poor thing, it feels like another lifetime and also recent, if you know what I mean.'

'I do. So this guy you saw, did he look like a zombie?'

'Leti, God.'

Her smile contracted. 'Sorry.'

'He just looked ordinary.'

'Was he a teenager?'

'No, he was around our age, in his thirties, I guess the age Nicky would be.'

'I can't imagine what Nicky would have looked like if he was our age.'

'Well, I would have said the same, but then there he was. This man looked just the same really, only older. And I felt a jolt when I saw him.'

'Of recognition?'

'Of something. Hard to explain.'

'And the guy you were with . . . ?' she said, raising an eyebrow.

'It's not going anywhere.'

'Ah, shame. You should have been with me for the bells.'

'I should have been with you, that would have been more fun.'

I wanted her to ask more about the man who looked like Nicky but she didn't. Instead, she started telling me about the party she was at, how a mutual friend had got very rapidly drunk and vomited into the hood of someone's new coat. 'I don't know what she had. One minute we were having a coherent conversation, the next minute she's like something from The Exorcist.'

'And then you got my text and thought here's another one.'

'Yeah, then I got your message and thought, well, Emily's wasted.' We slowed and turned our feet sideways as we reached a muddy slope next to a narrow waterfall. Already the light was going, the days snapping shut like clam shells at this time of year. 'Do you want to get food on the way back?' Leti said.

'Sure.'

We ended up eating a fish supper off our laps in the car while discussing previous unsuccessful relationships and making each other snort with laughter. Stabbing at my fish with the inefficient wooden fork, I tried to think of another way to bring the conversation back to what I'd seen. I could have just said I wanted to talk about it but the words didn't find their way out.

She asked me to come back to her flat for a drink, but I made excuses about having things to do at home. I wanted space to think. And I did feel there were things that needed doing at home. I had an unusual desire to tidy. The detritus from the previous year was starting to disturb me: the stacks of newspapers, abandoned socks and unsorted mail. I drove us back, dropped Leti off, and headed home to sit in my living room alone, cocooned in the lamplight.

I couldn't help searching for Nicky's name on the internet. My fingertips hung over my laptop keyboard. I didn't want to see anything about him dying. I don't know what I was expecting to find.

Of course the first search page simply brought up other Nicholas Harpers, since he had been dead so long. I found an academic, a joiner's website, a vet, an obituary for a photographer. I closed the browser. As I tidied, made cups of peppermint tea that kept my hands warm and tasted of almost nothing, the moment played on through my mind on a loop. This face appearing, bobbing, laughing, and that feeling of certainty like a piece of machinery clicking into place. It is, even now, hard to put into words.

*

A few days after New Year I started back at work. I parked my car in the shadow of a short, squat block of flats and stepped up the path between a couple of bare, spindly silver birches poking up through the concrete. Compared to the old tower blocks behind, the new block seemed gaudy, with patches of mauve cladding on the outside. Residents complained about the thinness of the walls. If you stood in certain spots in particular rooms it would sound like a stranger was suddenly in the room with you. I worked as a housing officer for an organisation that supported people who were 'vulnerably housed'. In practice this usually meant they were recently out of psychiatric hospital or struggling with addictions. Our job was to try to make our clients' home lives more secure. Most of the work was out and about visiting the people we were supporting, only nipping in and out of the office to sort paperwork now and again. We'd see each client every few weeks or months for up to a year, depending on their support plans, then they were on their own. I pressed the buzzer now and waited. I had intentionally planned my first session back with a client I liked. Nevertheless, a large part of me wanted to return to hibernation, for the client not to answer so I could have an hour of dawdling. But already Jim's voice was crackling through the speaker.

'Who is it?'

'It's Emily from StartingUp.' The electronic locking system hummed and I headed in. When I reached the top of the purple-carpeted stairs, Jim was waiting at his door, his grey hair standing up in tufts.

'How are you keeping?' he said.

'Just gearing up for another year.' The door opened into his living room. I stepped inside. Everything was neat in the flat but there was a sparseness, as if he had recently moved in when in fact he'd been there nine months now. The only obviously personal items were a row of wooden trains on the windowsill interspersed with potted succulent plants. He'd made the trains himself, complete with moving wheels, *years back*, he said, *when I used to do things*. He'd given one to me when I first arrived. We weren't supposed to accept gifts but I'd taken it home and kept it on a bookshelf in my living room.

'Recovered from your Hogmanay hangover?' he said.

I smiled. 'No need.'

'Aye right.'

I sat down on the couch. 'I'm too old for much of that.'

'You're just a bairn. You can't be thirty yet.'

'I can though, by a fair bit. How are you?'

He blew through his teeth. 'Wasn't as bad as I thought. New Year, watched the fireworks from the flat. As for the day of jollity and peace on earth, I just stayed in. Fell asleep for half of it, then got a Chinese.'

'Well, I'm glad if it was OK. How have things been since the holidays?' I said.

'A few problems. Want tea?'

'Yeah, thanks. What sort of problems?'

He gave a wincing half-smile. 'For one, the neighbours again. I got the recording you wanted so you know I'm not a nutter.' I reddened as he raked through a box to pull out a small digital tape recorder. Noise from neighbours was a surprisingly common hallucination; when clients complained of it we asked for a recording. Before he lived in this flat, he'd spent four months in a psychiatric hospital. He'd been signed in voluntarily after a second suicide attempt at a railway bridge.

'I don't think you're nuts,' I said.

He waved his hand. 'I know that.' He could be defensive with me but he never had the need some clients seemed to have to pre-emptively put me in my place. We'd been working together for a decent time now and he was one of my favourite clients, something about the way his spikiness hid a softness.

He set the recorder down between us and pressed play. Muffled voices started up, shouting, and a regular beat. The voices sounded like they were coming to us through a thick liquid. I felt slightly disorientated listening to them.

'It's not very clear, but you get the sense of it,' he said.

'Sure, clear enough. Did you make a diary of the times?'

He shook his head. 'I got caught up in other things.'

'If you can get that done then we can go somewhere with it. We need to show it's round the clock.'

'I just don't want any fucking trouble with the neighbours. Sorry, but you know?'

'I know, but they won't know any complaint came from you.'

'Pretty likely it would be me though, eh? And one of them is a big guy, I mean, seriously big.'

He was frowning. He poured steaming water into two mugs without looking at me. We spent a bit of time discussing his new medication, benefits changes and the visits from the community psychiatric nurse. I forgot my tea and drank it cold in sugary gulps.

'Take care of yourself,' he called as I left. He said it without his usual amused tone, almost as if I had worried him in some way. I gave him a wave as I was heading down the stairs.

I was already running late for the next client. As I drove away, the tower blocks seemed to watch me. It was a similar but not identical feeling to the one I sometimes got driving beneath the mountain back in the village. The rest of the day rolled by quickly enough and I found myself thinking of the past and of Nicky at odd moments during conversations with other clients. Flickers of memory just sliding haphazardly in and out of my mind like jumbled lines from a long-ago song.

When I talk about my childhood, the thing that stands out to other people is that I had a baby sister who died. This sounds devastating, and of course it was for my parents, but it didn't have the full weight of tragedy for me growing up because I did not remember her. I was two and a half years old when she died from a heart defect. My parents knew from the time she was born that she would not live, and took turns watching over the baby in the hospital and taking care of me at home. In the end, she survived for twenty-eight days. I was brought to the ward once. Apparently I was held over the plastic incubator and I touched her foot with my stubby hands.

As a child, I was loved and knew that I was. My parents were sad about my sister but I never felt that I had to live up to some ideal phantom sibling, I never imagined that they preferred her to me, I didn't have any sense of guilt about being the one who lived.

My sister's grave was marked with a brass plaque on a small white stone, and my parents visited it once a year on the anniversary of her death. She was buried on the other side of the country, on the east coast, in a family plot. My parents did not push me to go on these pilgrimages, always saying that she was not there anyway. For my mother, with her scientific mind, this meant that her small life had blazed and gone out, and she existed only in memories. For my father, this meant that she lived on in spirit in some way. I felt free to ask questions – *Did she have a middle name?* and *Would I have got on with her?* and *Do you think her hair would have turned dark like mine?* They didn't have time to pick but if they had maybe Grandma's, and we'd have got on sometimes and fought at others like all sisters, and who could say, it might have stayed blonde.

I have a lot of detailed memories from early childhood but they are all from the time after my sister died. I remember nursery, my first day, playing in the sand box with a plastic crocodile, a gale blowing at the window. I remember Christmases in the village, dragging a sledge up the back way to the Forresters' farm land, pretending it was a horse and the string was the reins. I remember much of primary school. When I was seven, our class began a school project about extinct animals. Dodos, Tasmanian tigers, moa birds, quaggas, passenger pigeons. I recall patiently drawing the stripes on a Tasmanian tiger with a fine felt-tip while Leti drew a moa bird. To me, the tiger in the photograph I copied had an angry expression, as if it already knew of its species' fate. The stories of the extinct animals played on my mind long after we dropped the project – I couldn't get past that full stop, the fact that nothing we could do would ever bring them back. The animals made such an impression on me that they came back to me in dreams when I was in my twenties, dozing on my single bed in my student flat.

I was eleven years old when Nicky's family arrived in the village. They moved into the big house at the end of our road, two doors down from us. It was a dry summer, the roads were coated with dust and there were more dragonflies than usual. I watched the new family move in. They brought the largest television set I had ever seen and a giant fish tank. Our house was one of a trio of terraced houses, each covered in white stones with postage-stamp front and back gardens. Nicky's house was a former manse, an old grey granite building. The back windows of each of the houses all looked out on to the mountain. When the moon was out the shape of the peak loomed through the dark. My room was at the back so the mountain's changing moods and colours were the familiar background to my childhood; gentle and green or dark blue and glowering or forbidding and perfect with snow. There was nothing but low hedges of dog rose between the separate gardens, and I sometimes watched Nicky kick a football around his lawn from my window. Occasionally I saw him climbing over the back fence in his hiking boots, heading up onto the rough moorland that lay below the mountain. Because he was a boy, and because he was older than me, we didn't speak at all for the first couple of months he lived there.

~*~

By the time a few weeks had passed after that Hogmanay, I had almost stopped thinking about the experience with the man who looked like Nicky. Other things had taken over, small worries and hopes for the year. Come late February, the weather was unexpectedly mild and the air had begun to get that optimistic scent in the mornings that hinted at the coming of spring. I had started to leave the house without gloves or a scarf. Then, one night, it began to snow. Tiny, elfin flakes drifting down in the dark as I walked home from the supermarket under the streetlights.

When I woke up on Saturday morning, there was a white glow radiating from behind the curtains. Beyond them the snow lay in a thick layer. I had arranged to meet Leti for coffee at a cafe a couple of streets from my flat. After heaving myself out of bed and into my clothes, I pulled on my hiking socks and boots. It had not properly snowed at all over the winter months so it was pleasing to see it lying like slices of royal icing on fence tops and car bonnets. As I turned onto the narrow street that I used as a cut-through to the cafe, I saw a snowball flying, then another. I heard a stifled squeal. A group of adults about my age were hiding behind cars, giggling and hurling clumps of snow at each other. I tried not to be irritated. I walked out into the middle of the road where they could see me. 'Wait,' someone shouted and the fight held off as if frozen.

I stepped onwards, the snow squeaking like polystyrene under my boots. As I passed a covered motorbike, there was a white blur, a stinging thump – a snowball hit my face. A shard broke off down my top and melted painfully against my skin.

'Watch it,' I called. A woman stood up, her cheeks pink from the cold like a little girl's.

'Sorry.'

The firing stopped again while I walked the rest of the way down the street. As I was turning the corner, another snowball hit the back of my jacket with a thwack. I whipped round to my left but no one was there. Then, to my right side, someone grabbed my arm. A man was next to me, wearing big ski gloves. His face close to mine, laughing, meeting my eyes like we knew each other. I stared. It was Nicky's face. It was happening again, the same face. Looking at me, clear eyes framed by dark eyelashes. His black hair and wide eyebrows, a heavy jawline and stubble – a man's face. But underneath that, a boy I knew.

'Where did you come from?' I said, the words bursting out of me.

He grinned, his fingers still squeezing my arm. 'I dug my way out.' He said this as if it was funny.

'What?'

24

He shook my arm just a little. 'I dug my way out.' There was a cool sensation in the centre of my chest, where the snow had melted. He let go of my arm and ran back into the snowball fight. Someone pelted him and he raised his arm in defence and disappeared behind a car. The snow glittered now as the sun came out.

I wrapped my coat around myself more tightly and carried on walking towards the cafe. I had no reason to stop and try to talk to him further, this complete stranger. His comment was a joke. Perhaps he had mistaken me for someone he knew, part of the snowball fight. He was not Scottish; he did not sound like Nicky had. It was hard to place his accent, if anything it was slightly American. Maybe he meant he'd dug his way out of a snowdrift. He had not meant that he'd dug his way out of a grave. Even though I knew that, it was what I pictured as I walked towards the cafe. Hands clawing up through earth.

The next street was wide and bright, people milling about with their shopping bags, two Italian greyhounds in tartan coats marching along on matching leads. Cars hissed by, spraying up slush. It didn't take me much longer to reach the cafe. Stepping inside, I kicked the snow from my boots on the metal grille. The tables were lit with candles inside lanterns though the sky outside was light. I was the first to arrive and managed to find one empty table at the back. I sat down, took my coat off and pictured the face I'd seen a few minutes ago. There was an old, old feeling jumping in my stomach.

Leti arrived a few minutes later, pulling off her hat and gloves. It was a couple of weeks since we'd seen each other; normally we met up every week but life and work had seemed to get in the way.

'How are you?' I said, giving her a one-armed hug.

'Pretty good, pretty good. You?'

'Fine, good. Something weird just happened though,' I said this with a small smile, not wanting to alarm her.

She widened her eyes in mock shock. 'Can it wait until I order a coffee?'

'Yes,' I said. 'Yes, it can.' I smiled more widely and my cheek twitched.

We ordered two coffees and a carrot cake and a chocolate fudge cake, and after the waitress was gone I said, 'I just saw the guy that looks like Nicky.'

'Like who?'

'Nicky Harper. You know, I saw someone who looked like him before.'

'Oh, right, yeah. This was the same guy?' Leti leant forward on her elbows and I nodded. 'Well at least that's cleared it up.'

'How do you mean?' I said.

'He was a real person, you didn't hallucinate him.'

'I never said I hallucinated him.'

'I thought you did. You said you were worried you were hallucinating or something when I saw you on New Year's Day.'

'I don't think I said that.'

'Well anyway, that's pretty freaky, if he looks so much like him. I don't know. Did you talk to him?'

'I couldn't.'

'Why not?'

'He was having a snowball fight. I didn't want to interrupt. Also, what could I say?'

'Excuse me, are you my old schoolmate back from the dead?'

I started to laugh but slightly choked. 'I suppose I could have said that.'

'Sorry. Anyway, now you know it was just this guy.'

'Well, yeah, but it was so bizarre. He looked exactly like him again. I mean he looked exactly as you'd imagine Nicky grown up.'

'That is strange but I still can't picture how he would look now.' Our order arrived. The waitress placed the coffees carefully in front of us and I began to eat foam off the top of mine with a teaspoon. We talked about Leti's work for a while. She was a high-school art teacher and she'd landed a particularly difficult group of boys in her class this year.

'I'm fed up with the school.'

'I know.'

She pushed her tongue to the side of her mouth. 'No really. Properly, deeply fed up.'

'Are you thinking of leaving?'

'To do what?'

'I don't know. Anything?' I said.

'I can't afford to retrain. We've been round this. And don't say painting.' She created her own artwork; she always had done, or had since we were in our teens. She never sold it. I wanted to ask if she'd started any paintings lately, but I could tell she was already ruffled. We talked a bit more about the problems at the school and I drank down to the bottom of my cup. 'So how are things with you anyway?' she asked, pulling her slice of cake closer.

'To be honest, I'm still pretty shaken by this thing.'

'What thing?'

'The thing with Nicky.'

She frowned. 'I just, I don't get what's bothering you about it. And it's not really anything to do with Nicky.'

'But he looks so like him.'

'Yeah, all right, but then what?' She put down a small forkful of icing and looked at me sideways. 'You don't think it's actually him because you're not insane, right?'

27

'No, I'm not insane. I don't know. It just rattled me. The past coming back.'

'It was a sad time.'

'It was,' I said.

'And a traumatic thing for kids to go through. Someone our own age dying. A hard thing to get your head around.'

'Yeah, yeah,' I said. 'You know theoretically young people can die but it's a whole other thing when it actually happens, like finding a trapdoor in your house that's always been there, but you didn't know it. I wish you could see this guy so you would know what I'm on about.'

'I might not see the resemblance.'

'I think you would,' I said. 'I'm not normally good at recognising people, that's why it's strange. It's another level of recognising. Like if he wasn't dead I would be certain it was him.' I could see the snow falling again through the windows at the front of the cafe; it felt like the year was doubling back. Like we were heading into midwinter again instead of heading out of it.

She scraped the last foam from the bottom of her coffee cup. 'It's funny when people ask about growing up in the village, and they ask what it was like, if it was exciting growing up surrounded by all that wilderness, and I tell them nothing ever really happened. But that happened, Nicky died, and it was a big thing.'

'Yeah, it was,' I said. 'It was a huge thing.'

'I suppose life was quiet outside of that. It was the only really big thing that happened. Though it always felt like something else was about to happen,' Leti paused. 'You know what I mean?'

'I suppose I do,' I said, remembering other things but not being sure if they counted as big in the same way.

We moved on to talk about a book we were both reading, then about a new pear cake recipe Leti had tried that had fallen apart in the oven. 'The middle just collapsed like a tent folding up.' The sky had clouded and our pale-grey shadows chatted on the wall as we spoke so that it felt like evening. There were moments when we giggled about people we both knew and we could have been our younger selves sitting on my bedroom carpet, as if no years had passed. Then out of a small silence Leti said, 'That time, with Nicky. It was so sad for Mr Fletcher too.'

'Aye, it was. It was,' I said. And there was a pause and then we were on to something else, a friend who had moved away. Soon we finished up, paid for our drinks and hugged goodbye.

When I left the cafe, I walked back by the same route and I thought about Mr Fletcher, the chemistry teacher with his ragged grey hair and serious eyes. One day at school, I'd vomited in front of him. This was when I had only been at the high school a few weeks. I remember running from the playground with a nauseous feeling and sinking down against one of the walls in the red corridor that led towards the science classrooms. A heat burned over the bone of my forehead. Then someone was saying, 'Are you all right?' Mr Fletcher's voice was unfamiliar in its sudden gentleness, losing its classroom sharpness. I tried to stand up. 'Now take a moment, don't get up right away.'

All at once the sickness was lurching through me, going from something I could try to keep down to something inevitable. I gagged and threw up on the floor.

'Take it easy. Better to let it all go,' he said. I did not look at him.

The nausea billowed again. The wave of it up through my neck. 'I think I'm going to—' and there it went, onto the floor, splatter.

'It's OK, you'll get to the other side. Deep breaths.' He was talking to me like a parent, not a teacher. His hand hovered over my shoulder. I didn't want him to touch me and he did not. The acid burned the back of my throat. I lay my head against the wall. Moisture ran from my nose, I started sniffling.

Already a feeling of clearness was coming over me. 'Can you stand?' I got up slowly and he let me do it without touching me. 'Let's get you to the nurse's room. Is your mum or dad at home?' I shook my head. 'But we'll have work numbers for them.' I nodded. 'You get home and rest. You'll feel much better in half an hour or so and you'll have the afternoon off at least.'

His kindness that day was the first thing I thought of when I heard that he was the one driving when Nicky was killed.

Making my way home from the cafe, the street where the snowball fight had been was quiet and empty and the morning's footprints were covered with new snow as if no one had walked that way all day. Piano music came from an open window somewhere high up. The fresh fall of snow was firm under my boots. A pink scarf lay abandoned under a car. The only marks were new tyre tracks, and tiny, hopping bird prints. I imagined what it would be like if I really was hallucinating this man who looked like Nicky; I would start desperately pointing him out and other people would shake their heads. I realised I had told Leti I hadn't spoken to him, which wasn't exactly true. I hadn't told her about him saying he'd dug his way out. It had felt like too much in the light of the cafe. As I walked by a row of tall, old Victorian houses, there was the sweet scent of wood smoke, reminding me of home.

By night-time, the snow had melted away, replaced by rain and slick, dark pavements, as if it had never fallen.

In the morning, as I set out to work, I ran over the strangeness of the previous day, the man with his sharp, recognisable features and the blue banks of snow that had vanished so quickly. My first client was Megan, a shy, day-dreamy teenager with straight black hair cut neatly around the line of her chin. She reminded me of a rabbit, something in her anxiousness combined with her small nose, the way her upper lip twitched when she was thinking. Her flat was full of clean, pale wood furniture. I had accompanied her on a shopping trip to a charity store to help her choose it all a month back.

'How are you?' I said, taking off my coat. Outside the window I could see the low grey roof of the flat opposite and a squirrel, holding a peanut, running across it.

'All right,' she said. 'How are you?' I liked that she asked every time. The younger clients usually didn't ask me how I was. They had enough problems of their own, of course, but I sometimes felt like I might as well be on a screen to them.

'I'm great,' I said. Her flat was a tiny studio so her bed sat behind the couch, only part hidden by a screen with a print of ferns on it. A collection of cuddly toys were arranged in a row on her duvet, leaning back against the far wall. Rabbits and teddy bears and a cat and a droopy-eyed dog.

Sometimes teenagers made me nervous. They were more likely to be openly sarcastic or eye-rolling. But she never seemed to have any of that hidden under her shyness. I suppose I was part-way between her age and the age a parent of hers might be, and sometimes I caught within myself flashes of an awkward, overprotective feeling towards her.

Today, her television was on in the corner of the room, though she was not looking at it. A jangling collision of noise streamed to us from an advert break while her phone pinged at her side. It was often like that in her flat – devices chattering away, as if a tiny, noiseless gap would frighten her.

'Mind if we turn the TV off? Or put it on silent?'

She turned the volume down so that the flickering continued to distract me. We went through her file, got up to date on her to-do list, then I made a call to her energy company for her, swapping the phone back and forth between the two of us.

She was wearing an unseasonable light yellow dress, the cut of which made her look like a younger girl, and I wondered where she'd found it, picturing her patrolling the racks of a charity store with her nose wrinkling happily. She had recently left foster care. We didn't get so many clients in that situation, the foster kids usually had a personal advisor from the council, but she'd left a tenancy after falling out with her flatmate and lived on the streets for a few days, so that qualified her for our help. While she spoke on the phone, I thought again of the weekend, the moment in the snowball fight and the hand on my shoulder.

Megan ended the call and gazed at me for a second. 'You look tired,' she said, smiling her shy smile.

'I am a bit,' I said. 'I hate talking to those companies. It's draining, eh?'

'Yeah. Thanks for your help.'

As I got my things together to leave, she was nibbling at her nails, and there it was again, that minuscule flash of a protective, almost parental feeling.

~*~

When I was seven years old I saw a girl in a yellow summer dress disappear off a cliff. I was with my parents in the car, heading to the nearest town to buy new school shoes. We passed a great lichen-stippled boulder with a little girl standing on it. Behind the rock was a drop down to the sea, the water smooth as a mirror. The girl had her hair in two braids and her skin was dark and her face held a look of concentration. As our car passed, she jumped backwards and disappeared. I was so surprised that I didn't say anything to my parents. It seemed such an unlikely thing that I kept it to myself, sure that in some mysterious way, it had not really happened.

A few days later, the same girl was standing at the front of the classroom in a cream dress and cream shoes, twisting a pipe-cleaner animal about in her fingers. Rain crackled at the classroom windows.

'This is Violet,' the teacher said. 'Everyone say good morning, Violet.' We gave out the familiar welcome chant. 'She and her family have come to live here from a country called Malawi.'

I wanted to know how she had disappeared. When the teacher asked, 'Who wants to sit next to Violet?', my hand went up along with half the others. We were always curious about new people. The teacher pointed to me. As the girl stepped down the aisle to sit beside me, I could see that the pipe-cleaner animal was a red horse. The girl placed it on her desk along with a ladybird pencil case. I had made pipe-cleaner animals with my parents, twisting out bodies and necks and legs, so I was hopeful that we could base our friendship on this.

The teacher began to write words with missing letters on the board for spelling practice. 'Copy these down in your best writing.'

'Who made him?' I whispered.

The girl reached out and closed her fingers round her red horse. 'Me,' she said, without looking round. 'And people call me Leti, not Violet.'

'Remember no talking until it's time to talk,' our teacher said and we became silent but began to take glances at each other as we copied down the spelling words. I worried she was angry that I had got us told off. At lunchtime she played with someone else.

At home that night I made a blue dog out of pipe cleaners with my dad's help. I brought it in to class the next day and placed it on my desk. Leti silently took out the red horse and sat it nose to nose with the dog. Over the coming weeks, Leti and I kept our pipe-cleaner animals on our desks, adding to them, creating a collection of them that had complex interactions with each other throughout the school day. We made up things together. She told me stories about her grandmother's house and the ghosts that lived in it. I told her stories about the magical creatures that lived inside the mountain. These were not local legends; I made them up for her. There was a sense at that time that we could twist the world to suit our daydreams, a sense that we could shape it together.

I learned how she did the falling trick, choosing a boulder that looked like it was on the edge of a cliff when in fact there was a gentle slope behind it. She'd whirl her arms and jump off backwards and crouch down on the landing so that it looked to anyone passing like she'd disappeared.

~*~

I didn't see the man who looked like Nicky again for a month or so after the incident with the snowball fight. Then, late one

34

spring night, Leti and I were leaving a birthday party for one of her friends. It was just after midnight and we were circling down the concrete staircase in the centre of the block of flats, the voices from the party echoing behind us. As we descended, using the peeling, putty-coloured walls for balance, we heard the slam of the front door at the bottom of the stairwell, new voices and chatter rising up. We turned the last curve of the spiral to meet a group of four guys walking close together. They took the outside track up the stairs and we edged round them on the inside, trying not to trip on the narrow steps.

As they passed us, the second of them, a guy with a black tunnel earring and an Edinburgh accent, offered a slurred, 'Evening ladies.'

'Evening,' I said because he seemed harmless. I turned for a second to grip the central column of the stairwell and as I looked back, I took in the last face in the group, tucked under a grey woollen hat. I waited until we were at the bottom of the stairs, then pinched at Leti's arm.

'Did you see, did you see?'

She stopped, turned to me with calm eyes, and I thought she going to say, *see what?* But instead, she said, 'Fuck me, that was him.'

'It was him.'

'It was.'

'Nicky?'

'Yes.'

We both looked up the stairs now, the smoke-grey stone spiral. The men's voices and footsteps receding and echoing as if they were disappearing into a cave. A door somewhere up there opened and closed and we could no longer hear their words. The door seemed to be on the right side of the building, opposite to Leti's friend's flat, leading to a different party. 'We better go,' Leti said. We took hold of the fabric of each other's coats and turned and opened the main door and pushed out into the night.

'It was him,' Leti said again once we were outside, her voice rising now, as we picked up our steps.

'I know.' We hurried along the road. The night air was sharp and we were cold in our dresses.

'But it really was him, eh? Like you said. Not like him but it was him. Though obviously it isn't him.' She laughed and shook her head.

'Yes, yes!' I said, the strangeness of it smoothed by the rum cocktails we'd had. We were both laughing, the clip of our shoes echoing off the tenement walls. 'That's the thing. It bloody is him, even though it can't be.'

'Obviously it can't be.'

I stopped in the street. Wheeled around, faced the other way. 'Where are we going? Should we go back? Confront him! Ask what business he's got coming back from the dead.'

'No. Yes. We could get another look. Should we though?' She was holding my arm, like we were partners in a dance. She bobbed sideways suddenly and caught me for balance. She was drunker than I was.

'We should get another look at him, right? I mean, aren't you curious?'

'But it can't be him,' she said.

'I know but I want to see him again at least, while you're here. Why not?'

She looked at me wide-eyed, as if this was a great joke. 'We can't.'

'Why not?'

'It'll seem weird, we don't even know the people he's with or the flat he went into. I'm not sure I'm drunk enough to do this.'

'You're plenty drunk enough. Believe in yourself.'

We were doubled up laughing. Something in me turned from the darkness of the real memory, the horror of a sudden death by a roadside, and spun it into this game. 'Yes, all right, let's go back, just for a sec,' Leti said. We turned, retraced our way along the wet, dark pavement, stepping over drink cans and crisp packets. A Dickensian haze hung around the streetlamps. This was play-acting, sneaking big steps as we got closer. I was swaying a bit, more in the pretence of being drunk than anything else. If I could persuade myself that I was too intoxicated to feel self-conscious, it was going to be easier to do this. We found the chipped main door and rang the buzzer for Leti's friend Morna. We had to lean on it three times; it seemed they didn't hear us over the music. Then Morna's voice crackled through the holes in the metal speaker.

'Who's there?'

'It's us. We need to come back in. We forgot our hats.'

The door buzzed open. Leti put her hand over her mouth, laughing. 'Now we have to go in and steal two hats,' she said.

'We could just tell them.'

'That we thought we saw someone who'd come back from the dead and we wanted to double check?'

'That we saw someone who looked like someone we knew.' We climbed the stairs. When we reached the door across from Morna's flat, we stood still. The stairwell was dark apart from one strip bulb, which guttered like a candle. There was music coming from behind the door, bubbly pop clashing with the low beat emanating from Morna's place. We both giggled but my breathing came narrowly through my throat. 'Let's knock,' I said.

'No. Come on, this is too much, let's not.' Leti was suddenly looking more sober.

'You brought us up here! Go on, you knock,' I said.

Leti bit her sleeve and shook her head. It was a gesture that reminded me of her as a kid in primary school. 'You do it then if you want to. You knock.'

I watched my hand move forward. I banged on the painted wood panel. Louder voices, steps. The door opened, music spilled around us. In front of us there was a man with a pink paper party hat, the kind you get folded inside Christmas crackers. He was younger than us, flushed, clutching a cider can, ginger hair standing up inside the circle of the paper crown.

'Hello, hello!' he said happily.

'Oh, is this the right place?' I said.

'I don't know,' he said.

'Is this Morna's flat?' Leti said. We both craned our necks to see past him. There he was. The man who looked like Nicky, facing away from us. I thought so anyway, recognising his hair, the cut and colour, somehow the shape of him and the slant of his shoulders, the solidity of his neck.

'Nope, 'fraid not,' the pink-crowned guy said.

'Oh, sorry,' Leti said.

'You probably want across the hall.'

'Oh, aye, sorry,' I said. The man made as if to close the door. An impulse struck me. 'Nicky!' I called. The black-haired head looked round. He was the only one who turned. He glanced square at us, expressionless, then turned away again.

'Are you coming in or going away?' said the man at the door. We shook our heads, stepped back. 'Wrong party,' Leti said.

'Suit yourselves.' The door swung shut.

Leti turned to me. 'Shit!' she said. 'I saw. I saw.'

'Shit,' I whispered. 'It was him, wasn't it?'

'And he looked round at us when you said the name.'

Then the blue door to Morna's flat opened and her girlfriend Shelley leant out and said, 'Are yous lost?' A repetitive beat blared behind her.

'Nope.'

'Come back in then.'

'It's OK. We found our hats.' We stepped back, feet shuffling on the concrete floor.

She rolled her eyes. 'All right then. It's cold, I'm shutting this.'

'OK.'

'Have a good night.' The blue door closed, the music dulled. We were left alone in the stairwell, in the shivering light of the strip bulb.

When I heard that Nicky had died that first day, dizzy with flu, I didn't cry. Instead, a stillness came over me. The world had a muted quality, as if everything was covered in dust cloth. I talked to my mum and dad, I watched television, we ignored the phone ringing, I ate dry toast with the butter spread cold. In some way I believed that when the distancing, bleary sensations of my flu had lifted, this strange news would lift too. It would be gone and everything would be back to normal.

It was three days later, when I woke to clean, bright morning light streaming across the bedroom floor, my nostrils clear and throat no longer burning, that I knew it had really happened. The garden birds chattered near my window and the fluey cotton-wool feeling of being separated from the world was gone, and I understood in a different way. I got up and put my feet on the familiar bobbly carpet and suddenly I was sobbing and coughing and gasping for air. My mum brought me a glass of water and a square box of tissues and kissed my forehead. 'It's the unexpectedness of it,' she said. I got back into bed and slept for a long time and woke again feeling calm. I thought that the worst of it was dealt with; I'd been through the realisation of it, and come out the other side.

Nicky's funeral was held in the Catholic church, down in the dip of the valley, at the point where the river frothed highest. A little white square of a church with cheerful blue paint along the eaves. My black clothes, the cashmere top borrowed from my mother, the trousers newly bought from Fort William, hung itchy and heavy on my limbs. People had to stand at the back of the church because the place was so full. White lilies were packed into vases at the front, a multitude of them, seeming to multiply even as we sat there. I had never been to a funeral before. I had seen funerals take place often enough in one of the three sparsely attended churches in the village but only the cars outside, the people in black. I was at home, with a relative babysitting me, when my sister's funeral took place. It seemed impossible that all this was for Nicky.

It is hard to describe my relationship to him. I knew him from school, from living nearby, from his having lived with us for a brief time. But I could not say we were friends.

The PE teacher who'd taught the boys to climb arrived soon after us. I swivelled round to look at him until my mum elbowed my shoulder. As he passed us, he seemed to be wrestling for a blank expression. A scabby area of pink skin sat just below his ear and it looked as if he had been scratching at it. I felt a stab in the stomach for him, something I didn't want to feel, and I looked away. People were whispering about the accident not being his fault, which, if he heard them, probably made him feel worse.

I had not been inside a Catholic church before. To the right of us, a pink-cheeked Mary statue in a blue hood was affixed to the wall. The air had the same smell as the Church of Scotland kirk down the road where I attended school services, though the notes of dust and book mould were heightened. I knew the priest from the village. I'd once heard two teachers at the school joke about his female housekeeper, whether she wasn't an elderly mistress, whether he was into older women, and the kids said he was gay, something they said of every adult they didn't understand.

There was a soft sort of dizziness hanging over me. Robin, the boy who had been with Nicky when he died, was sitting three pews in front of us. He was in my year at school. I studied the back of his head, the shaved stubble on his neck, the trio of red spots near the curve of his shoulder. He sat stiff and slight between his sturdy parents. He had not been back to school yet. I wanted to catch him saying something, some whispered comment, but he remained silent.

Further up ahead, I could see Hailey, the girl Nicky had been dating. Some of the other girls at school called her cold because she had only taken two days off after the death. To be fair, she didn't seem to act any differently as she wandered the long corridors with her group of friends, like a swan sailing onwards. Now, she wore a black velvet dress and her long dark hair was brushed out smooth down her back so it shone in the buttery light of the church. Sometimes she turned to one of the girls next to her and I saw her sharp pretty features in profile. She was not crying as far as I could see.

The funeral began. When the coffin arrived at the door, the priest sprinkled it with holy water and I felt a downward pull, but also thought of how hungry I was, of the potato stew my mother had said she'd make that evening. I did not cry. There was a shadowy sensation brewing inside me somewhere in my ribcage, but when I tried to focus on it, it shifted and hid.

Once the service was over and we had made our way back out of the main doors, someone was standing on the other side of the church wall, over by the fence that ran along the back road. 'He should go home if he has any sense,' my dad said, and I looked again and saw that it was Mr Fletcher. He didn't go home, or come closer; he just stood still watching as people climbed into cars or began walking to the graveyard. I turned to see what Nicky's parents would do but they only wandered out onto the flat tarmac in front of the church, looking at a point on the ground ahead of them. Perhaps they had not seen him. It was hard to believe no one would say anything to Mr Fletcher but no one did. My parents and I began heading up the road towards our house, in the opposite direction. I took one more look back at the chemistry teacher. He was just standing there, loose jacket flapping in the breeze, looking like a scarecrow. Something sad must have happened in his life, to make him drive into the village drunk. Even at my age I understood that.

We did not go to the burial. My parents said it was only for close family, though I learned later several schoolmates had gone. When we got home I changed out of my black clothes immediately and kicked them under my bed where they lay like discarded snake-skins. The day became ordinary again with the kettle boiling and the radio chattering and the dog wagging round our feet but all the time I had a dim awareness of holding something back, of not looking at something. At dinner both my parents were red-eyed. I pretended I'd not noticed as I ate my hot mouthfuls of potato.

Two weeks after Nicky's funeral, I visited the graveyard with Leti. The new cemetery lay in a dip at the foot of the mountain, behind a row of shabby farm buildings. You could not see the graves from the road. A large black and white pig watched our arrival. We had planned to put picked flowers on the grave, something we'd discussed together with a sense of our own seriousness and adultness.

But when we actually found the gravestone what I felt was an absolute and complete repugnance. Standing there in front of Nicky's grave, that two-foot-wide, freshly dug patch of dirt containing the body of a boy I had known, the new turf clearly demarcated from the old grass, it seemed I was going to fall through the earth and keep falling.

Leti bobbed forward and put her daffodils on the cut turf and bowed her head. I made the same movement and placed my flowers – a mix of daffodils and flopping crocuses past their best. They lay there flat, their stems tied together with white string. The emptiness of what we were doing bore into me, putting soon-to-rot flowers on that blind strip of earth. It was as if what I thought of as reality had been ripped and I was looking through it onto the actual world underneath and it was empty and dank.

'Should we say a prayer or something?' Leti asked. The birds were trilling and chirruping behind us.

'OK,' I said. The mountain rose up into the sky to our left. Today it was lit with shifting patches of sun, giving it an otherworldly appearance. I still felt that it had taken him, because he had gone there to climb and he hadn't come back home. I understood why mountains were sometimes thought of as gods; it seemed to watch us, perhaps to dimly judge. Looking back at the ground, I noticed now there were dips in the earth, what looked like shallow trenches between the newer graves so that the graves themselves stood out. It felt like the bodies were directly underneath those mossy lumps, as if I could sense them, un-coffined, only millimetres under the blades of grass, though I knew that was not the case.

Leti spoke. 'Dear God, please take care of Nicky in heaven. Please help his family. I don't know what else to say. Amen.'

'Amen.' The grave nearest Nicky was Mrs Henderson's, an elderly lady who had died a year or so back. Her name and dates were written on a black marble heart in gold lettering. The writing only covered the left half of the heart. I guessed the other half of the heart, the blank half, was for Mr Henderson,

44

whenever he died. I didn't like that, half an empty gravestone waiting to be filled.

'It's cold,' I said. 'Let's go.'

'All right.' From behind us there was a low grunt. I jumped. Leti started laughing and I wanted to thump her. It was the black and white pig in the far field. My shoulders contracted to my neck involuntarily.

As we wandered back along the track, someone was burning leaves and other damp vegetation on the farm land. We passed a low, smoky fire, which my mind transformed into a funeral pyre. An insistent hammering came from the new farm building, a man was working on the roof. We cut across the bridge over the river to reach Leti's house.

In her bedroom, we watched a stand-up comedy video, something we'd taken to doing a lot now that she had her own small television set. We laughed but a numbness was spreading across my face, down into my neck. The comedian's forehead shone with sweat. The audience laughter bubbled and rose. Nicky was shut in a grave at the foot of the mountain. We were watching television, and Nicky was in his grave. Leti turned to me and said, 'You're not watching it.'

'I am,' I said, facing forward, my eyes towards the screen.

'You know what I mean,' she said.

'I don't.'

'You're not paying attention. Are you freaked out about the graveyard?'

'No,' I said.

'If you are then you are.'

'I'm not. I'm just tired.'

'You shouldn't let it bother you. He's not there, it's just his body, not his soul.'

45

'What if it's all of him? Doesn't it bother you, the thought of lying in the ground forever?'

'No. Either there's a heaven or there isn't and then there's nothing so there's nothing to be scared of.'

'Nothing is one of the worst things I can think of.'

'You are freaking out.'

'I'm not. I'm just tired. I think I'm going home,' I said and I gathered up my wool hat and gloves and left without saying anything more.

In my flat one evening, a few days after Morna's party, I was half-heartedly wiping dust from the skirting boards when a small piece of the wood crumbled away. Underneath it a few daubs of paint seemed to form an image. I knelt down. The daubs coalesced into a simple black outline of an animal with a large yellow eye, almost like the kind of illustration you see on the edges of medieval manuscripts. It looked like a fox or perhaps some kind of wild cat. I stared at it. I could just about make out a couple of faint stripes on its back. It could nearly have been my Tasmanian tiger from the school lessons on extinction. Perhaps the last person who lived in the flat had painted it, or the person before them. It was like a small gift that someone had left to me. I put the splintered piece of wood in the kitchen drawer, feeling uncomfortable about throwing it out in case I wanted to glue it back. I liked my creature, my little tiger. It was a rented flat, but I thought of it as mine for as long as I paid for it and so the tiger was mine for now.

The weekend after the party, I set out to a performance of Twelfth Night. It was a second date. I'd met the guy online and we'd got along well on a first meet-up at my local pub so I'd booked the tickets for the play. He was training to be a vet after quitting a financial job he'd hated. He had a slim build with a long straight nose, no hair, and an easy smile. I was slightly concerned that a play was too intimate an experience when we hardly knew each other but I'd seen a review of the production that had made me curious. I'd mentioned it to him and he'd sounded enthusiastic. On the way in, as we were squeezing through the lobby under the glow of the oversized chandelier, I had a light feeling, as if something had been lifted off me. We were laughing about a television show we'd both seen the night before. Just then, I noticed a dark head in front of us in the crowd. A denim jacket and dark hair. I craned my neck to see. The tick of my pulse started up. But the face turned to the side and it was someone completely different, a woman actually, with a short, choppy haircut. I'd missed the last thing my date had said but I laughed along because he was laughing.

As we filtered our way in to the auditorium and settled into the red velvet seats, I found my eyes flicking over the gathering audience. People chatted in groups and shuffled past each other with drinks and small tubs of sweets. The expectation continued to buzz in my mind, that I was about to see the man who looked like Nicky, even though I had no reason to suppose he was in the crowd.

My date and I talked for a bit about the worst shows we'd been to. He told me about an ill-judged improv gig with an audience of five that seemed to last for days. I had just begun a similar story of my own when the lights dimmed and I made a face and fell silent.

The curtain drew up. The sound design used deep, rumbling music at key moments. The production was aiming for a darkness that I hadn't expected. I had an odd sensation of floating in my padded seat as if the chair had risen off the floor. For minutes at a time I forgot I had someone else beside me. During scene changes the speakers blurted out whale noises and jangling underwater sound effects. Blue, rippling lights moved over the stage and the audience. I felt disorientated and had an urge to get up out of my row, out of the darkness, to be somewhere bright and normal.

In the interval, I turned to my date. 'Are you enjoying it?'

'Sure.'

'It's quite good, isn't it? The whale noise is bit much though,' I said.

I rose to go to the toilet. As I waited in the line packed tight next to the bar queue, my eye was drawn again to a sudden flash of a dark head over by the main doors. I froze, focused. But as the shoulders turned I saw it was an older man with weather-beaten cheeks.

Once I had made my way back to my seat, I smiled and slid into place next to my date. He started telling me about a trip he'd been on to Chile but one of the actors walked on stage and began sweeping the boards with a broom and the crowd fell silent. The theatre darkened and the next act began. Every time the low music played, the fibres of my nerves seemed to vibrate. I kept tuning out of the words themselves and lost track of where we were in the plot, missing great chunks of dialogue. My date slid his hand onto my fingers and I moved my arm away absent-mindedly and then froze with embarrassment. I hadn't wanted to reject him but somehow I couldn't bring myself to reach for him now.

When the lights came up he forced a smile and we walked out together, not saying much over the chatter of the exiting crowd. Once we were outside, he said he was going to head home because he had an early start. We made vague promises to message each other but I didn't think that would happen.

As I walked home under dull streetlamps, someone cycled past in an anorak and luminous armbands. An older man with wild grey hair who splashed through a puddle and soaked me.

I don't think he even noticed, and I was almost amused, as if it was a final, absurd touch being added to the night by the universe. The man reminded me of Mr Fletcher, something about the rigid way he rode his bike and his fly-away grey hair. I turned down my own dark street as the puddles shimmered with light, and I thought about the chemistry teacher, about high-school days.

~*~

A few weeks after Nicky's death, a condolences book was set up in the high-school library for Nicky's parents. A red leather-bound volume like a family photo album with Nicky's name embossed in golden print on the front of it. I climbed the metal steps to the library to sign the book during my free study period. It was placed open on a table around a corner in the quiet reading area behind the science bookshelf. I crept in and stood looking over the pages. On the far side of the shelves, I could hear voices. I knew that Mrs Andersen, the librarian, and the head teacher, Mrs Richardson, had not heard me come in because they continued their conversation.

'Gregory apparently went down there and tried to get Paul to speak to him.' I pictured Nicky's dad standing in the front garden of the chemistry teacher's house.

'God, what happened?'

'He went all round the place, banging on the windows. Jill saw the whole thing from her car. He was shouting for him to come out. Paul had all the lights off, hiding in there. Or, I suppose, he wasn't in.'

'He must be losing his mind.'

'Who?'

'Well, both of them.'

'Paul will probably go to prison.'

'No one ever goes to prison.'

'Yes, well, maybe. But people do, don't they? For things like this.'

I stared at the entries in the book, the varieties of handwriting, narrow scrawls or looped, babyish letters, and listened intently, imagining my ears were turning and pricking like a doe's. The library windows looked out onto the brown-brackened foothills of the mountain. In its dun, spring cladding it appeared ordinary, almost drab. The lush greens would not come for another month or so.

'It's a nightmare,' said Mrs Andersen. The way she said it implied it was not her nightmare but a lurid dream someone else was describing to her.

I picked up the pen but I couldn't think what to write. Seeing his name so many times twisted something in my stomach. I wrote *sorry for your loss*, like a hundred other people, and signed underneath. I couldn't imagine his parents being happy to receive this book. There was something about the absolute bleakness of it, the kind of thing you could only be given if your child had died. A few of the girls from his year had written long messages in tightly packed writing. I could find no message from Robin, or from Hailey. A few pages back I saw Leti had written, '*with deepest condolences*' and I felt satisfied that it was no better than what I'd written. She had put a kiss after her name but I didn't feel like I could do that, as if his parents were friends of mine.

The conversation round the corner had faded out. The two women must have heard the faint crackle of the pages turning because the headteacher suddenly walked round the side of the bookshelf and said calmly, 'That's nice of you, Emily.'

'I didn't know what to write.'

'No one does with these things. I'm sure whatever you've written is fine.' She smoothed her hands over her cheeks. 'God, it's miserable.'

'It is,' I said. Occasionally the teachers fell into talking to us as if we were real people. I closed the book so my message wasn't the first one anyone would see. The bell rang for break.

In the playground, a group of kids were gathered near Robin, their coloured jackets forming a semi-circle. It was his first week back since the accident. His face flamed red under his red hair. Leti stood at the edge of the group and I shuffled into a space next to her. In a solemn speech from the deputy head we'd been told not to ask Robin about the accident, to wait until he chose to speak. But of course, some of the kids had asked about it from the moment they saw him.

'Fucksake, already told you,' he was saying in a low voice as I arrived, 'I went to get the ambulance. That's it.' His hands were thrust deep into his pockets.

Suzanne, one of the girls in my year, said, 'Yeah but was he already dead then?'

A boy called Cameron said, 'Jesus Christ, Suzanne.'

'What?' Her round fish eyes flashing.

'You can't ask that.'

'I don't know,' Robin said. Leti and I glanced at each other silently. Robin was gazing straight ahead to where a seagull chased a chip carton caught in the breeze. 'I don't know. Maybe he was.' Robin wore a small, silver cross on a chain. His hand moved from his pocket now and he held onto it lightly, two fingers curling around it.

'He doesn't want to talk about it everyone,' Suzanne said in a loud, mock-serious voice.

'Jesus Christ Suzanne.'

'What?' Suzanne let her mouth fall into a pretend *oh* of surprise.

'It's fine, I don't care,' Robin said.

'Did you cry?' Suzanne said. *You are so stupid*, I thought. *Why don't you just shut up, you stupid, stupid bitch?* Rain began to spit down and the group of us shuffled under the roof of the science block, like pigeons huddling together. The nearest classroom was chemistry. Inside the scuzzy lights were on and a substitute teacher was taking bunsen burners out of a box, unwinding their rubber tubing.

'No. I went to get the ambulance.'

'Why didn't you come back to school?'

'I would have but they told me not to.'

'Why though?'

'I don't know.' As they were talking, I found I was clenching my teeth, locking my molars into each other. But I also had that slightly cut-off, behind-glass feeling, as if I was watching the conversation through a one-way mirror.

'Is it cos you were depressed, Robin red breast?' Suzanne said.

'They just told me not to come back straight away.' The puddles around us began to jump with the rain and the corrugated iron overhang of the science-block roof started to rattle.

'Did you see him get hit?'

'For fuck's sake, just shut up,' Cameron said.

'No,' Robin said. 'I didn't see it. I was looking the other way.' Later, I'd learn he wasn't sure whether he'd seen it happen or not. There'd been the blur of tree branches and the tarmac and a thud and maybe the screeching of brakes and maybe he had seen Nicky crumple down and away and maybe he hadn't.

~*~

53

Robin and I hardly knew each other when Nicky died but some time after that day in the playground, we gradually, cautiously became friends. I sought him out really. I'd felt sorry for him, seeing him surrounded by the others, an object of curiosity, angry and harassed. After our initial awkwardness had shifted, I found I could talk to him in a way I hadn't talked to any boy before. It wasn't that the awkwardness went away altogether, but it thawed enough for us to realise we had things to say to each other.

We started to talk about what we believed. What was possible in the world and what was not: ghosts, gods, miracles. 'I've always been kind of into supernatural stuff,' Robin told me one day early on, which was something that fascinated me too at the time. He knew a lot about Catholic saints. A picture of him in a white suit with a pudding bowl haircut sat on the kitchen mantelpiece in the farmhouse and when I'd asked him what it was, he'd mumbled, 'My confirmation day,' with a mix of pride and embarrassment. His patron saint was St Andrew.

'St Andrew was supposed to have brought a woman back from the dead,' Robin said to me one day after school. We were walking by the river in the bands of light between the trees.

'You don't believe in that kind of thing?'

'No, but you know there's lots of stories of it. I don't know.'

'It's impossible,' I said.

'Yeah, I know. Why impossible though? I mean, you can resuscitate people. They can be dead for a time and come back.'

'But after a point they're just gone.'

'Why though?' At that age, I couldn't answer him, I didn't know about irreversible cell damage, oxygen starvation; I couldn't put into words why it seemed certain a person could not come back.

'You don't believe in miracles though?' I said, whacking at the riverside grasses with a stick.

54

'Well, I'm supposed to and that. Do you?'

'No. Not miracles exactly. Well, I'm not sure,' I said.

We carried on walking until we split up to go to our separate houses. I watched Robin make his way on up to the farm. His sloped shoulders and his gangly frame. There was no romance in it but the romance of friendship, of gradually finding out more about another person, of them learning things about you.

Around two weeks after the theatre date, I did hear from the trainee vet again. Arriving at the office on a Friday morning, my phone blinked with a message from him saying he was going to a gig that night and would I like to come? I felt a little glimmer of something, maybe just pride that he wanted to see me again. In my lunch break, I sat in the car and looked up the band. I played a short clip of their clashing music, a video from a live gig showing their eager faces shining with effort in a small, boxy club space. I didn't really like the music, it didn't have enough melody for me. A heave of tiredness came over me at the thought of going out that night and being in the hot, frantic atmosphere of a club. I sent a short message turning the gig down but saying that I'd love to meet up with him again.

OK no worries, came the reply as I still held the phone in my hand. For a brief moment I pictured him somewhere, probably in one of his veterinary school classes, his lit phone in his palm like mine, a slight frown on his face. I put my phone away, gathered up my work things and headed off to my first client of the day.

The thought of the message stayed with me though. When I parked up at lunchtime, I texted him again and suggested we go out to an Italian restaurant I liked at the weekend. No message came back, though I could see he had read mine.

My second last client that day was Jim. I stood outside his building and rang the buzzer. There was a cool wind blowing, whipping round the corner of the block so that I tucked my hands into my sleeves as I waited. Finally, Jim's voice came on the intercom, cheerful enough.

'Come on up, Em.' He'd never called me Em before; it was a nickname that annoyed me.

I climbed the stairs and Jim already had the door open for me at the top. 'Hello, how's you?' he said.

'Not bad. How are you?'

'Not great.' He was grinning tightly.

I stepped inside and he closed the door behind us. We made our way to the kitchen. 'So how are things? Is the music still a problem?'

He winced, and for a moment I could see the boy in his fifty-year-old face, puzzled and overwhelmed. 'It's weird, it seems like it's coming from underneath now. A different flat. But the same music. Thump, thump, thump.'

I watched his hands as he filled the kettle. There were grey marks on his fingers I'd not noticed before. I wasn't sure if they were faded tattoos or fresh pen marks. He'd been a joiner, before he got ill. We were not encouraged to open up past stories, but he had talked to me about that work sometimes. How he'd loved it and been exhausted by it, bored and elated. How a finished project gave him a feeling of peace. *It would fill a hole in my head, if you know what I mean.*

'Do you want to do anything about it? With the floor below?'

'Not just now. But it would be a bugger if they stopped it upstairs and someone else started doing it.' I nodded. As I was talking to him now, I became aware of a pressure behind my eyes. I rubbed my forehead. Maybe I was getting a bug of some kind.

'Well, if someone else is doing it, try to get a recording,' I said.

'You think I'm going nuts.'

'I don't. It's just we need to have—'

'Yeah, yeah, I know. But the thing is I am going fucking nuts.' He pulled the teabags out of our mugs and dumped them in the flip-top bin, trailing thin brown rivulets onto the lid.

'It's been rough lately?'

'I feel like I'm sinking into a bog.' He carried his cup into the living room, sat back down and pressed two fingers to his eyes, as if there was a pressure there too.

'Are you feeling suicidal again?'

'I said the wrong catchphrase, didn't I?'

'Are you though?'

'No. It's more like I'm winding down, like one of those jump-rope rabbits. I don't want to kill myself. And if I was going to I wouldn't tell you because I don't want all that palaver ending up at my door again. Police and ambulances and they do nothing for you.'

My throat tightened a millimetre. 'Well, you know that worries me when you say that because then how do I know you're not just pretending not to be suicidal?'

'Good point. But honestly, honestly I'm not. I think you'd know if I was lying.' He looked at me with eyebrows raised, almost playful.

We talked for a while longer. Under his bravado I could sense him slipping and, as I often did in these circumstances, I had both a desire to help and a desire to detach, to escape the choppy water of his life.

I left with a heavy grey sensation but I didn't believe that he was in any immediate danger of making a suicide attempt. I called in a report of what he'd said anyway, phoning my manager about it from the car before driving away.

Tony, my last client of the day, lived on the third storey of an old sandstone tenement block like mine. I waited outside his door on the small landing. The space was bare except for a loft hatch up above me. He sometimes took a while to get to the door and, as I was waiting, I found I pictured Nicky beside me. The boy I'd known, standing in jeans and a dark jacket, half leaning against the wall. He just slid into my mind. I could almost see him there, though I couldn't get his face exactly clear. I almost mouthed, *What are you doing here?*, when Tony's door opened and he smiled at me through the gap and I blinked the image away.

Tony liked to wear an eye patch like a pirate. He had a mild learning disability and had been referred to us after a psychiatric hospital stay. He had trouble with his concentration and often got confused about money and bills. His jet-black cat Penny, who he had adopted from a rescue centre, strutted and purred around my feet as I stepped into his hallway. I sat down on his compact couch and opened my folder as I sank into the springless base.

'How have you been?' I said.

'All right. She's good, isn't she?' He stroked the cat.

'She is,' I said.

'You had a dog when you were wee, didn't you?' It was one of the habits of his conversation that he repeated questions he knew the answer to. He had quite a good memory so it was more about reassuring himself that the facts were still in their places.

'That's right,' I said. 'How's your computer class going?' He was signed up for a technology class aimed at people with learning disabilities.

'Your parents have a dog now but you don't.'

'Correct,' I said. 'How about your class?'

He nodded. 'It's going OK. People are nice. Are you going to get yourself a dog?'

'Not right now.'

'Or a cat?'

'Not just now. But we're not really here to talk about me, are we?'

'You should get one. You'll be lonely without a pet.'

'Maybe we can have a look at what we need to cover from your file.' I tapped at the plastic folder. His cat rubbed herself against my shin again and I let my fingers rub along her back. Her eyes were so green they almost glowed.

'You'll be lonely,' he murmured again as I started leafing through his paperwork.

Leaving his flat half an hour later, I thought of the farm cats that lived in the barn next to Robin's house. At one time there had been a jet-black trio, all sisters. And then I thought of Oscar, the feral cat Leti and I had fed, the one who used to live in the abandoned house up by the pine wood.

~*~

We had a kind of den for a while, Leti and I. By the ramshackle look of the building, you might imagine it had been abandoned in the nineteenth century but the woman the house belonged to had died only a few years before I was born. Her children, living down south, hadn't taken it over, but they hadn't sold it either, and gradually the elements had crept in like vandals. The two front windows were gone. Ivy had eased itself into cracks in the mortar. When I was little, we used to pass by it often on family walks. My mum would joke about people living there, saying, 'They've got no windows, they'll be cold,' every time we passed, which always made a pricking sensation start up my spine, as if there was someone watching from the empty windows of the house. As if they really were cold, waiting there in the damp, with the things that must grow and live in an abandoned building.

One afternoon, when we would have been about eleven, Leti and I arrived to find the cracked old door was completely off the hinges. It had not been like that before.

'Want to go in?' Leti said.

'I dare you to go in,' I said.

'You first.'

'I dared you first.' And so she waded towards the door over the tangle of wild grass and bramble stems, which tore at our jeans and formed half-loops that caught our feet. She carefully sidled through the doorway and I followed her. The first room we entered was the old kitchen. All the appliances were still there, the brown oven and the cream fridge and the large horizontal cabinet freezer. A thick black mildew climbed up the walls above the cabinets in repeating fan shapes.

'Cool,' I said, though I was disgusted by the stains, feeling somehow as if they would touch me or I would be unable to stop myself from touching them. I stepped through to the living room, crunching over dead leaves and God knows what. It was bare of furniture, even the carpet and underlay were taken up, leaving nothing but grey mulch-strewn concrete. Leti cut ahead of me and into a corridor. I followed her along the dank space and on to a bedroom. The furniture here was gone too. At the end of the corridor next to the bedroom there was a bathroom with a salmon-coloured suite of sink, toilet and bath. The tub was marked brown near the plughole and contained a small amount of peaty water. It made my skin creep and I felt oddly guilty for the creeping sensation because this had been someone's home. Perhaps the woman who'd lived here had been happy in this room, sitting in bubble baths reading magazines, or playing with her children. Still the creeping continued.

Over the next few weeks, the place became our hideout. At the time we didn't tell anyone else about it. Leti and I got on fairly well with most of the other kids at our school but we were never so close to anyone else and, to begin with, there was no one else we wanted in our den. With each visit in the first few weeks, we were nervous in case there were signs of other intruders, drink cans or cigarettes, like the markings of an unknown animal. But as the weeks passed, we relaxed. After a while we left two old folding chairs there and we'd bring sweets and sugary drinks. We started to leave food out for the feral cat who appeared behind the house. He was thin and striped and he moved with a considered caution. We'd buy canned cat food for him and put it in a breakfast bowl borrowed from my house. Sometimes we'd play games in the house; sometimes we'd just talk.

One evening as the light was fading from the sky, Leti said, 'What would you do if you fancied someone and you knew they didn't fancy you back?'

'How would you know they didn't?' I said. We were sat in our deck chairs with gnarled leaves crunching under our trainers.

'Say you just knew.'

'Well, there's nothing you can do then.'

'Wouldn't you tell them anyway?'

'Not if I knew they weren't interested.'

Her look was hard for a second. I didn't know who she was talking about, though I understood it was not just an idle question. My mind ran through all the boys in our year, but I was shy of asking her outright and she never offered the name.

We called the cat Oscar after Oscar the Grouch. He never let us touch him but we tried to get as near as we could, holding limp pieces of ham in our fingertips, whispering his name which he did not know. This was around the time Leti started with her art. Often, she would sit and draw in pencil on a wide watercolour notepad, looking out of one of the wind-smashed windows on to the network of tree branches that surrounded the house. Frequently I felt annoyed, like she entered a special world with her drawing and even though she was beside me I could not completely reach her. I tried not to show my frustration, pretending I was busy with something of my own, playing with a deck of cards or scribbling notes onto paper.

The basement room was full and heaving like a lung. There was a band playing electro-swing music, violins mixed in with guitars and an electric keyboard. I hadn't been out dancing in a long time, almost a year. Though I could rarely be bothered now, I realised I had missed the freedom of it. I'd arrived with Leti, her friend Morna and Morna's girlfriend Shelley, a few hours ago. We danced and kept dancing and I became hot and tired, but tired in that way that makes you want to keep going, because the tiredness itself is pleasurable. At about half one in the morning, I pushed my way through to the bar to get an orange juice to cool my throat, and as I looked over the crowd, a tiny shudder went through my body before I registered why. There he was. There was the man again. It was really him this time. I saw him from the side, standing in the bar queue and I knew him instantly.

He was separated from me by two rows of people, in a parallel queue. The space of the club was filled with dry ice so that it looked as if we were standing in a rising mist on a moor. There was that clicking feeling again. And yet the place was so familiar, years back we would go there often; I knew the old sticky floors and had memorised half the graffiti in the toilets, it didn't feel possible anything incredible could happen there. I was slightly drunk and so I elbowed towards his place in the queue. Once beside him, I watched my hand reach out and touch the pale-blue fabric of his shirtsleeve. He looked round at me, frowning in mild surprise. Shouting over the music, I said, 'You know who you look like?'

'What did you say?' The shock of being so near him washed over me and away, and with the drink and the music it all seemed almost funny, like a game.

'You know who you look like?' I yelled.

'Who do I look like?' He smiled in an irritated way now, like he thought I was flirting and he didn't fancy me and didn't have the energy to pretend he did.

'You look like someone I knew from high school.'

'Could be I am someone you knew from high school.' His accent again was hard to place. There was an American or even Canadian cadence mixed up with the occasional slight Scottish intonation. His eyes found their way to mine now.

'Well you can't be because that person is dead.' The music quietened down to a break between tracks. I had expected him to look fazed but he just nodded.

'Could be I've come back from the dead.'

'Like Jesus?'

'Or Dracula,' he said. He had reached the front of the queue. The woman on the bar took his order. For a moment, as he turned his head towards her, he looked beautiful. I hadn't properly noticed it the other times I'd seen him; he was beautiful, and in the moment of noticing I also felt a repulsion, in the literal sense of being pushed away.

'Dracula didn't come back from the dead. He was undead.' I was saying all this haphazardly, like it was a joke, blotting away the darkness that surrounded the real memories.

'Similar thing,' he said. 'Maybe that's me, maybe I'm undead.' He leant his arm on the bar, trailing his sleeve in a wet patch without seeming to notice. 'Maybe I found my way back.'

Though surely he was joking, cold dots ran up the back of my neck.

The bar woman started placing drinks in front of him. He focused on her as she scooped ice into a final glass and I didn't think he'd say more but after he had paid and the woman had tipped silver change into his palm, he turned to me and said, 'Maybe I found my way back to life.' My smile must have faded because his did too. He gave me a serious, or mock-serious look. 'Maybe you did know me and maybe I died and I'm back now.'

That feeling of recognition was so intense. The set of his eyes and his nose and his cheekbones. 'I know you,' I said.

'You've told me that already.'

'But you look so much like him.'

'Must be him then.'

The fuzzy heat of the club seemed to swirl over my skin. 'Nicky Harper?' I said.

'Sure, why not?'

'You're joking?' I said.

He looked at me, lips parted slightly, then said, 'Maybe I know you. Did you live down the road?'

'Are you joking?'

He smiled. The clashing of drums had started again. He picked his drinks up in a clump, squeezing the middle glass between the outer ones, and returned to his friends. The crowd closed up between us. I headed back to my group. Leti was away at the toilets. 'What's in that?' Shelley said, pointing to my glass.

'Orange juice.'

'Rock and roll.'

Morna leant over to me and said, 'Do you know Nicholas then?'

I stood still. 'Who?' I said.

'Nicholas, that guy you were talking to.'

'That's his name?' The beams of light casting out from the stage seemed to enlarge then shrink the room.

'That's his name. Do you know him?'

'No, not really, he just, he looks so like someone. Someone from school. How do you know him?'

'I work with him,' she said.

'You work with him?'

'I do. Why were you talking to him?'

I raised my voice over the music, trying not to spit on her. 'I just thought I recognised him.'

'Were you chatting him up?'

'No.' I couldn't at that moment remember what Morna did these days. I tried to call it to mind. My head felt cloudy, as if the dry ice had sifted into it.

Leti emerged from the crowd beside us. I caught her wrist and said, 'That guy who looks like Nicky is here.'

'It's like he's following us,' she said.

'Or we're following him.'

'Where is he now?' I looked around but I didn't see him or the people he was with. The place was still crowded and there was another floor upstairs that he could have moved to.

'I want you to see him too so you know I'm not going mad.'

'I saw him the last time.'

'Yes but each time I think I must be going nuts.'

'OK let's look for him,' she said. We broke off from the others and burrowed our way through the crowd, getting elbowed and shouldered, occasionally spattered with droplets from plastic beer glasses like fine, sticky rain. We tried upstairs. The second floor was hung with paper lanterns and largely deserted, except for a few drunk couples dancing lopsidedly as if they were on a ship sailing in rough weather. Circles of light floated over our faces. Leti took my arm and said, 'Let's leave it.'

We headed back downstairs. Now we couldn't find Morna and the others. I was feeling suddenly too hot, and also more drunk than I should be, given how much I'd had. 'Want to get some air for a sec?' I said. We squeezed our way out of the main door and into the cool April air. Outside, we leant against a brick wall a few metres away from the smokers.

'Look at the stars,' I said. We both gazed up. It was a clear night in the city. More stars appeared the more we looked. Pin holes in a dark sheet.

'Is that a planet?'

'I don't know, could be.'

After a while, we saw three guys heading out, piling into a taxi. I grabbed the lace shoulder of Leti's dress. 'It's him,' I said. He was the last of them. They were three flesh-and-blood men, all slightly drunk, in shirts and jeans and dark leather shoes. Unconsciously, I started to pull Leti forward.

'Get off,' she said, tugging her dress from my hand. At that moment he turned, gave a one-handed salute.

'Goodbye, Em,' he called. *Goodbye* and an extra little syllable, bouncing into the night. The taxi door rolled shut. The car drove away.

Leti stepped out from the wall, straightening her dress. 'Well that was definitely the guy from before,' she said.

'He said my name, I didn't tell him my name.'

'Did he say your name?'

'Yes, he said *Goodbye Em.*'

'Nobody calls you Em. You hate being called that.'

'That's not the point.'

'You must have told him your name,' Leti said, taking another step back towards the door.

'I didn't. I'm sure I didn't. And you saw him, again, how he looks?'

'It is weird, I'll give you that. He does look like Nicky. I do have this weird feeling, almost like . . . the same atmosphere as when Nicky was around. But obviously it can't be.'

'How did he know my name?' I said again.

'I don't know. Maybe he said something else. Maybe you told him. That's probably enough of this now, let's go inside, it's getting cold.'

We headed back in to the warmth of the club, it took us a while to find the others between the shifting bodies, and when we did, they were leaving so we headed off too, deciding to walk back, as we were only a few streets from my flat.

When I arrived home I was hungry. I heated up a pot of instant porridge and ate so rapidly I burned my tongue. I thought about what the man had said. That I *lived down the road*. Was that just a random guess, based on the assumption that I'd lived nearby? But I had lived literally down the road from Nicky. As I was putting the porridge packet in the bin, I dropped my spoon. I knelt down to get it and as I did I noticed a tiny mark on the wood surface underneath the kitchen cupboards. I peered more closely. It was another painting. But this time it wasn't a tiger. It was a pigeon. A grey-coloured pigeon painted with pink dots for feet. A passenger pigeon maybe, I thought; an extinct animal. It had one black bead eye. The closer I looked, the more it lost its detail and became a very simple series of paint marks. A daubing that could be any kind of bird. The tail was just a single brush-stroke.

That night I dreamt I'd woken in my own bed, and at the end of the mattress, there was a dodo, just looking at me. It tilted its head, its alien-grey eyes blinking. Taking a few steps around the bed, it opened and closed its implausible beak. I woke up soon afterwards, the room still pitch dark.

When I was a student, I'd started to become plagued by extinct animal dreams. They began abruptly and tended to involve the creatures walking through the walls of my bedroom. They might have been set off by the environmental protests I was going on at the time, the protests about climate change, about animal and plant extinctions. I dreamt of dodos, great auks, passenger pigeons, quaggas, Tasmanian tigers. All the creatures from those school lessons years ago. The animals would look at me with dark eyes, pace round the toe of the bed and then vanish through the far wall. Sometimes I'd try to reach out and catch them. On rare occasions I'd attempt to follow them through the wall and find that I couldn't. Other times I was afraid of the animals, so that I'd wake clutching the quilt, knowing it had been a dream but not moving for a while, in case something wild and uninvited was still in the room. The dreams had stopped after I dropped out of university. Now here they were, back visiting me again.

The next Monday, after I'd returned from work, another little arrow from the past arrived. An email from Robin. Seeing his full name in the address line made me utter a soft, startled noise alone in my flat. Though Robin and I had become friends after Nicky died, the friendship had faded out in our later years of high school so over time we became no more than passing acquaintances. There was no harshness between us, just a gap. I had hardly spoken to him in the years since. The last time I'd bumped into him had been at bonfire night in the village two years ago, when I'd said hello almost shyly as he passed by carrying a couple of mulled ciders. He'd nodded and smiled at me through the smoke and disappeared into the crowd. Hearing from him now, I had a sense of the past opening up like a nesting doll. I clicked to open the message.

Hi Emily,
Is this still your address? It's been ages. How are you? Hope you and yours are doing OK. I'm in Edinburgh these days, think you are too . . . Would you like to get a coffee sometime? Not a problem if you're busy.
Robin

I wrote back to him, and as I typed, I found it became a long email; I found myself talking about the past, mentioning Nicky and Mr Fletcher, explaining things that had happened in my life. I read it back out loud then I deleted it all and wrote a few breezy lines, saying I was well, and yes it would be nice to go for a coffee. The days passed over the next week and I did not hear back.

After the moment at the nightclub, it took me a while to ask Leti which company Morna worked for. I was worried she thought I was reading too much into the encounter with this man. I asked her on a sweet-scented evening at the end of April when we were heading back home from a film.

'Why do you want to know?'

'She's told me twice before, I can never remember. I don't want to seem like I haven't listened to her.'

'You haven't listened though.'

'Yes, well . . .'

Her eyes widened. 'You're going to look up that guy, aren't you?'

'Ah, maybe. To be honest, I'm curious.'

'It is odd, I can't deny that.'

'But also I just feel bad not remembering.'

'Honestly, don't go chasing this guy.'

'I'm not insane. I'm just curious.'

She told me the name of the company, a law firm. When I arrived home, I searched for their website. The brightness had stayed in the sky, speckles of evening light pushed through the blinds and lay on the computer screen. His employer was a large Scottish property law firm, with three branches in three cities. There was a separate page about the staff. I clicked on it and scrolled through rows of photos. There was Morna, in a black suit coat, looking absurdly formal as she never did whenever I met her. She worked in their admin department. I scrolled further. Down on the right near the bottom of the page, it was him. I stared at his face. *Nicholas Blackburn*, it said next to his picture. He was a property lawyer. He was wearing a white shirt and blue tie, smiling toothily. It was definitely the man I'd been seeing, and yet I didn't have that clicking-into-place sensation, that hard knowing. There was a kind of blankness to the image. I put my finger up to the screen, actually touched his face. It was him, but the resemblance to Nicky wasn't obvious.

Perhaps the sense of knowing I'd felt in person had come from seeing his face in three dimensions, seeing him move, seeing the shape of his nose and chin in the round, not flattened on a screen. I tried looking away from the picture and then looking back suddenly, almost taking the image by surprise, but I still didn't get the click. There were no individual email addresses for the staff, but there was a branch email. If I wanted to contact him I could presumably address something for his attention. But it would have to be something plausibly business-like. Instead I copied the link into a blank email. *What do you think?* I wrote and sent it on to Leti.

Outside, a loud group of men clattered past my window, probably on the way to the pub. I liked the fact that my window was so near to the street, but people couldn't see me in any detail through the frosted glass. It gave me a feeling of being a kind of ghost, watching without being watched. I sat up with my browser open for a while, flicking aimlessly from one thing to another.

The next day at work, I was in the office for the morning and I kept clicking onto the property law firm website, studying the picture. The shape of the nose, the height of the forehead, the line of the lips. It was like a magic eye puzzle, like I was trying to see something in or beyond the photo. One of my colleagues, Julie, saw me looking and leant on the corner of my desk.

'Are you planning on buying your own place then?'

A little of her tea dripped near my keyboard. I almost told her the truth but instead I said, 'Yeah, I've been thinking about it.' So we began a slightly absurd conversation about flat prices and the merits of different areas until the phone rang and I lurched to answer it.

I made a little progress with Jim's noise problem. A council worker got back to me to say they'd had a discussion with the people living above him and they had agreed to cut down on the music. I rang Jim to tell him but the line was so blurry I couldn't make him out. Eventually I had to apologise and hang up. It was slightly eerie, his voice coming to me as if from underwater, but his tone sounded upbeat at least. My manager had spoken to his doctor since I'd flagged up the risk of suicide and had decided he was safe enough, so I wasn't worried about him generally.

In the afternoon, I drove out to visit Megan, the teenage girl. The first thing she told me was that she had split up with her boyfriend. She sat on her bed, swinging her legs, a heap of damp tissues next to her like a pile of snow left over after a thaw. Her eyes were puffy and marshmallow-pink at the edges. In the corner of the room was a small animal cage that had not been there before, the kind with a plastic base and white wire bars. Shredded paper filled up one corner and there was a faint, pleasing smell of wood shavings.

'He wouldn't say why.'

'I'm sorry. People are like that sometimes. It doesn't reflect on you.' As I spoke, I realised I was saying more than I should. Perhaps it did reflect on her.

'I keep texting him, asking him why and he won't message me back. Do you think I should go round to his and demand to know?'

'No, I don't think so,' I said. We weren't meant to give personal advice, but the comment wouldn't stay in.

'I'll try not to. That's Bertie, by the way. He's a guinea pig.' She tilted her head towards the cage.

'Good idea to get a pet.'

She slid off the bed and stepped over to the cage and I got up to look too. A small ginger bundle was huddled inside at the far end, a dark berry eye peering out from under a fringe. The animal was making a soft sound like the word *weak, weak*. I was amused since I'd pictured Megan as a rabbit. I almost wanted to tell her that, but I didn't in case she would take it as a slur on her appearance.

'It's something to hug,' she said, squeezing a piece of carrot from a dish between the bars. 'He scratches me though.' She pulled up her sleeves and showed thin red lines on her forearms.

'Ooh, take care with that,' I said.

We spent half an hour going through her application for a college course in childcare. She was so much a child herself, her big eyes and her soft voice. I pictured her working in a nursery, like an ungainly doll looking after other, smaller dolls. At one point she glanced up from the screen and peered at my face intently.

'You look tired again, by the way,' she said in her quiet, dreamy voice.

'I'm fine. Maybe a bit of a late night, but let's focus on you.' She cast her eyes obediently back down at the application. I had been up late after looking at the legal firm website, not doing anything in particular, just distracted by one thing and another while the hands on the clock clipped round until it was so late it didn't seem to matter what time I went to sleep.

Before I left she started crying about her boyfriend again. I wanted to give her a hug and also to shake her and tell her to stop being so silly. But I remembered the intensity of those feelings, those crushes as a teenager, how real they felt, how overpowering.

Mr Fletcher's classroom was long and low and angled so it didn't get much sunlight. I was in his class for first year general science. It always smelt of lemon cleaning fluid and chalk dust. Mr Fletcher spoke quietly and usually seemed tired – his voice was flat and that made it difficult to listen to. Sometimes after he'd spoken for a long time, I felt my own throat was dry, my gums tingling. It would never have occurred to me that he drank. He lived with his wife in those years; I often passed his house on my bike and saw her in the garden sometimes, kneeling on a foam pad, weeding a circular flowerbed, fighting a losing battle with the wilderness. She was from Cornwall originally and moved back there when they separated, the year before the accident. She tended to wear long flowing skirts and tops with repeating patterns that seemed to come from another time. A cloud of citrusy perfume trailed after her quick step when she walked around the village shop.

Mr Fletcher didn't have that need to humiliate kids who misbehaved in the way that some of our other teachers did. When he asked pupils to leave the class for talking or causing a nuisance, he'd only sigh and point a finger at the door and say, *Get out*. He liked to wear sand-coloured suit jackets and pastel ties, though none of the other teachers wore suits at all. On the wall beside the blackboard, he had tacked up an astrological chart, decorated with ornate line drawings of the zodiac animals: a goat, a ram, a lion, a bull. It seemed out of place in a science classroom – when we asked if he believed in star signs, he said it was a bit of fun.

Mostly I remember a peaceful kind of boredom in the chemistry classroom. I did love playing with the blue flame of the bunsen burners but we didn't get to use them often. The classroom was cold, though the radiators were usually too hot to touch; somehow the heat never spread through the room. When we asked about it, Mr Fletcher joked that there were separate laws of physics operating in his class.

One day he took us outside to show us an experiment. We trooped out in a crocodile line; he made us bring the scratched, yellowing plastic classroom goggles, which we wore pushed up into our hair. Behind the school, where the river ran black under the trees, he had set up a large tank full of water. 'Here's one I made earlier,' he said. We jostled for space among the brambles and ferns on the riverbank. Leti and me eyed each other before pulling our goggles down. Mr Fletcher was wearing purple rubber gloves. He unscrewed a beaker of sodium and upended it into the water. Woosh. A plume of light and droplets exploded out. Further up the bank a blackbird startled into the air. The children gasped, stepped back, Leti gave a half-scream then immediately put her hand over her mouth. We all stood around laughing and scowling; our school clothes were spattered with water, our vision suddenly mottled and refracted by the droplets on our goggles.

'You didn't expect that, did you?' he said. He smiled like a kid getting a card trick right for the first time. The memory of that day and his small, easy moment of joy, was another thing that made me sad for him when the accident happened.

The day after Nicky died, the chemistry teacher was charged with causing death while driving under the influence of alcohol and given bail. The trial was set for the autumn of that year. Many of the kids, maybe all of us, wanted the drama of seeing Mr Fletcher in school while the trial was still pending, but the following Monday, the head teacher stood up at the end of assembly to announce in a blunt monotone that Mr Fletcher had left his job and would not be returning. In response to the murmur of questions that followed, she took off her glasses and waved them in her left hand while pinching her nose, meaning we were to shut up.

~*~

On a warm afternoon in May, weeks after I'd sent my original message, I received a reply from Robin. It was full of details about his life now – his work, family and friends. Full of apologies for not being in touch sooner. He said he was busy with his job, supervising staff for a chain of hotels. It turned out he was living permanently in Edinburgh now and so I sent him a reply suggesting a coffee. There was a friendliness to his message that made it feel easy to meet up.

I chose the same cafe where I usually met Leti. An apprehension crept over me for the first time as I was walking down the pavement. We hadn't properly spoken in so long. I started to imagine that the friendliness of the emails was false, that I'd be met by someone as sullen and awkward as a teenager. We arrived almost at exactly the same time, a gust of late spring storminess blowing through the door with us. There he was. So much time had passed and hardly any. He was smiling, wearing a dark-red jumper that clashed sweetly, perhaps intentionally, with his hair. I slid into a plastic seat across from him, making a split-second decision not to offer a hug.

'Emily. How are you?' he said.

'Good, good. You?' His expression was genuinely warm, if slightly embarrassed. There had been an intensity to the friendship we'd developed as teenagers. Some of the memories made me wince but I tried to push them aside and be my adult self with him.

'I'm well,' he said. 'Parents are still crazy.' He grinned. I'd never thought of Robin's parents as crazy. A bit strict, maybe. I remembered his father giving us fierce looks a few times as we ran giggling to the barn – perhaps he thought there was something sexual going on between us – but they'd always seemed like decent, solid people. Quiet in their way but also as much a part of the life of the village as the river or the mountain.

We talked for a while about our jobs and the awkwardness eased. A tiny cross hung over his jumper, this one made of wood, about the size of a thumbnail. He had an affable, social air that he had not had as a teenager. When a waitress with sparkly green eye shadow came to take our order, he chatted with her in a mock-flirtatious way, which she reciprocated cheerfully. Robin's highland accent came and went, like mine, becoming stronger when we brought up home. I studied his face, his mouth and eyelashes, the set of his nose, the scattering of freckles on his cheekbones. Would I have recognised him if I hadn't seen him since he was sixteen? He had filled out a bit, a mother-of-pearl sheen had appeared under his eyes, his fashionably shorn hair somehow changed the shape of his forehead. I couldn't say for sure.

Robin told me about how he ended up in hotel management. How he liked figuring out what to do with disagreements and grievances. He was almost pleased when there was a tangle to sort out. I bit into the sugar-coated shortbread I'd ordered, crumbling some of it onto my lap as I listened. He asked me about my job and I told him bits and pieces. When a small silence fell, he leant back in the chair and looked at me side on.

'You know, I'm glad you wanted to meet up, because a weird thing happened recently,' he said.

'What kind of thing?'

He was still looking amused but something else crept into his expression. 'I want to tell you but you'll think I'm nuts.'

'I won't. Try me.'

'It's about Nicky, to be honest,' he said.

'Nicky?'

'I've been thinking about him a lot.'

'Yeah, me too actually,' I said.

'Funny thing is, I've seen someone who looks like him.'

'How do you mean?' I tried to keep my face straight.

'I know it sounds like nothing. But I've seen this guy in the city a couple times and he looks so much like him it's disturbing.' The background noise of the cafe, the hissing of the coffee machine and tinkling of cutlery, seemed to heighten and blur.

'I think I've seen the same person,' I said.

I watched his eyes; they did not widen or narrow. 'You have?'

'I have.'

'No way, that's too much.' He laid his hands palm down on the table as if pressing it towards the ground.

'Where did you see him?' I asked.

'While I was out on a walk by the canal. He was feeding the ducks then he looked right at me and I was so shocked, I just walked off. But I saw him again, it was a few weeks later and he was ahead of me in a queue for cinema tickets and I got the same feeling, pure shock. That sounds like nothing when I say it like that. But fuck me, it was weird. It was so like him.'

'You know I'd eat my shoes if it's a different person to the guy I've seen,' I said.

'I guess we'll never know.'

'But we could. I know where the guy works. I'll send you a picture of him.'

'Really? Jesus. Where does he work?'

'He's a lawyer. His picture is on the company website. Honestly,' I said, 'I don't know. Leti saw him too and she agreed. It's so strange. It's like at the back of my mind, I wanted another opinion, and here you are saying you've seen him already.'

'That is bizarre.'

'The thing is, I've spoken to him . . .' I said.

He was looking amused again now, lines gathering under his green eyes, and I was almost annoyed because I wanted him to take it seriously, but I found my smile matching his, as if it was funny, because maybe it was. The cafe was growing warm, I took my cardigan off. More people came in and took up tables near us and for no clear reason we both lowered our voices.

'What did you talk about?' Robin asked.

'About Nicky.'

'Christ, he knew him?' His mouth pulled in at the edges for a split second.

'No, actually . . . he told me he is Nicky and it freaked me out.'

'What the fuck, he told you he is Nicky?'

'OK, I asked him,' I said. 'I mean I told him he was like this person I knew who died. We were in a club, I guess he was just drunk and he thought it would be funny.'

'He was just winding you up?'

'Well, he must have been. But it was so bizarre, I've found it hard to stop thinking about it really. Poor Nicky. It was such an awful time.'

His animation finally subsided and he slumped back. 'Yeah, yeah, it was. The worst time of my life really.' A toddler on the table next to us started banging a cup in a repetitive rhythm and we both looked round for a second, then back.

'You were such good friends,' I said. 'I suppose I never really was his friend exactly.'

He nodded slowly. 'We both got good at climbing together, you know that was when we got to know each other. I think he respected that I could do it. I surprised him, I surprised myself. Nicky would do kind little things for other people when that sort of thing wasn't cool. I remember dropping a bag of chips on the ground by the river at school lunchbreak and he gave me all of his, just went without lunch.'

'That's sweet.'

'It was a funny sort of uneven friendship though.'

'Oh yeah?' I said. Robin was speaking with an openness that he had not had as a teenager.

'He could be a shit to me. He'd just get into these moods. You probably didn't see that. You know, he pretty much told the whole school I was gay. Were you there?'

'I don't think so.'

'We were sitting in the lunchroom and someone had brought in a newspaper, this was back in the days when they still had breasts in them, they'd bought it to look at the boobs, and the next page has some story about a gay couple having a kid by surrogacy or something, and one of the boys said it shouldn't be allowed, and I said, to my shame, *It seems kinda weird*, and Nicky turned to me and said, *Really, Robin, but I thought you were bent? Are you not?* Just grinning at me, like it was hilarious. I don't know why he did things like that. Or how he knew.'

'Kids are horrible.'

'They are. But you know, it was kind of the start of me thinking, maybe people know underneath everything. And if people
know, then that's the worst that can happen, and I'm still alive.'

'The little shit, though.'

'The little shit. My face was burning. I wanted the ground to
swallow me.'

'That makes me want to cry,' I said, thinking of his young
face, the way he blushed then.

'So yeah, he was a funny mix of things, wasn't he? But I suppose we all are. It's so weird . . . us both seeing this guy. I don't
know, I don't know. It's brought a lot back, to be honest.'

'This guy, we could arrange to meet him, set that up somehow,'
I said. 'Find an excuse for it.'

'Why?'

'Just to clarify the whole thing, I don't know.' He was looking
at me with an expression that was hard to read so I said, 'There
was something else. This will sound nuts, but he knew my name.'

'Really?'

'He said *Em* as he was leaving the club. I thought he did
anyway. I want to know if he was just winding me up. I mean,
of course he was, what else could it be? Maybe I misheard. But
I want to talk to him again.' There was a pause, Robin's look
was a little worried. Behind us the coffee machine whirred
and hissed.

'But what would we say? He'd think we were crazy.'

'Yeah, I know, but still.'

'We can't do that. I mean, how would it work? And it's obviously just a wind-up.'

'Yeah, I know. No, of course.'

'It could be interesting but . . .'

'You're right, you're right,' I said, feeling something inside me
winding down, running out of energy, Jim's jump-rope rabbit

maybe. We switched to talking about other things, the places we'd travelled to, events that had happened in the village over the years when we'd hardly seen each other. People came and went from the cafe and we stayed at our table ordering cups of coffee. I was used to only having one cup at a time and as we carried on talking I gradually became aware of my heartbeat. As we finished up, I promised to send him a link to the law firm website where he could see the picture of Nicholas. We parted at the door, went for a hug and I sort of head-butted his shoulder, forgetting how tall he was now.

On the way home it was raining. Damp vegetation poked up through the cracks in the pavement. I passed the street where I'd been hit by the snowball. No one was there but soft piano music was playing from somewhere high up again. The leaves on the tree on the corner shivered over my head. The piano stopped abruptly on a bum note and then a phrase was repeated and I imagined someone sitting there doing their practice. If I called out or applauded they would hear me through the window, this invisible person, but I didn't do that; instead I carried on walking, thoughts of the past again filling my head.

~*~

Mr Fletcher pled guilty to causing death by careless driving while under the influence of alcohol and was sentenced to four years in prison. After he went to jail, I cycled by his house a couple of evenings a week. I told myself I cycled all over the place so why not there as much as anywhere else? But I also knew what the word voyeuristic meant. The house was on its own, away from the village, surrounded by thin silver birches that did not obscure the view. Each time I passed by, I slowed my bike but didn't stop. My skin prickled to think of the empty house, the stale air, the nothingness inside. The furniture with no one to sit on it, the bed unslept in.

His house remained the same as the ambers and browns of autumn turned into winter proper, as we hazed back into spring. One morning in July when all the air was laced with sweet plant scents, as I rolled past the garden on my bike, I noticed something dark on the lawn. It looked like a head and a torso. I slowed my bike and let my feet brush the ground. The thing was black and dark brown, and whitish in places, burned. I could see it clearly between the bright lime-green of the birch leaves. Charred bits sticking up in blackened spikes. I stared at the rounded, mangled shape. A body. I blinked, focused. It didn't change. I thought it would become something else soon enough, my eyes would pick up something recognisable and familiar, but there it was still. For a crazy moment, it came into my head that it was Nicky's body. Someone had dug him up and put him there. My limbs jerked unbidden, as if to get away, to get the bike moving again. I kept staring. It was a body but strangely proportioned. A torso, in a frayed old shirt and burnt jeans, with a large head. There were bits of something poking out from the skin. I squinted. Bits of straw. Individual strands sticking out of the body and strewn across the grass.

It was a scarecrow. Someone had set a scarecrow alight and dumped it in the teacher's garden. Straw compacted into a shirt and trousers, a head formed of mesh. My hands tightened round the handlebar grips. I felt the pattern denting into my palms. I thought of Mr Fletcher's hand hovering near my shoulders while I was sick in the school corridor and I felt not sympathy but a longing never to have known him. The animal part of me wanted to get away from what still looked like a charred corpse. I jumped back onto the saddle and cycled on, the wind whirring in my ear canals.

In those months, Nicky's parents had stopped meeting up with anyone and another neighbour had started to bring their shopping to their house for them. Their cars rarely left the drive. My mum took on walking their family labrador with our dog. She'd pick it up first thing in the morning. Over time the dark-green privet hedge at the front of the house began to spill over into the road and people moaned about it but did nothing. They just allowed the branches to thwack their windscreens as they drove on past. I sometimes saw Nicky's father out striding alone at dusk but he never had the dog with him, as if he could no longer tolerate the animal's good-natured grin.

I did end up going out for another date with the trainee vet. We met for a comedy show that he'd suggested, two months after our first date. He'd messaged me three nights before and I'd replied after a few hours, taking a while to decide if I really wanted to go. When I saw him standing on the stone cobbles outside the venue, there was that lightness again, that weight lifted off. The gig was in an Irish-themed pub in a barrel-shaped vault that was not usually a comedy venue, which made me a little suspicious of the quality. It seemed as if the heating was jammed on because when we got through the doors, the warmth was already like something you could slice.

We filed in just as the last seats were filling and realised too late that we'd have to stand. The space was so tight we had to position ourselves one behind the other instead of side by side, as if we were in an airport queue. The bar stayed open during the show so the comedians had to compete with shouted orders. It was a mixed bill with seven different acts. The first comedian was mildly funny but predictable, the second act lost his confidence and turned sarcastic with the audience. By the time the third act was on, the men seated at the table next to our standing space had become drunk and talkative. I could only catch every second line from the stage over their chatter. I wanted to tell them to shut up but there were five of them and I could imagine how it would go. A tall woman across the other side of the room had an extremely loud laugh and she cackled at every line from the stage regardless of how funny it was. The men started commenting on her, saying she was a robot. My ear on the right side began to hurt off and on like a blunt sewing needle was being poked into it. I turned to my date and smiled, rolled my eyes. As we stood there, I found that now and again I thought of the man who looked like Nicky, imagining I was standing with him instead. It wasn't that I'd prefer to be on a date with him, he just crept into my head, as if he was standing behind me and I could sense his presence and turn and make eye contact with him if I wanted.

When the show was over and we were bundled outside with the rest of the crowd, the cool air was a relief. The light of the streetlamps spilt across the cobbles as we walked together to the bus stop. There was a moment where we faced each other and I made a tiny head movement towards him to kiss him, just to see what it would feel like, and he didn't move and so I stepped back as if nothing had happened. His bus arrived shortly afterwards. As I walked home through the familiar streets, I decided not to give it another try with this guy.

When I was getting ready for bed, a text arrived from him. *It's been lovely to get to know you but don't think there's really a spark.*

I texted back, *I feel the same. Good luck with everything! X*

I was annoyed that I hadn't been the first to send the message. I was annoyed I'd put a kiss. I sat on my bed and sent a text to Leti.

Ended things with the vet guy

A line at the top of the screen blinked, showing Leti was reading, then typing.

Hope you're OK? But didn't sound like it was going anywhere

I typed, *Yeah, just feel kinda relieved*

89

I put my phone away without waiting for another message. I found myself looking at the lawyer's website again. That face, in the still photo, the resemblance was there but it wasn't quite Nicky. The living, moving face, however, in the club, that had been him somehow, the essence of him.

~*~

One wet afternoon early in the holidays, the summer before I started high school, I was out walking by myself along a forestry commission track that led into the mountain above the village. I would have been eleven at the time. I came to the marshy ground where the pine forest stopped, bordered by a tall wire deer fence. The sky was overcast, the ground oozing with mud. After walking a short way along the line of the fence, a movement up ahead made my heart stutter before I could understand what it was. A flash of red-brown, a shape making sudden jerks, the motion neither natural nor mechanical.

I took another few steps forward. The rocking shape became a deer that had hooked its torso onto the top wire of the fence. Every couple of seconds it bobbed forward as if to leap the wire, then bobbed back into an unnatural roll, becoming further enmeshed.

Breathing through my teeth, I crept towards the animal. I stepped carefully onto marshy tussocks, until I was about two metres away. The thrashing reminded me of a worm on a fishing hook. The animal's eyes rolled, showing the whites. I wanted to save it and I wanted to be nowhere near it. Rain began to fall. A hard rain that came out of nowhere and was painfully sharp against my skin within a few seconds.

I looked round behind me without knowing why, perhaps I'd subconsciously picked up the sound of a boot squelching in the mud. There was someone on the path. The person was a blur of black raincoat in the downpour. I called, 'We need help here,' my voice coming out shrill. *We*, as if the deer was an acquaintance of mine.

The figure waded closer and I saw that it was Nicky, the boy who lived at the manse. He made his way over towards me, the marshy ground sucking at his boots. We stood side by side, looking at the deer. There was a stillness for a few seconds as the animal rested and panted, its beautiful black nose and white chin parting to gulp the air, then the jerking movements began again.

'Maybe we should get someone?' I said.

'Let me try.' He stepped forward just as the doe lashed upwards against the wire again. I had the sense that I was about to see something horrible. The rain stinging into my face, soaking my hair, I half closed my eyes.

Somehow he put his hands either side of the animal, avoiding the dagger hooves, and gave a heave of a lift, and there was more scrabbling and tangling and I closed my eyes to the point where I was only looking at the blur of my eyelashes. I heard a crash and clatter and a grunt. I opened my eyes. The deer was still attached to the fence. Nicky lifted again and again and each time he did the deer became more frantic. He pushed forward and upwards once more and the deer fell backwards and so did he. For a moment the doe was on top of him, neck twining like a sea serpent's, legs pedalling the air, and then she wriggled round the other way and was up on her feet and galloping. She had a cut across her chest; I could see the pink flap of skin as she fled by, like a strip of wallpaper hanging loose. She disappeared behind us into the haze of the trees.

Nicky lay in the mud where he had fallen. I was blinking hard, the rain dripping into my eyes and mouth. He started

struggling to get up. He was scowling, like the deer had been a
pet of mine that had strayed.

I didn't know what to say. 'It didn't kick you?' I tried.

He looked down as if checking he wasn't blood-spattered.
'Nah.'

'Thanks, thanks for doing that,' I said.

'Why are you thanking me? I didn't do it for you.' He said
this with amusement, without malice, but I was easily mortified
at that age and fell silent. 'Stupid animal,' he added.

'It's not stupid,' I balled my hands inside my sleeves.

'It wouldn't have got stuck on the fence if it was clever.'

'It doesn't think like a human,' I said.

'It doesn't think at all. Anyway, you'd better head home.'

I had intended to. The track back down to the village was
getting so wet I knew it would run like a river soon enough.
Water was already bubbling into my shoes. But now I didn't
want to move.

'I'll go home when I want,' I muttered.

He looked amused again. 'Please yourself but if you're just
going to stand here, you'll get washed away.' Painted with mud,
he began heading on further up the mountain, towards the gate
in the fence. Why should I go back if he went further? But I
knew how impassable the track could get and so I waited for a
count of a hundred, as if we were playing hide and seek, letting
the rain drum into the crown of my head, and then I started
down the track again, not turning to look at him.

Back home, over dinner, I thought mostly about the doe, not
him. I didn't mention it to my parents. It felt like a secret, not
with Nicky but with the deer itself. I tried to imagine it healing,
as if my thoughts would help it. When I went for my bath, I
realised I had picked up a couple of ticks on my shin, shiny and
round like tiny black berries. I sat on the bathroom floor and

carefully plucked them out with tweezers. Rain fell against the window and I imagined it soothing and washing the deep cut on the deer's chest. I imagined my healing thoughts feeding into its cells. The edges of the frayed skin slowly knitting back together. Only later, late at night, did Nicky come into my head.

~*~

Midweek after the date at the comedy club, I was due for my next visit to my client Jim's flat. I stood outside the main door and pressed the buzzer. There was no answer, the grille on the entry system stayed silent. I spoke into the mute lattice of dots, just in case. Nothing. I pushed on the door; it didn't give. Then I noticed there was a button at the bottom with a hand-written label saying *services*. When I tried it, the door open-ed automatically.

The hall was littered with the leaf-fall of flyers for a new take-away. I made my way up the stairs, shaking a leaflet off my foot. The window in the stairwell looked onto a grim crematorium-like church. I stood by Jim's door and knocked. There was no response and I tried again. I listened at the panel of the door as if listening for a heartbeat in a chest. No noise came from any other flat, the place was quiet as an abandoned building.

It wasn't rare for a client to miss an appointment, but Jim had never missed one so far. I walked back down the stairs. As I left by the front door, a noise made me look round and up. A window was open and loud music was coming from it. A tinny melody and a lower thump, thump, thump. Strange that I hadn't heard it in the stairwell, unless they had just started it right then, the moment I'd stepped out of the main door. I guessed those were the upstairs neighbours, the ones Jim complained about, but it seemed from where I stood like the sound was coming from Jim's floor, even from Jim's flat. I stood on the pavement and tried ringing his landline on my mobile. After twelve rings I hung up. I made a report to my boss and went on to my next client.

I took a week's annual leave at the end of May, two weeks after my failed attempt to visit Jim. I had planned to stay at home in Edinburgh, going to films in the evening, getting small jobs done during the day. But as the time approached, I found instead I wanted to go home. *Home* home, as we would say. Back up north. I felt unsettled and, with it, a pull to be home like the draw of a lit doorway on a wet night.

I drove, setting off late so that it was evening by the time I was halfway. I'd started out with the radio on but soon turned it off and continued in silence. I took a break in the same cafe I always stopped at. As I got out of the car, I could smell the change in the air that indicated I was heading north; it always hit me around that point. Sometimes I tried to work out which combination of plants it was: bog myrtle, pine needles, heather, rhododendrons. Individually none of them fit. Inside the cafe, I sat and ate chips and drank a coke, watching people come and go, families and couples and lone travellers, trying to guess their reasons for being there. When I returned to the journey, the evening sun was still high, gold light frittered over my eyes as I drove the familiar road between two slopes of Scots pines.

I arrived fairly late at night, but the sky was still a fading blue. The lamps were on in my parents' house. There was no sound except the river running. At the end of the row, the house that had been Nicky's was in darkness. His parents had moved away a long time ago and a young couple lived there now. Still, to me the house had never stopped looking like a place of bereavement, its garden overgrown, the grey-bricked front marked by damp, island-shaped patches.

My mum and dad had a new dog, Solly, now a year old, a labrador cross, who was already barking at the sound of the car. When I stepped over the threshold, the dog jumped up at me, all scrabbling claws and friendly teeth. I sat up talking with my parents and drinking a glass of sickly sweet sherry, something that had become a tradition whenever I arrived home.

Over the next few days, I did the usual things. I went walking, and I took a drive up the loch-side, after which red insect bites gathered on my hands and wrists. I met a couple of friends from school in the hotel bar, but the atmosphere was subdued and I left early. Leti texted me to ask what, if anything, was happening in the village and I texted back to say nothing much. I was tempted to ask her to look out for the man who looked like Nicholas, to let me know if she had seen him again, but I felt that might sound a little obsessive.

On a few mornings I sat in the garden to read when the sun was warm enough, the hedge so full of sparrows at this time of year it seemed the branches themselves were alive. Once a stag got inside the boundary fence and started stripping the bark from a sapling my parents had recently planted. It stared meaningfully at me for a moment before it leapt easily over the low wire fence.

As these lazy days passed, an intention was seeding at the back of my mind. I began to have an urge to see the chemistry teacher, Mr Fletcher. I started to feel that just seeing him would settle something in my head. Like checking for your passport when you're in the taxi to the airport even though you know it's in the zip pocket. After he'd been released from prison, after serving two of the four years, he returned to his house beyond the village and stayed on there. He didn't get his job back at the school but he carried on living in the house, taking out the bins, working on the garden. He neither became a hermit, nor quite resettled himself into the life of the village. Apart from a few mumbled *hellos*, I had hardly seen him since the time of the accident.

Looking back, it seemed incredible that he would continue to live nearby, having caused the death of a child. He'd not been born in the area and did not have family there. But the community could be surprising like that, not so much forgiving as absorbing. The population was around four hundred and so it was possible to be known and unknown at the same time. He was banned from driving for five years after the accident but managed to arrange food deliveries with the local shop. He often cycled out to the shop, too, on weekday mornings when the place was quiet. My parents said he didn't particularly have friends. No one ever saw him buy alcohol. As the years went by, I would notice him sometimes making the long bike ride home from the shop in the rain, backpack on, wearing what appeared to be the same heavy blue overcoat he had worn during my school days, though surely it wasn't.

I had heard that he made his money now by writing advertising copy for companies online. He seemed to make enough to keep the house, or there may have been money from somewhere else, some family fund perhaps.

As I sat alone in my old bedroom, watching thin strands of rain on the fifth morning of my break, I felt an irresistible urge to talk to him. Beyond the window, the grey granite patches on the mountain were picked out in the sun. The thought that I could speak to him burrowed at me, but curiosity came with guilt. Was I just wanting to gawp? The more I tried to talk myself out of it, the stronger the urge became.

So I cycled past the chemistry teacher's house a few times, just as I had done as a teenager after the accident. It was a pretty route anyway; it led on out to a small stony bay, an inlet of the sea loch with slanting views out across the water towards the distant layered mountains. I could kid myself I was just exercising, just going this way for the fresh air and the beauty of it.

The third time I reached Mr Fletcher's house, there he was in the garden, strimming a hedge in grey overalls, like a mirage I'd conjured up, yet also solidly mundane. Just as I drew level with the front path, he had the clippers switched off, and was adjusting the flex. I slowed my bike. The day had brightened to a real warmth, seagulls wheeled overhead. He did not look up despite the squeak of my brakes.

'Hello,' I said loudly. He glanced round. The baggy grey overalls gave the unfortunate appearance of a prisoner on some kind of day release.

'Are you looking for something?'

I thought he had mistaken me for a tourist searching for the cafe or the hotel. Flustered, I said, 'I maybe look different but it's Emily Stroud.'

'I know that,' he said. 'Are you looking for something?'

'I just saw you and I wanted to say hello.' I was picturing my own face now as it must look to him, plastered with a fake smile, my hair blown about like straw from the bike ride.

'Hello then.' Mr Fletcher glanced round at the door of his house, as if someone was in there who would come out to tell him what to do. 'Do you want to come inside?'

'No, no. I wasn't wanting to bother you . . .'

'I could get you a cup of tea.' He said this like I might doubt his ability to source tea. I turned my body so I was half facing the road.

'You're busy with the garden, I wouldn't want to disturb you. I just meant to say hi.'

'It's no problem. I can take a break. If you want a cup of tea.' Close up he seemed older than I expected from seeing him now and again around the village, his cheeks softened inwards. I wanted to go and also my curiosity turned, a screw spiralling down into place. And I did want a cup of tea; my throat was dry.

'All right then,' I said.

He threw aside the flex and laid the clippers where he stood on the grass. I followed him into his house. It was a bungalow, built in the fifties or sixties. The hallway smelt of the eighties, of the houses of the village I had visited as a child for birthday parties and sleepovers, I suppose our house smelt the same. Perhaps it was a mix of cleaning products everyone used and the recipes that were popular then. I had a sense of having fallen out of the sequence of time, like a dropped stitch.

We stepped through his hallway, across the carpet with its swirling tendrils of brown, red and orange. He made for the kitchen so I slipped into his living room, saying, 'I'll wait through here, shall I?' I couldn't think of anything else to do and didn't like the idea of us both squeezing into the small kitchen. The living room was dingy and had the same time-frozen air, somehow augmented by a loud brass clock ticking above the electric fireplace. I stepped around in a circle, taking in the mismatched furniture until he returned with two cups of tea and sat down in an armchair. I took a seat opposite him on a green felt sofa. For a moment it was like I was in one of my client's homes and I felt as if I should be drawing up a list of helpful things I could do for him, asking if he'd like new furniture, new carpets.

'How have you been?' I said.

'As well as anyone. I hope you're well? Your parents?'

'Yes, aye, all good. The new dog's settling in well,' I said, as if he would know all about it, as if he was still part of village life.

He gave a calm smile and said, 'And why are you here?' He was cradling his cup, one hand underneath it. His tone was different to how I remembered, more boyish or playful. It was as if he'd grown younger and older at the same time. I took a breath to try to cobble together some answer and he spoke again. 'I guess you want to ask me about the car accident.'

'Oh no, I wasn't going to.' My face suffused with heat.

'Ah, I think you were. Anyone from the school, sooner or later, that's what they want to ask about.'

'I was just passing.'

He nodded. 'You wanted to talk about the car accident. It's been on your mind, at least.'

'Well, yeah, it has, I have thought about it. But that honestly wasn't why I came by.'

His eyes crinkled, gratified. 'Why has it been on your mind?'

I thought of the man who looked like Nicky but mentioning the whole thing out loud in this room seemed impossible. 'I don't know. It's hard to explain. Maybe just getting older, thinking of the past. I didn't mean to bring back bad memories.'

'It's not a memory to me, it's always present.'

'Of course, I'm sorry. That was a daft thing to say.'

He shook his head. 'It was a perfectly reasonable thing to say. It is only a memory for all of you. That's why I think you've seen or heard something that's put the whole thing to the front of your mind.'

The tone of this disturbed me very slightly like finding a crack in a cup as you're drinking from it. 'It was a big thing for us kids, of course. You need to make sense of your past, I guess.'

He tilted his head to one side, nodding slightly again as if to an internal question. Then he said, 'He didn't die, you know.' I sat still with my cup in my hand; the couch seemed to have disappeared from under me. He repeated himself. 'He didn't die.'

99

'Why do you say that?'

'Because it's what I believe.' He bent forward to put his cup down on the carpet, then straightened and looked at me steadily.

'I don't know what to say to that.'

'No one does. It's not what you expect to hear.'

'It must have been very hard for you,' I said, helplessly. I wondered if he was about to launch into some description of a conversion to religion, talk of heaven or reincarnation. But I knew that was probably not what he meant.

'Of course it was hard. But eventually I realised the whole thing goes a lot deeper, that it wasn't about me.' For a moment, it seemed I was standing out on a diving board, about to drop down into a different world. Then he said, 'His death was faked. His parents were involved in covering it up, I believe.' Everything snapped back and I was listening to a man who wasn't well. 'No one wants to hear it,' he continued as I pictured the faces of Nicky's parents at the funeral. How I sometimes saw his dad out walking afterwards and he was always staring straight ahead as if he could see through the landscape to some emptiness beyond it. 'No one actually saw him die,' he said.

The room softly dulled then lightened as a cloud passed over the glen. 'But you did, and Robin was there.'

He shook his head. 'I didn't. I hit something. I didn't see him die.'

'But Robin was there, and the ambulance. I mean they took him to hospital. The doctors saw him. The funeral people.' He smiled, shook his head. 'Who did they bury then?' I blurted out.

'It was another boy, I think. One who'd gone missing.' He was looking behind me now at the off-white wall with its repeating rose emblems, as if watching slides of the evidence he thought he'd gathered.

Something tugged at me to get up and walk out of the house. I felt vaguely unsafe there now, not that he would hurt me, but more a sensation that the tattered house was about to fold up and squash us both like the House of Usher. He continued, 'I believe it was a deer I hit. Some animal that was already dead. The impact shocks you so much. And then there's the boy lying there and everyone is saying it's your fault, it's your fault, so of course you're going to believe that.'

Some of his thoughts were the kind of thoughts that had slipped in and out of my mind since I'd been seeing the man who looked like Nicky. But I had told myself they were just daydreams, that I was really only curious about the man. Now, hearing another person say them out loud, linking it all into some kind of conspiracy to do with Nicky's parents, it all seemed deeply unhinged. I understood I shouldn't argue with him, that was part of my training at work. I was trained not to get into arguments about what was real with people who weren't well, but I couldn't help saying, 'Why would anyone do that?'

He sighed and said. 'I don't know for certain, but I have my theories.'

I looked about the room. The clock above the fire, an impressionist print of the sea in a gold frame, a few small ornamental animals parading across the mantelpiece. What I'd seen as boyishness now seemed to be a kind of feverishness, with the light from the window catching the whites of his eyes. I tried to find a way to set him on a different track. 'Well, it was a hard time for everyone. I shouldn't really have brought it up.'

'You didn't. I asked you. But I think you wanted to talk about it. I've seen you going back and forward.'

'Like I said, you know, getting older, some friends have got kids now, you look back . . .' This wasn't really true, none of my close friends had kids. We all seemed to live similar, studenty, free-floating lives. I was suddenly exhausted.

He was watching me with bright-blue eyes, the piercingness of which I didn't recall noticing in the time he taught us. 'That's not the real reason, I think.'

'It is. Really there's no reason.' Now, in the white-hot light of the teacher's intense belief, I wanted to forget all that wondering about Nicholas Blackburn. Of course he was not literally Nicky. I told myself I had never thought so.

'Human beings don't do things without reasons, there must be something you've seen,' Mr Fletcher said.

I shook my head. 'No, really. I'm sorry I've given you the wrong impression.'

I was like a child that had poked at a dead animal only to be surrounded by flies. His mouth subsided slightly as he watched my face.

'I'm sorry. I didn't mean to scare you. I know all this sounds absurd but I've researched it meticulously. I'm trying to talk to you now like you're an adult because you are. Look, if you want to know more I could email you something.'

'Really, that's kind of you but I'm not going to look into it further to be honest. We all make the best sense we can.' From the mantelpiece, the animals watched me; fox cubs and kittens, an elephant and a stag. Perhaps they were chosen by his wife.

'You think I'm insane, of course.' Crinkle-eyed smile again.

'I don't, I don't, I just probably see things differently.' I took a huge slurp of tea, trying to make it disappear. There was a silence then that he didn't break so I blurted out, 'Do you never think of moving away?'

He nodded gently. 'It must seem weird to you that I stayed. It seems odd to me too. I was happy when I first moved here but then it became a miserable place. Over time the landscape, the mountains, it all seemed to oppress me. I want to live sur-rounded by the sea now. Not that sandwich slice of sea loch but really on the coast, somewhere clear and blue, an island probably. That would make a difference, I think.'

'Why don't you?'

'I feel like I'm stuck here. It's hard to explain. Nowadays I listen to Hank Williams a lot. I don't know if you know the lyrics: *I jumped in the river, but the doggone river was dry.* A man tries to drown himself but he can't. Can't escape, not even to die. Do you understand me?'

'I think I do,' I said. I remembered the recent workshop I'd been to with my job, about suicide prevention, and I wondered if I should ask him about suicidal thoughts but I wanted to be outside and away. I didn't want to say anything that would open up a longer conversation. I drank the last dregs of tea. I felt so tired, as if the drink was making me drowsy instead of more alert. Like a chalice in a fairy tale. 'Really I should go. I don't want to take up more of your time,' I said.

'You mean you want to get away.'

Something sparked. I stood up and smiled. 'That's about right, yeah. I want to be getting on.'

He nodded. 'That's understandable. I'm sorry I blurted all that out. I see how it sounds. It's too much in one go. It wasn't fair to you.'

He walked me to the hallway, asked after my parents again. Outside the door, midges hung over the step in a small golden cloud. Deep in the garden, a blackbird was singing in elaborate trills. I picked up my bike at the end of the path and hopped on it, catching my shin on the pedal as I scrabbled to get moving.

I was sitting at the top of the stairs in my pyjamas when a boy turned up in the kitchen. He clattered through our front door with a duffle bag to the sound of my dad's low voice. He was going to be staying with us for an unknown amount of time. I was eleven years old and had only been told about this half an hour before. My mum's voice rose to meet the two of them, saying, 'There you are now.' I shuffled down three steps from the top of the staircase and leant forward to get a better view.

'I'll get you something to eat,' my mum was saying. I sat there, fingers gripping the edge of the step. It was late on a summer night, the sky was navy blue outside the windows and I was wearing my furry slippers. I heard the shush of the fridge opening and closing, the kettle clicking on and bubbling, the fan over the oven whirring up like an aeroplane starting. Nicky's voice was a murmur, a muddle of low syllables. I slid down another two steps. From there, through the bannisters, I could see the side of his face. I saw him often enough of course, living two doors down, but the incident with the deer was the only time we had really spoken. I was curious about him but I did not want him inside my house.

My mum's voice again. 'You must be hungry. Where is Emily? Where is she?' It was well past dinner time, we had eaten fish fingers and boiled potatoes and peas. I was not coming down to eat another unnecessary dinner with Nicky at the table.

When I heard my dad's footsteps moving towards the stairs, I hurried into the bathroom and shut and locked the door. I stood on the toilet and opened the high window and sniffed the fresh night air as a moth imprinted itself on the glass. 'Emily!' my dad called. He tried the bathroom door handle. Rattle, rattle. I would pretend I was going to the toilet. If I was going to the toilet, there was no way I could answer, what was I supposed to say, *I'm on the toilet*, so that Nicky could hear me? My dad rattled the door again. 'Are you in there?' I stared at the rectangle of sky through the narrow window. I could just make out a bright star which might be a planet. My dad's footsteps moved away.

After Nicky had been lodged in the box room at the front of the house, after a fuss had been made about putting up the fold-out camp bed, I sat on my bedroom floor near the door and listened to footsteps on the stairs again. My bedroom door opened slowly and my dad's moustached face appeared. 'I hope you're not put out. You know Nicky's staying with us for a wee while. It's all had to be decided a bit quickly. Now you need to be kind to him. If you were staying with strangers, you'd want their kids to be nice to you.'

I wanted to ask how long he'd be staying, how much of my life would be ruined, but I felt there would be no answer to this; if there was one it would have been given already.

The next day I got up before him and ate breakfast on my own. I asked for jam sandwiches to take out for lunch and ate them at the end of the garden, hidden by the bramble bushes. During our first evening meal together, I did not speak. My parents didn't force me, they just directed polite questions towards Nicky about his school subjects, his favourite sports, any wildlife he'd seen. He answered my parents' questions with a tone that suggested they were irritating him, which made me hot with anger.

When he was having a bath that night, I walked deliberately past the bathroom door, knowing there was crack in it. I saw a flash of pale skin and a blur of blue towel, the steam rising from the bath. With the gurgle of the water draining away, I hid in my room and sat listening to his footsteps on the stairs, listening out for the box-room door closing so that I could breathe more easily.

The next day I watched him out in the garden. He read a gaudy-looking sports magazine for a while, then ineptly began sharpening a stick from our willow tree with a penknife. I knew my parents wouldn't allow him to have a knife and I kept that information to myself in case I needed to blackmail him.

He didn't speak to me at all until the second night, when it was late enough that the house was made cavernous by lamplight, and I was heading upstairs to bed. We met on the landing by the bathroom, the moon a chip of porcelain through the window.

'Have you ever seen a dead body?' he said to me. He stood sideways on with his back to the wall so that there was space for me to pass by but I did not. My parents were downstairs with the television on in the living room, I could hear the lapping waves of audience laughter.

'No,' I said.

'I have.' He said this in a flat way, as if he was not showing off, but I knew he was.

'I have to go.' I stepped towards my room. My mum had seen dead bodies as part of her medical training, but I didn't want to think about that.

'OK.' He shifted out of my way. I took another step towards my room. But I felt the threatening tug of not knowing. I turned.

'How did you see a body?'

'It was my auntie. She was younger than my mum. I saw her in the funeral home. She died of cancer. She looked like a wax doll but also like herself.'

'That's sad,' I said, not feeling sad at all, feeling instead a kind of unpleasant twisting. I stepped forward into my room to get away from him. He had passed me a memory of his that he didn't want; like a clump of mud, he had put it into my hands.

After this incident I started to look at him more. I remember watching him eat cornflakes and thinking I liked the shape of his nose. I didn't feel attraction but something akin to it. A fleeting sensation whenever I saw him, like those tiny spots of water that land every now and again before it has started to rain properly.

Leti came around on the first Sunday after he arrived and we hid in my room and ate chocolate biscuits and played board games and talked about him.

'Why is he here?' she said.

'I don't know.'

Later that day we found him asleep on the couch, his mouth open like a small cave. We sprinkled glitter into his hair without him stirring. He never did mention it and must have washed it away though I noticed a tiny piece next to his eye two evenings later.

As the days passed, I talked to him more when we were alone, mostly about animals. 'Saw a hawk,' he told me one morning.

'I saw a fox in the MacKinnons' back garden,' I said though this was a lie. I had never seen a fox; they were rare in the area.

One day Mum and Dad were out in the garden and I bumped into Nicky on the upstairs landing, gazing upwards.

'What are you looking at?'

'That.' He pointed at the panel that led into the loft. 'How do you get up there?'

'A ladder comes down when you push the trapdoor with a stick.'

'What's in there?'

'I don't know. Old stuff. The Christmas things. Suitcases from my grandparents.'

'Let's go in there.'

'We can't. I'm not allowed.'

'Where's, you know, the stick for opening it?'

'In the drying cupboard.'

He opened the cupboard door and fished the hooked metal rod out. When he jabbed it against the hatch, the panel suddenly swung down with a whistling weight so that he had to duck and I flinched. The ladder was attached to the back of the hatch and he used the stick to pull it down in two stages as if he'd done it before. It slid down easily with a metallic shoosh. I could hear my parents' jumbled voices from the garden.

'After you,' he said with mock formality. Then added, 'It's your house.'

I was about to repeat that I was not allowed, but instead I put my foot on the first rung of the ladder. One glance at him then I began climbing, careful my feet didn't slide in my slippers. Hands then feet, hands then feet. When I reached the hard flooring, I flicked on the light switch I'd seen my dad use. The light fluttered like the wings of a moth. I hauled myself up onto one of the wooden boards. Everything smelt of dust. Nicky climbed up behind me. We walked under the low beams and a cobweb strung itself into my hair; I swiped it away but it stuck to my fingers. The attic was another world within the world of the house. Through the single skylight I could see fluffy clouds passing by at speed. Nicky unzipped a few suitcases, I opened the Christmas box and looked at the glinting Christmas things; out of their season they seemed startled by my gaze, the baubles and felted robins, plastic Santas and the ballerina-fairy for the top of the tree.

After a few minutes, Nicky said, 'Let's go back down before your parents come. I don't want to get thrown out on the street.' It had not occurred to me that my parents would throw him out. I didn't think that was possible but I said nothing in case he was joking.

When we climbed back down he effortlessly pushed the first section of ladder into the second. He brought a chair from my parents' room and stood on it to push up the double section until it clicked into the mechanism and folded away with the hatch closing behind it. He put the chair back in its place.

Looking serious, he said, 'We can go up there anytime. No one will know.'

The city was full of fading blossom, the browning petals filling up the gutters like spent confetti. The week I arrived back from the highlands, work seemed to blur by with clients hitting one complication after another so that I ended up covering a few extra hours. During those days I repeatedly tried to get hold of Jim but I couldn't. I let my boss know my concerns. Another client was admitted to hospital and an old woman I worked with had her flat flooded and I didn't have much time for daydreaming on the job. Things calmed down towards the end of the week. With nothing scheduled, I took back the overtime and headed off around midday on Friday. I arrived home for lunch and checked my email while the oven heated. There was a message from the chemistry teacher with the subject line *Some info for you*. For a second, my fingers recoiled from the keyboard. I wasn't sure I wanted to know what was inside. I left the computer, switched on the oven and I read a newspaper for a bit. When the oven was hot, I placed some leftover lasagne in a roasting tin and returned to the computer. I sat there with my hands hovering. After a few moments, I clicked the subject line and opened the message.

It read, *Got your address online, thought you might find these interesting*. A list of websites followed. I didn't know where my email address could be found online. I tried searching for it myself under my name but I didn't find it. He must have had to dig for it. I drew up my shoulders and shuffled them back down again, took a deep breath, then clicked on the first of the links, then another, then another, flicking through them like pages in a strange book.

They were all standard-issue conspiracy theory websites. Everything was on there, from the secret services to crop circles to black helicopters. There was nothing I could relate back to Nicky in any rational way. Still, the image of a boy walking away in the rain, away down the loch road, came into my head. A boy heading away from the scene of an accident. I blinked hard, shook my head and closed all the browser windows at once. Behind the laptop, a spider was weaving its web on my bookshelf. I let it be, stepped away from the computer and headed back into the kitchen to check on the oven.

As I ate lunch, I thought about Nicky, his walk, his face, short sections of memory playing on a reel.

After eating I headed into town to buy a few things. I picked up some shoes, a scarf as a birthday present to send to my mother, a new shower curtain because the old one was getting tatty. As I was ready to head home, it occurred to me that I could cut by Nicholas's office on my way back. I'd seen the name of the street when I looked up the company website, it was a pleasant route to walk and not far out of my way. I knew that I probably shouldn't do this and also that I wanted to. I thought of the chemistry teacher's words and how unwell he seemed and how I did not want to be like him. But I wanted to see the place where Nicholas worked. And I wanted to see him, to just look at him really. Since Robin had told me he'd seen him too, I'd had this odd hunger to find him again. I had not heard anything back from Robin; he had not replied to my email. Still, at the time, in the cafe I had felt his shock about seeing this person who looked like Nicky. Something had struck him in the way it had struck me.

I stopped in the street for a second, wondering what to do, the bag of shopping twined around my hand, digging into the soft pad of my palm. The sky hung low and grey between the buildings like faded linen. Someone bumped into the back of me, muttering their objections, and I snapped to and made my decision.

On the walk over I told myself that I was just wandering and that coming this way was only a coincidence. Once I reached the street, the sun had broken thinly through, and it softened the appearance of the wide paving stones in front of the Georgian terraces. I looked up at the doors and windows. Most of the old houses were businesses or rental offices now, the majority of the huge bay windows bore a logo for an accountancy firm or lawyer, a private dental practice or else some completely opaque company name that hinted at large financial dealings.

It began to rain through the thin light and I put up my striped umbrella. As I passed a forbidding-looking estate agent, a familiar figure appeared in front of me. She was wearing a suit coat too light for the weather and walking with a slight frown, her body angled against the rain. It was Morna. I dropped my gaze, pretending not to see her. She'd told me Nicholas worked there, so she might guess I was there because of him. There was a split second where we passed and she raised her head and then looked quickly down again and I guessed she was also pretending not to see me. Maybe she was wrapped up in something personal and didn't want a half-friend, half-acquaintance treading into her thoughts.

I carried on as the sky darkened again around the cathedral spires. Three more doors and there it was. Nicholas's office, the company name stamped in blue lettering on the window. I paused for a second. The rain opened up and I pulled my umbrella down so it almost sat on my head. I looked around behind me. I could just see Morna crossing the road at the traffic lights. Back at the window, a woman carried a stack of coloured folders to a desk. I felt like a stalker. I headed on past the windows, past the next building, until I was in line with a narrow alley.

And there he was. Nicholas was halfway down the lane, leaning against a wall. He was not doing anything. Just leaning there, looking slightly upwards, though the wall above him had nothing on it, nothing to see. He had no umbrella or hood and the rain was falling against his face, even into his eyes. It was as if he couldn't feel it. I stood, watching him. There was the old feeling, in the pit of my stomach, a turning, a flipping. The nose, the chin, the angle of the shoulders. If he was to look round he would see me. I gave myself another beat of a pause to stare and then walked on past.

On the way home I bought chips and carried them tucked warm against my chest. A rainbow appeared above the castle rock. I made a wish inside my head, I wished for what I always wished for when I saw a rainbow; a happy life. It was my childhood, catchall wish, used for rainbows and birthday cakes and white horses.

Back at the flat, I told myself I should not do that again. It worried me that he might have seen me. I told myself he was just an ordinary person, but that thought wouldn't quite sink in. The image of him staring up into the rain stayed in front of my eyes. That night I felt tired, as if I was coming down with something again, and I went to bed early. I dreamt of a Tasmanian tiger. It was curled at the foot of my bed, I could feel the weight of it across my shins, its amber eyes glowing, watching me.

~*~

Three days later, after work, I was piling my laundry into the machine when my phone buzzed. It was a text message from Robin.

I saw him again and it is him. Everything about him is like Nicky.

Where? I typed and hit send.

In the park this morning, just walked by.

I typed, *Why don't we meet him?*

I pressed send on the message before I thought about it. What did I hope to achieve? I didn't know but the desire to meet him kept bobbing up in my mind like a cork in a bottle of water. No more messages came for a time. I wandered through to the kitchen and picked at some grapes, searched through the fridge for something for dinner. I sat listening to the burble of the radio for a little while, then the phone buzzed again. I swiped at the text.

How?

I thought about it then wrote, *You message him at work. Say you think you know him from high school & does he want to meet up?*

Another message arrived so fast that I hardly knew how he had typed it in the time.

He'll think I'm mental. What will I say when we meet?

I put the phone down. I pulled a packet of halloumi out of the back of the fridge and sliced the plastic open and clattered dry pasta into a pan. After wiping my hands on a dishcloth, I typed another message.

I'll turn up too and we can figure out what to say when we get there. You could just say you were mistaken. See what he says.

He probably won't come. What if he asks for details? The school name?

Worth a try, I typed.

A few minutes of nothing. I set the pasta boiling and started heating oil in a second pan for the cheese. Another buzz of the phone: *All right. Done it.*

I typed: *I can't tell if you're joking.*

Neither can I.

There the messages stopped. I finished cooking, sat down to dinner, ate at my table with the radio on in the background, some programme babbling about online dating. Every so often I glanced at my phone. No more messages came.

A week and a half went by, I heard nothing more from Robin and somehow couldn't bring myself to ask what was happening. Then I received a text out of nowhere one afternoon at work when I was packing up to leave the office. All it said was:

I'm meeting up with the Nicholas guy on Sun. Want to come?

Yes, I did want to come.

The day before I was due to meet Nicholas with Robin, Leti and I drove out from the city for an afternoon walk. We set off from that place where the river ran through the woods. The water was high and churning. We cut along the main path through the trees, then wandered down a side route. The hum of the distant motorway traffic mixed with the babble of the river so that it all seemed like natural sound. The track was dry and rutted after a few days of June sun on previously muddy, boot-dimpled ground.

'How's school?' I asked Leti.

'I've decided my life would be so much better if I could just kill three of the children, just three boys, no questions asked.'

'Only three?'

'There's more I'd like to kill but with these particular three out of the way, my working life would be seventy per cent better, at least.'

'How is your own art work going?' I asked cautiously

'It isn't. I haven't really done anything myself for months.' Her eyes dropped to the path for a while. I remembered as a teenager, the first time Leti wouldn't come out cycling with me because, she said, she was going to paint – how hotly annoyed I was. I started to realise Leti had a passion and talent for art in a way that I didn't have a passion or talent for anything. I had envied her then, and in an odd way envied the art itself for getting her attention. Even as an adult looking at her pieces – the small, square canvases with thick dark paint scraped away to reveal brightly coloured lines representing abstract figures – I felt I could never say the right things, never admire them in the right way.

'That's a shame,' I said, 'I hope you find more time.'

We fell silent for a bit then I said, 'I met up with Robin.'

'Oh yeah?'

'Yeah. He's living here now.'

'How is he?'

'Good, good, I think. He asked after you.'

'Well give him my best, if you see him again.'

I realised that he hadn't asked after her but there seemed no point in correcting myself. Instead, I said, 'But do you know what's really strange?'

'What?'

'He's seen the same guy. The guy who looks like Nicky.'

'I suppose it's not massively unlikely. Edinburgh can be like a village sometimes.'

'And he had the same feeling I did. He was so certain it was him,' I said, wondering whether I'd tell her about the pub meeting plan.

'But, I mean, it can't be him.' We climbed over arching roots, gripping tree trunks for balance. I took a breath to speak then didn't so Leti continued. 'You don't actually think it's him, do you?'

'No, no. But you thought it was him when you saw him. I mean you were shaken by it.'

'That is true but we were drunk, both times.'

We ducked under some holly branches as I said, 'But we weren't that drunk. And you said it yourself, we went searching for him so you could see him again.'

Leti stopped and looked at me. She was doing a particular kind of smile that meant she thought whoever was speaking was stupid but she was being kind. 'But you're not taking this literally? Really?'

We passed by a small family group, two adults, a child and a dog, some kind of setter that had been in the river. We squeezed ourselves against another spikey bush as the dog shook its red coat. 'I'm not, I'm not. I'm just finding it strange. Intriguing maybe.'

'You know it's so long since we actually saw Nicky and people do look like each other sometimes. I read an article once about two guys who thought they were long lost-twins – they knew they'd been separated from a twin when they were adopted and they looked just like each other. When they got DNA tests, they found out they were completely unrelated. But the resemblance was uncanny. And what, I mean, did he fake his own death? Then why turn up in a city where he's probably going to know people?'

'He knew my name.'

She curved her lips over her teeth for a second. 'I'm not saying that isn't a bit creepy. But I didn't hear him say it.'

'Mr Fletcher thinks his death was all faked,' I said.

'I know that.'

'You do?'

'Yeah, my mum told me. He's been going around saying that for years. Some mad conspiracy theory. Imagine how awful for his parents if they ever got to hear about it.'

'They're long gone,' I said. I meant they had moved on, not that they were dead. I had heard they'd divorced by the time we were at university, his mother had gone to England and his father had moved further north and neither of them had been seen back in the village.

The light around us cooled and faded as the sun dipped behind a cloud. Something was burrowing at me. I didn't know how to answer her question, whether I thought it was him. What does it mean to say you believe A is B? You can feel something is true and also know that it is not true, in the same minute. Right then, I honestly couldn't say what I believed.

I had seen other friends often enough over the past months, but I had not mentioned anything to them about Nicky and this man. It seemed too strange, too hard to find a way in. It felt like something fragile, like an object made of sugar glass, that other people could crush. Now, with Leti being so scathing, I started to wonder if I was having some kind of paranoid delusion, some low-level psychotic episode, a linking of things that were not really connected. I didn't say that to Leti in case she agreed. I decided I wasn't going to mention the pub plan.

We passed by an old graveyard on our route back to the car park. The birds sung above us and the sun reappeared, hazing through emerald leaves. I glanced over the graves. Ornate Victorian stones mottled with different coloured lichens, they were old enough to seem like part of the landscape rather than a reminder of death. The graveyard was empty except there were four magpies, one balanced on a stone, three hopping on the ground. I remembered the rhyme: one for sorrow, two for joy, three for a girl, four for a boy. I thought about what the chemistry teacher had said about another boy being in Nicky's grave. The thought disgusted me in a muscle-deep way.

When I returned home, I began to read up on paranoia. I came across the term 'non-clinical paranoia' in an article. It argued that we are more or less all paranoid some of the time. This everyday paranoia was linked to episodes of depression and anxiety. I sat at my computer. Could that be what was happening? I didn't feel sad or anxious. But I didn't feel ordinary. There again was the hint of dizziness, of congestion, as if I was coming down with a bug. And I felt like I might just pull the bedroom wall aside like a curtain and find another world behind it.

One weekend when I was fourteen, about a year after Nicky died, I woke up in a hospital bed. I remember opening my eyes to white sheets, and my mother reading a nature book out loud on a chair beside me. Further away, a television was playing a morning chat show. A drip with clear liquid in it was attached to the back of my hand.

'Oh, you're awake again,' my mum said calmly.

'When was I awake before?'

'You've been waking and sleeping all day, don't you remember?'

I shook my head. I scrabbled back for memories, but retrieved nothing and nothing. There was a sense of time passing, that memories were there to be had if I could reach them, but they slipped away like minnows slipping through a child's fingers in a cloudy bucket.

'You spoke to me, you chatted to Dad.'

'I don't remember that. Where am I?'

'Shush, everything's fine. We're in the hospital.' She said this as if I was panicking but I did not feel the slightest sensation of worry. Like my memories, any concerns were just out of reach.

Over the next few days, I spent hours lying with my head on the pillows, looking at the detail of the white folds in the sheets. I felt fluey and achy but otherwise untroubled, or more accurately, unable to be troubled, as if the world's volume had been turned down. For a patch of time it seemed fascinating and joyful, the way the sheets rose over my legs and feet, they seemed to create a landscape made of snowy peaks and caves. Small details held my absolute attention. The glass of water next to the bed and the tiny bubbles that formed in it, the way the light rested inside them as if it could be contained. I didn't know what had been wrong with me and for days I didn't ask. It didn't seem important. My mum stayed beside me reading silently to herself because I couldn't follow anything she read aloud. My dad swapped places with her and also read silently. It didn't bother me that I didn't understand things; nothing had any weight. I often fell into a half-sleep where I seemed to be inside the television programme that was playing on the screen in the next bay. I'd benevolently watch over the presenters in a gardening show, floating above them, the colours of the flowers popping out in three dimensions, or I'd drift round the set of a quiz show, flying above the contestants' heads, nodding approval to the answers.

I have no memory of the journey home from hospital but I do remember being back in my bedroom, the white sheet replaced by my patterned duvet. For a few days I was in a similar state, sleeping and waking and becoming absorbed in the details of small things. I played my old music box with its tiny spinning elephant on a golden spring, over and over.

I remember Leti being in my bedroom for a time and an awareness that I was frustrating her. I couldn't hook into the real world enough to think of things to say. A heavy flu-like sensation and shooting pains remained in my arms and legs. I had more or less forgotten about Nicky and then in the second week of recovery I began to talk about him obsessively. When my parents were there I talked to them about him and when they were not there I talked quietly to myself. I went over the accident and the memories I had of him. I went over what people at school were saying about him. This ended as abruptly as it started. One day I stopped talking about him, a self-consciousness creeping back in.

I met Robin at the bar he'd chosen, which turned out to be a place I'd known well as a student. The carpets had a deeply stale odour and the walls still smelt of nicotine despite the many years since the smoking ban. We took a seat by the yellowed window. The pub had always allowed dogs and a large brindle lurcher was curled on the sofa in front of us sound asleep, its paws faintly twitching.

'So what did you say to him?' I asked once we'd sat down with our drinks. Robin was wearing a dark-green jumper. His cross was tucked away but I knew he was wearing it because I could see the band at the edge of his neck. He looked younger somehow than the last time we met.

'I said I thought we went to school together and would he like to meet up for a drink, like you suggested. He got back the next day saying all right then, and when and where?'

'That's a bit crazy isn't it? You could be a serial killer. Did you just use your own name?'

'Yup. He said he thought he remembered my name.'

'Maybe he thought it was a date?'

'Maybe. He didn't say.'

Robin seemed buoyant. It felt strange in the context of the misery that was behind this, the way Nicky's death had flattened him as a teenager, but I found myself playing along, speaking rapidly and jokily, meeting his comments with wide eyes.

Though it wasn't exactly as if we were teenagers again – he was a changed person, far easier to talk to than he was back then.

'You told him I'm coming?'

'I said another school friend called Emily is coming.'

'What did he say?'

'That he thinks he remembers an Emily.'

'Well I suppose every school had an Emily.'

We waited. A heavy rain came on, battering at the window behind us, giving the pub a cloistered feel. People dashed through the doorway with half-opened umbrellas or slick wet hair. At first we turned to stare at the door each time it scraped open. Eventually we stopped looking round. We bought a bottle of wine to share. 'He's not coming,' I said. Robin kept lifting his phone from the table, flicking it open, putting it back down. There were no messages.

We ordered chips and ate them too hot, blowing on them then taking small bites. I stabbed at mine with a fork to let some of the heat out. We bought more wine. Everything in the pub started to seem alive and inviting; the glasses of wine on the table shone like dark jewels. Robin powered through his portion. Perhaps because it was a place well known to me from the past, many of the faces that came and went through the door looked half familiar.

'Do you go back to the farm much?' I asked.

'Quite often. I still help out a bit.' I liked this, picturing him in his fashionable clothes covered in mud in those bracken-speckled fields.

'Did you ever really think you'd be a farmer?' I asked.

'Yes, all that time I was growing up.'

'But you escaped.'

His smile slipped for a second. 'I don't see it like that. It's a good profession. It is its own world.'

'Sorry, I just assumed it wasn't your thing,' I said.

'It's more complicated than that. I did love parts of it.' I remembered then, his obvious pride in the animals he owned, and felt ashamed of my assumption.

After a while, I stood up and stepped over to the bar to order more food, fishcakes and mushy peas. 'It looks like he's not coming, so what are we going to do?' I said. 'Could you message him again or do you think that counts as stalking?'

'I'm not doing it again. You can try next time. You email him. You've met him.'

'We probably should stop,' I said. Little burnt patches were forming on the ridge behind my teeth from having eaten the chips too hot. Full of food and wine and sitting in a warm, people-crowded place, the whole thing seemed like a fantasy, like we were just there to clear up the last bit of it. He hadn't arrived; it was over.

The sound of the rain faded against the window behind us. We talked about the gap between how we thought our lives would go and how they had turned out. We talked about Leti; Robin was keen to see her though they hadn't really got on when we were younger. He remembered liking her artwork, he said. I wasn't aware he even knew about it. We talked about Robin's family, what was happening with the farm finances; not good news, for the umpteenth time they were considering selling it.

'But I think they never will. Or maybe I just want to think that.'

'Maybe they'll find a way through.'

Just then, Robin looked past me over my shoulder and said, 'There he is.' He raised his hand in a half-wave. I pulled myself up through the slight fog the wine had created.

'Hello,' someone said, right behind my back.

I turned around. It was him, Nicholas.

'Hello,' I said. Nicholas, leaning to shake my hand. He had obviously been drinking somewhere else. His breath smelt of hops, his eyes were unfocused. I had the same sharp jolt as before, looking at his face.

'I'm supposed to be meeting someone. Rob, is that you?'

'Robin. That's me.'

'Sorry I'm late, I got waylaid.'

'No bother, no bother. This is Emily. She came with me.'

'I think we might have met somewhere,' Nicholas said. I could feel my smile fixing in place. The silliness of what we were doing. Robin got up, shook Nicholas's hand, offered to get him a drink. The way Robin moved, eager and bouncy, reminded me of a schoolboy but not him, not his small subtle movements as a boy who didn't want to be noticed too much. I had the feeling if I got up I wouldn't be able to stand very well, both from the drinks and from that slightly fluey feeling returning again. They headed to the bar together. Robin kept glancing at Nicholas when he was looking the other way, staring at him like he was something impossible, a moving painting. I wondered what Robin was telling him, what he was asking.

They returned with their drinks. 'So,' Robin said, 'Emily thinks, and I kind of agree, you are a friend of ours, back from the dead.' There was again a tipping strangeness, to see Robin joking about it like this. A memory flashed of his face as a boy, grimly set, as the others in the school playground were talking about the accident.

Nicholas laughed. 'All right . . .'

'Shush,' I said, swiping at Robin. 'We just thought you look like him.' Robin was smiling.

'But maybe I am him,' said Nicholas, smiling now too.

'You're going to claim that again?' I said.

'When did I claim that before?' he asked.

'When we met in that club. Do you remember? You told me you were him.'

'Well if I said it, it must be true.'

'Why did you come tonight?' I asked. 'A stranger says he recognises you . . .'

'I'm lonely,' he said with mock seriousness. 'I don't know anyone.'

'In Scotland?'

'Anywhere.'

He smiled and just like that he changed the subject. He looked at his phone and said he was tracking prices on a flight to Japan and then we were talking about travel and then Japanese food, which I knew nothing about so I could contribute nothing. Robin seemed to know a lot. Filled with the soft glow of the wine, I just nodded along. I studied Nicholas's face. The likeness and the clicking feeling were all there. The pub became louder, a smooth change as if someone was just gradually turning up the volume. Their voices were straining now over the noise. I tuned out for a while, short images fluttering through my mind from the past. Robin got up to get another drink. I leant forward.

'What was his last name?' I said. I had taken Nicholas's eyes for grey before but now they seemed blue. It was like they had brightened, though it was probably just the lighting in the bar.

'Harper,' Nicholas said. I focused now. The voices around us made a web of sound so that no single strand made sense.

'How did you know that?'

'What?'

'How did you know?' My throat became tight with straining to be louder, I could hardly hear my own voice.

He leant forward across the table. 'You told me.' Some tiny spots of his saliva landed on my cheek.

'Did I?'

'Didn't you?'

I thought back blurrily to the time I met him at the bar queue. I had told him, hadn't I? I'd said Nicky's full name. I slumped back. 'That's right, I did. So you're just putting it on? You're just winding us up?'

'Of course not, I'm telling the truth.' Nicholas looked at me quizzically. 'Are you ever in touch with the teacher?'

'Who?'

'You know who. Listen, I know I've not been here long but I'm probably going to head.'

'Which teacher?'

'I always felt sorry for him. I know he didn't mean to do it.' He got up and started patting his pockets.

'Wait, wait, what? Are you winding me up? You've looked that up, right?'

'You lived down the road from me, didn't you?' He stepped towards the table again, leaning in slightly.

'You said that before.'

'How far away? Two doors down?'

'Are you guessing that?'

'Yeah, that's right, two doors down, the houses all in a row.'

'You're guessing.'

He put a hand on the table. 'In between it wasn't like being in the sky. It was like being under water.'

'In between what?'

'The time in between, in between living.' In the light of the small hanging lamps on the ceiling the shadows were suddenly, comically, demon-like under his eyes, beside his nose.

'For fuck sake, would you stop this?' My voice came out jokey, trying to hide how flustered I was getting.

'This has been fun. I really have to get going.' Robin was just arriving back with some pints, placing them gingerly. The liquid slopped onto the table despite his efforts.

'Wait, stay a second,' I said.

'Don't you want your drink?' Robin said.

'I'm off. You have it. Nice to meet you both.'

'Bye,' Robin said. He was slurring a bit. He looked sleepily happy. Once Nicholas had pushed his way out of the bar, I reached my hands towards Robin but he did not reach for mine.

'What do you think?'

'Don't know,' Robin said. 'Life's so weird. God, I'm tired.'

'He seemed to know things. I don't know. About my house, my street. Could it be cold reading? Like television mediums do?'

Robin's eyes were half lidded. 'Don't know. Looks so like him, eh?'

'He does,' I said. Robin was so drunk, it wasn't really worth discussing with him now, and I felt somehow drunk and sober, both at once, like everything was hazy but also coming into focus.

My dad attended a séance in the village once. This was about six or seven months after Nicky died. It was called a séance, though what it turned out to be was a few of the adults playing with a Ouija board. The event took place in the back room of the hotel bar in a private space they sometimes rented out for birthday parties. There had been no advertisement, no notice in the newsletter, as there usually would be for any little thing that happened in the village. I watched my dad getting ready to head out, putting on his scarf and hat.

'Can I come?' I said. I was sitting at the kitchen table surrounded by maths homework.

'It's just a bit of fun.'

'It's a load of nonsense and you're not to involve her,' my mum said.

'I'm not,' he said.

'I really want to go,' I said.

'No, no. It's just adults being silly, you'd be bored.'

'I wouldn't be.'

'You're not going,' said my mum with a finality of tone she didn't often use.

So I stayed in the house. I finished my homework. I watched television, read for a bit, had an argument with my mum about whether I could in theory go on holiday abroad by myself in two years' time. The rain stayed off and I stepped out into our front garden for a while, the air smelt of pine needles and I could just see the lights from the hotel down the hill, the dull haze made by the ceiling lamps, like the lights on a faraway ship.

When my dad came back it was late. My mum had gone to bed to read. He hung up his coat and hat. 'Did you hear from any ghosts?' I said in a tone that I hoped made it sound like I thought it was a joke. He went to the fridge and took out a lump of cheese and began unwinding the clingfilm.

'It's only a bit of fun,' he said. He took the cheese to the counter and cut off a matchbox-sized piece.

'But did anything happen?' The dog, our springer spaniel Lily, meandered happily between us both, her tail hitting our legs, hoping for crumbs.

'It's only adults messing about, Emily. It's not anything to worry about.'

'Why would I worry? I didn't say I was worried.'

'Well, not anything to take notice of.'

'Why did you go then?'

He sighed. 'Just for something different to do.'

'But tell me what happened. How does it work?'

'It's nothing.'

'Well you must have done something. You didn't all just sit there doing nothing all evening.'

He put a slice of bread into the toaster and, with his back to me, said, 'There's a pointer, a plastic thing; it's meant to move around a board, point to letters, spell things out.'

'And did it move?'

'Well, yes.'

'What, it moved by itself?'

'You put your hands on it.'

'Oh. So someone could have pushed it. So what did it say?'

'Just gobbledygook.'

'Who else was there?'

'Och, a few people. I don't really remember. I'm tired.'

'But you must know who else was there. I mean, who was sitting next you?'

'Keep your voice down, your mum's asleep.'

'No, she's not, she's reading. You must have seen who else was there.'

'That's their business. I didn't know all of them. Really, Emily, you should get ready for bed.' The toast popped up then and we both jumped.

As I lay in my bed that night, with the edge of the door the only faint source of light, I imagined that something had followed my dad home. That it had slipped invisibly into the house as he opened the front door upon his return. Something had followed him and was lurking in the corners of the house. The idea was fun and then frightening so that I lay in the dark with my eyes open and was too scared to reach my hand out of the quilt to turn the light back on.

I wondered if my dad had hoped to hear from my sister. Or even if perhaps he'd thought she had contacted him and wasn't telling me. The rain started up again, whipping at the roof. As I was falling asleep, I could hear my dad, busy downstairs, making seemingly random noise. It sounded like he was moving the furniture about, pulling plugs out of the walls and putting them back in again.

At school the next day, one of the girls said her mum had attended the séance. 'Nicky's mum was there, and the pointer moved and spelled words and it said a male spirit was with them. It said he was young and he'd died violently and that he couldn't tell his name. Then the wine glass in Nicky's mum's hand smashed and her hand was bleeding. My mum was pure freaked out.'

'Bollocks,' another girl said, leaning back, arms folded, against the playground wall.

The first girl continued like no one had spoken. 'Then Nicky's girlfriend, you know ex-girlfriend, came and stood in the doorway. She didn't say anything; she just glared at them from the door, then went away again.'

'She's a cold bitch, she's never shown any emotion about him dying,' the other girl said.

I wanted to hear more but they fell into talking about something else, about someone's boyfriend in another village, and I was not brave enough to bring the topic of the Ouija board back up.

~*~

The first Monday in July, I was sitting in my car with the rain pattering on the window, filling in case work for a client, when an email arrived from my boss about Jim. She said he had gone missing. I'd not been able to get hold of him since the unattended appointment. Apparently Jim's doctor had finally managed to get him on the phone and he'd said something about planning to take an overdose. It had all escalated quite quickly and the police had broken into Jim's flat but didn't find him there. I sat and watched the rain pool at the lining of the car window. I hadn't expected things to go downhill so quickly for Jim. I imagined his panelled front door being forced, strangers tramping through his small living room. His collection of wooden trains sitting silently on the windowsill. He was officially a missing person. Somehow it felt like it was partly my fault, though I couldn't think of anything I'd have done differently. I began to think he might be dead though I had no real evidence for that. Clients had gone off the radar before, but I'd not had someone disappear in such an absolute way when they were talking about suicide.

I drove past Jim's block of flats several times on my route to other clients that week. The windows of the block flashed in the sun or reflected a grey sky. I thought about the upstairs neighbour and the issue with the music, the way he had seemed to feel threatened. I'd mentioned it to my boss who'd mentioned it to social work, who'd hopefully let the police know. Now I imagined this neighbour keeping Jim's body in his flat upstairs. An image of the body rolled up in a carpet, stuffed in a bath, folded at odd angles. I didn't want to picture that but it came to me uninvited.

Over the next weeks, I began to search the local newspaper's website for headlines with the word 'body' in them in case he turned up dead somewhere. Doing this led to my reading a string of disturbing stories I wouldn't otherwise have heard about. I'd messaged Robin about Nicholas the morning after the pub meeting, asking for his thoughts, but I had not heard back from him. I had this odd sense of things spiralling. There was a spell of dry heat and at night I sometimes set out for walks on my own in the blue light, wandering round the city gardens, past the chatter of open sash windows, an unexpected energy itching at my feet. I found I was looking out for both Nicholas and Jim, as if they might appear at any moment.

At the end of the month, I went out with someone new a few times. He was an engineer for a large company. A short, stocky, dark-haired guy with a square jaw and a square head, who I'd met through a friend of Leti's. English was his second language and we bumped around a range of gentle misunderstandings. We went on a couple of dates and then he stayed the night at my flat. While we were in the kitchen sharing a bottle of red wine, he noticed the animal drawings, the little pigeon-like bird on the skirting board and the striped cat further along. 'Did you do this?' he said. I shook my head. 'I don't like them,' he said. 'Sorry, I wasn't going to say if you did them, but since you didn't, I don't like them.'

'What don't you like about them?'

'They're ugly, I can't explain.'

'I think they're kind of cute.' I didn't know why I'd said that. They were not cute. But I was annoyed that he was so openly hostile to them, when they belonged to me.

After the wine, we had sex. I climbed on top of him, let my hair drape over his chest, all the time feeling like I was play-acting. He had no hair on his chest and I found myself wondering, in the middle of it all, if he shaved or waxed or just didn't naturally have any. He had a tattoo of a tiny triangle on his shoulder and I wondered if it symbolised something and it worried me not knowing but I didn't ask in case I didn't like the answer.

That night, as we were falling asleep, I had a warm, happy, spinning feeling as if I was falling in love, but it didn't feel connected to the man I was sleeping beside. I dreamt about Nicky, that he was still sixteen, but he lived on my stairwell and as I passed him on my way to work, I kissed him on the lips. I, my adult self, and him a boy. I woke from the dream not knowing who was beside me and I had to lie still for a while breathing evenly until it came back to me.

In the morning I got up first and had a shower then started on breakfast. The guy I was with wandered into the kitchen after using the bathroom and put his hands lightly on either side of my waist and kissed me on the neck as if we were a settled couple, but the sensation was uncomfortable instead of sensual, his mouth too wet or too soft. I wanted to wipe the kiss away. I made the fancy breakfast I had planned in advance with berries and honey and pastries, which I heated in the oven. Our eyes met over my small dining table and it was like there was a joke shared between us. The joke seemed to be that we both knew there wasn't any real connection. We chatted pleasantly and ate breakfast together, letting the pastry crumbs fall all over the table like tiny brown autumn leaves.

After we'd washed the dishes side by side, I nipped to the bathroom and came back to find him holding a picture I'd printed out of Nicholas Blackburn from the legal firm's website, though I didn't remember leaving it in the sitting room.

'Is this your other boyfriend?' he said. I took it from him, feeling protective of the picture somehow.

'No, just someone I know.' He smiled a small smile and I grinned broadly. We did not go for another date.

~*~

After Nicky died, I came to think that I was in love with him. It didn't happen right away but gradually over months. That mad, pure teenage desire that looks for an object to latch onto and attaches to it like a sea urchin suckering on to a rock. For me, that desire latched on to a dead boy. In my defence, I know a guy whose first crush was Elvis, despite the singer dying six years before he was born. Arriving at school every morning to see a large memorial picture of Nicky in the trophy cabinet by the front doors, I began to feel a kind of longing. His face was in a silver frame with his dates printed under it, a boy frozen in time, next to a shinty trophy and a clay model of a Celtic standing stone made by one of the sixth years.

As I walked along the clamouring red corridors, the period bell echoing in my ears, I would think about what I would say to him if he was still alive. What he would say back. As if we were having long conversations about life and the world. The words flowed more lightly and quickly than in the real talks we'd had in my parents' house. He lost some of his sharpness in these imagined exchanges. The more I held these conversations, the more it began to seem like he was still a presence in my life. Throughout the school day, through the tang of the gym hall and the exacting slowness of maths class and the jangle and clatter of the lunchroom, he was there in my mind. It wasn't that I had no self-awareness, that I didn't understand in some way that this was related to the tripping of a switch in my brain, to hormones. I was observing myself indulging a fantasy and also it seemed real.

The memories I had with him, the moments in the house or the time the deer was caught on the fence, became flooded through with meaning. I'd lie on my back on my bed, gazing up at the stuccoed ceiling, mulling over scenes with him like they were religious visions.

And I sought out the closest person to Nicky who I could reach; Robin. I didn't just become friends with him because I felt sorry for him; I wanted to be nearer to Nicky somehow. We were not in most of the same classes, but I passed him in the corridors, we mingled in the same groups in the playground. Robin, with his red hair and small monkeyish ears and blaze of freckles across his cheeks that gave him a look of always being slightly angry or embarrassed.

One day after school, I saw Robin by the river, guddling a stick around in the pond weeds. I ambled down the bank and stood beside him. 'Hi,' I said. I stared into the brown water watching the mackerel pattern the light made, as if the river was what I had really come to see.

'Hi,' he said with a downward tone, like that was to be the end of the conversation. But I had a list of questions in mind. I asked him how his parents' farm was getting on, whether he liked working there, then whether he owned any of the animals. Having a set of questions was something I'd seen suggested once on a talk-show episode about dating. I did not want to go on a date with him, but I assumed the same tactics would work. The questions at least made him more animated than I had seen him for a while. The farm was doing all right, he liked working there better than school, seven of the sheep and two of the cows were his, he had chosen them and bid on them at auction. He rode over the farm on his dad's quad bike, checking on his animals, before and after school. I made a point of remembering the breeds so I could bring them up again; Boreray sheep and Shetland cattle and a Whitebred Shorthorn. When I ran out of questions, I said, 'See you later,' and made my way back up the bank while he continued to swirl the stick in the water.

The next time I saw him alone he was behind the shop, chaining up his bike between the metal bars that were hidden by a clump of woody buddleias. I tried again, adding to the ladder of questions, until he asked me a question. Did I have any animals at home? Yes, a springer spaniel called Lily. He probably knew that, had probably seen me out walking the dog, but I appreciated that he'd asked something. I asked him whether he'd been abroad, he said no, and asked me the same question back. No, I had not, I'd never left Scotland. Then with a hard blink he asked me where I would go if I could go anywhere. America, I said. He said he would choose the same, because it had lots of space, a lot of different kinds of people there; you could sort of disappear. The skin behind his freckles flamed and faded. 'I'm going into the shop now,' he said and left me in the shade of the buddleias.

Gradually, effortful turn by effortful turn, it came to be natural for us to fall into conversation if ever we were alone together, though not if we were in a group of kids because that would lead to accusations of fancying each other and we tried hard not to cause one another embarrassment.

Soon enough I took Robin to the abandoned house. The third time I brought him there, Leti was already sitting in the foldout chair in the living room. Oscar was very near her feet, but he ran when he saw us.

'Hiya,' I said.

She looked at us both. 'I'm heading off,' she said.

'Stay,' I said.

'I was going anyway, I'm not going cos of you.' She gathered up her sketchbook. I caught a flash of a pencil drawing of a black and white bird, another of a thin face, before the book fluttered shut. Leti stepped delicately over the leaves and debris to make her way out. I guessed that she was jealous; I knew that I wouldn't have been pleased if she had brought someone to the house we had found for ourselves. But I was not going to chase after her in front of Robin.

He and I took up the two seats. He had brought a pack of cards. We used an upturned bucket as a table and played poker with a packet of tiddlywinks as currency.

After a series of meetings like these, Robin told me that he thought Nicky's dying had been his fault. He said it out of the silence one day as we were sitting in the den, watching a mouse flit in and out from under a doorway. 'I keep thinking it was because of me. It, like, sticks to me.'

The wind shivered the leaves in the trees around the house. The sound seemed to hide us, to form a barrier between us and the outside world. 'That doesn't make any sense. You weren't driving.'

'But that's how it seems.'

'It can't be your fault.'

'I know, but.' I realised I shouldn't argue; he was giving me a secret by telling me this and I had to just hold on to it.

I didn't see Leti for weeks after the pub and the meeting with Nicholas. One thing and another got in the way of us catching up. When we finally got together, it was a Saturday afternoon at our usual cafe. The city was crowded for the festival, a haze of coloured backpacks passing the window, fringe posters staring at us from the walls. I told Leti what had happened, what Nicholas had said, and she sat silently for a moment. When she did speak, she said, 'You know I used to have a crush on him?'

'Nicky?'

'Yeah.'

'Really? When he was alive?'

She looked at me like I had just suggested she put a spoon up her nose. 'Of course when he was alive, when else?'

I shook my head. 'Of course. I didn't know you had a crush on him.'

'You didn't always notice things. Sorry but you didn't.'

'I suppose not. You must have been really heartbroken when he died, then?'

'I was more sad than I let on, but a few weeks after he died it was like something snapped and I understood that the crush had never been anything real because we'd never really known each other. Not properly. It was like a crush on a popstar. But I was sad, yeah, sad in those early days, I remember crying a lot and being angry.'

'God, I wish I'd known that.'

'Yeah. I hid in the bathroom and cried those first few days and then it just faded like something fading out in the wash.'

'I thought we told each other about most stuff in those days.'

'But we didn't,' she said flatly. 'There were things you didn't see.'

'I guess there were.'

'Your experience of the village was not my experience. You weren't an outsider there. I had to notice things more.'

'You could have told me anything.'

She rubbed her fingers against her temples. 'It didn't entirely feel that way. I'm not saying that's your fault. The whole point I'm making is teenagers have strong emotions.'

'Well, I'm not a teenager now.'

'Exactly.'

A heat crept around my jawbone. 'Leti. You saw this guy too. It's weird, he seems to know things, and we're just trying to find out more.'

'I'm only saying take care of yourself.' She spoke the words softly, so that my anger had nowhere to land, and I changed the subject.

~*~

One Halloween in primary school our teacher Mrs Oakley read The Monkey's Paw by W.W. Jacobs to us. We were about nine years old, sitting cross-legged in rows on the patterned story carpet. I was entranced by the part where the mangled son returns and drags himself to the door. The way the father takes up the monkey's paw and wishes him away just in time, before they have to look at him, before he gets inside the house. We sat quietly listening; it was a slate-grey October day with the sky outside the classroom windows potentially laden with witches on brooms. We might have been too young for that story; one of the girls reported nightmares the next day. I did find the tale creepy, but more than that I found it unbearably sad. It was something in the well-meaningness and sweetness of the parents, followed by their brokenness. Leti was off that day so I told it to her the next time she was staying the night at my house. I made my version as creepy as I could, focusing on the gory parts, but halfway through I started crying, hot lava tears spilling from my eyes as I half hid my face in my sleeping bag. I was embarrassed, I'd never cried in front of Leti before. She didn't comment on my crying but went down to the kitchen and came back with two chocolate digestives.

I thought about that story again after Nicky died. How his family must wish him back. I'd imagine him returning to their door, or mistaking the house, and arriving at ours. It fascinated me, that idea of calling someone back, and the question of whether you would take them at all costs.

~*~

Not long after talking with Leti, I headed up to the village for a few days again. I hadn't the money for a holiday abroad that summer and I decided I'd rather just be up north. A feeling adjacent to homesickness was hanging about me. The sky stayed blue until late, the August moon a chalky daub above the hills. When I arrived at my parents' house, the mountain was ringed with white cloud. I was too tired to sit up and chat with my mum and dad. A strange exhaustion gripped me and I headed straight to bed and slept like a dormouse in a teapot.

I spent a lazing morning at the house and caught up with my parents over breakfast. I didn't mention Nicholas; instead I told

tales about those of my friends that they'd met. As we were putting the dishes away, I saw a figure I knew pass by on the street.
It was Hailey, the woman who had been Nicky's girlfriend. She
was striding past the end of our garden, in the direction of the
village centre. Her tall figure and business-like step, her ponytail
bouncing on her shoulders. Hailey had become a midwife in the
intervening years since high school. She ran about the single-
track roads in her small blue car, dotting between the villages.
Coaxing babies into the world, one after another. She was one
of those people who had become milder, more approachable,
as they'd aged. I'd overheard her in the hotel bar once saying
how heartbroken she had been when Nicky died, how it had
seemed she'd been unable to breathe at first. It was us, the other
children, who had projected indifference onto her. Certainly I
had; I suppose I was jealous of her.

After breakfast I headed out for a walk despite the rain coming
on. I was wrapped in a waterproof coat and waterproof trousers
that rustled as I stepped. I cut onto the road that led to the graveyard at the foot of the mountain. I hadn't been planning to go
there but once I was in front of the gate my fingers itched to open
it. I had to use two hands to get the screeching iron bar to budge.

On the other side of the gate I knew I was going to go and
see Nicky's grave. It was almost like I was teasing myself. I
knew it would disturb me to look at it, but I couldn't help going
anyway. I wondered if it would jolt me out of the whole thing,
standing over the place where he was actually buried. I stalked
down the line of graves from the oldest at the back to newest
at the front. The rain ran into my sleeves when I reached up to
adjust my hood. Soon water was tracing down my elbows, along
my shoulder blades.

I couldn't find Nicky's grave. It was not in the row I thought.
I remembered the stone. It was carved from black marble, low

and wide, with sloping shoulders like those of a boy, the letters inlaid with some kind of silvery material. In my memory, the row was next to a rowan tree. And here was a rowan tree, gnarled, thicker than I recalled, but the grave wasn't there. Over the years since Nicky died, I hadn't been back to the graveyard. I'd passed it many times but I'd had no reason to step inside.

I was almost laughing as I searched through the graves. Of course it would be there. I stumbled along another row. These stones were mainly for old people I'd half known. One for the death of a baby I hadn't heard about, a sleeping cherub carved on the granite.

I knew I had just got mixed up, but I decided to abandon the search. It was too unsettling, my feet slipping into the mud between the stones as the rain slid down my neck, ran from my hair into my eyes. I hated the dips and mounds between the graves. And Nicholas came into my head, his amused face in the pub. His talk about being under water between his lives. Suddenly I didn't want to be in the graveyard and I also didn't want anyone to see me in there, as if I was doing something shameful by being there at all.

I left along the fast flooding track. Because there was no one around to see me, I broke into a run. Away, past the gate, past the farm where they still kept pigs, and on, feet slapping and slipping in the mud. Soon I was back to the village and on my way up the road to my parents' house where the dog was barking, barking, as if someone unknown was at the door, though it was only me.

That night I dreamt about my baby sister. In the dream she looked around sixteen years old and she was living with me in my parents' house. I was in the kitchen and she came downstairs carrying a basket of laundry. Her hair hung over one shoulder in a dark caramel tangle, wet from the shower. She was wearing my pale-blue slippers from years back. With no sense of urgency or worry, I said, 'You used to be dead.'

She shrugged, curled her lip a little in a look of amusement. 'That was ages ago.'

That's strange, I don't even remember her coming back, I thought. I tried to recall when she had returned, how people had reacted, but I couldn't. I woke from the dream feeling peaceful and then gradually a metallic fear came over me as the gloom of the room solidified. I opened the curtains and let the fresh reality of the garden ease the dream away.

The day before I was due to head back to Edinburgh, I saw the chemistry teacher in the local shop. It wasn't entirely a coincidence. I knew he was often there on quiet weekday mornings, and I'd found a reason to go to the shop on each morning of my visit. Recently it had been hard to stop going over what Mr Fletcher had said the last time I saw him, about a different boy being buried in Nicky's grave. It was such a grotesque concept. I both wanted to see Mr Fletcher again and was also slightly repelled by the idea.

And then there he was; he didn't seem to notice me at first. He wore a pale suit under his blue overcoat, a neat grey tie pushed up to his throat. He studied the shelves as if he was a chef carefully selecting ingredients even though he was only picking between identical packs of oats. Poking out from his basket were a family-sized packet of crisps and the top half of a bottle of Ribena.

I wandered around the opposite shelves, the assortment of random things, from children's tennis sets to an unsold Halloween mask from last year. I bought a newspaper and a syrup flapjack.

Mrs Morgan was at the till in the bee-patterned apron she always wore. 'How's Emily?' she said. I sensed Mr Fletcher behind me, aware of me now if he hadn't been before.

'Very well.'

'What are you up to?'

'The same as always. Keeping busy. Here for a few days then back down.' It was an exchange we'd had a thousand times before.

I left the shop to the sound of the tinkling bell but lingered by the door. I couldn't help it, my feet wouldn't begin walking back home. I pretended to study the signs tacked to the glass pane on the back of the door. A wheelbarrow, and border collie pups for sale, a sign-up sheet for the children's plastic duck race down the river. At last the door flew away from me and the teacher was standing there.

'Hello,' I said.

'Were you waiting for me?'

I decided it was wiser to tell the truth. 'Yes.'

He stepped outside, letting the door shut sharp so that the bell jangled loudly. 'What did you want to ask?'

'I just thought I'd catch up with you since I saw you in the shop.'

'And?'

'I was thinking about what you said again.'

We started to step away from the door. 'About Nicky,' he said.

'Yeah, about Nicky.'

'Did you look at the websites?' He stood still with his shopping bag hanging from his fingers.

'Not really, to be honest.'

'I don't think I'm going to convince you of anything. What more can I tell you?'

'I was thinking about that boy you mentioned, the one you said went missing. The other boy. What was his name?'

'What other boy?'

'You said, someone else was buried . . .' I kept my voice down, there were people I knew at the end of the path. 'You know, in the grave.'

'I don't recall his name off the top of my head. But you would know it if you heard it. When he went missing it was all over the regional news. You kids were all talking about it. He was last seen walking over a cattle bridge into the hills further up north, way north. You might remember?'

'I've no idea.'

'I'll find his name, I'll send it to you. You might as well walk up the road with me. I'll wheel my bike.' I did not want to walk with him, but I stayed beside him as he unchained his bike and put his shopping into his rucksack. 'Here's the thing I was going to say. You don't believe me, what I told you last time about a conspiracy, do you?'

'No, I don't, to be honest.'

He nodded. 'Yeah, I'm not surprised you don't. We're taught not to look behind things. It's the school system.' He tapped his forehead as if this was a joke against himself. 'The thing is his dad was in the secret services, but he left. That's why their son was taken. I don't know for sure but I believe it was the Americans.'

'Why would they do that?' The sun was in my eyes and I was squinting up at him. Wilting leftover wild garlic lined the hedgerow next to our feet. He began wheeling his bike and I walked along beside him.

'He was a genius. They wanted to use him.'

Whatever the answer was, I was sure it wasn't this. However, in the awkwardness of the moment I gave a tiny nod. Not looking at him, I said, 'But he didn't do amazingly at school. I mean I'm sure he was smart enough but I don't remember him being especially brilliant at anything.'

'Well of course, of course, he hid it. I think it's why they chose me too, they knew I drank, but I think the main reason was that I saw something in him. I liked him. They knew that it would crush me, to think I'd killed the boy. They knew I'd go away and be quiet.'

We cut sideways up the road that led in front of the school. I wondered if he'd react to passing the old building but of course he saw it all the time and he didn't even glance at it. We walked in silence for a bit, past the thick bramble hedges already dotted with berries beginning to turn from red to black. I wondered about the steps that had led to the teacher's belief, wondered how it had formed. I couldn't help myself asking, 'What first made you think this had happened?'

He gave the tiniest huff of a laugh. 'Dreams.' He put up his hand to stop what I was about to say. 'I don't believe in psychic dreams or anything like that. I'm not off my head. Though I know you think I am. But I had a series of dreams in which he wasn't really dead and it gave me pause. The unconscious is smart.' He tapped his temple again. 'The unconscious knows things we want to push away. The dreams started me thinking. I hadn't actually seen him dead. Two parents both in government jobs. This unusually bright boy. I had been reading a book on the deep state. Yes, roll your eyes if you like but there's a lot of evidence, for people who care to look.'

I was suffused with that sense of repulsion again. Above us a flock of small birds passed over and shivered down into a tall hedge. 'A lot to think about, I'm sure,' I said.

'Your parents have probably told you I'm nuts.'

'They wouldn't say that.'

'But they'd strongly imply it.'

I laughed out loud at this. 'I suppose they think I can make my own judgements.'

'You think I'm mad then.'

'Or just that you have an unusual viewpoint.'

'That's the same thing to most people. But here's what you should know – it is not the same thing. The boy buried in his grave. I've lost the information. I'm getting forgetful but I will send it to you when I find it.'

'Thanks,' I said, wondering why I didn't just tell him not to bother.

'I've said all I can, to be honest. I'm going to jump on my bike and get up the road now,' he said.

'All right then, take care.'

'You take care,' he said, meeting my eyes for the first time in a while. It took him a few fumbling pedals to get going. He swayed from side to side then took off surprisingly fast.

As I walked on up the tarmac road, something was firing, a tiny sliver of memory. I passed by a row of familiar, cluttered gardens, tangled with football nets and chicken mesh. I no longer knew the families in any of these houses. I realised that I did remember that story of the missing boy. I vaguely remembered some conversation with my parents at the time, that it happened somewhere further north. Once I was back at the house, I couldn't quite bring myself to ask them about it. Still it stayed in my mind, the grotesqueness of it, the wrong body rotting in the wrong grave.

I drove home to Edinburgh on the Sunday night and when I arrived back at my flat I was so exhausted I fell asleep in my clothes. I dreamt that I had a key to Jim's flat; I let myself in and found him hanging there dead. He was facing away from me but his body was spinning round, feet pointed down like a ballet dancer's. I was standing there, waiting to see his face, thinking coldly, *It's interesting that people's feet go like that when they hang, must be something to do with the spine.* I woke far too hot and rushed through to the bathroom and stood gulping a cup of cold water.

The next morning, my first client was Megan.

'I have a new boyfriend now,' she said, talking into her sleeve as we sat down on the couch. Her nostrils flared, giving her nose a rabbit-twitch. She looked happier than I'd seen her before. It felt like an effort to pull myself back into the world of work after the time away but I pushed myself to focus on her.

'That's nice.'

'He's amazing,' she said, her features forming into a shy smile. Beside us on the carpet the guinea pig's cage was full of limp lettuce leaves and smelt of dampened wood shavings. 'You were right that I shouldn't confront Cam. I realised that would have been a bit obsessive. I deleted his number from my phone.'

'I'm glad,' I said. 'I wasn't meaning to tell you what to do. It's just these things don't usually lead to any good and people have a right to leave a relationship.'

'But it's the way he did.'

'I know,' I said, getting out my folder, my list of things we needed to talk about, hoping we could gently slide the conversation away from her relationships. I was desperate for a cup of tea, but I knew that she didn't make tea or coffee or keep them in the flat. I wouldn't have at that age either, wouldn't have known how to make one even. I started to think about Mr Fletcher's conspiracy theory again. It was absurd and would involve so many people lying. Still the thought of it rotated round in my head. I realised Megan had said something so I nodded and said, 'Mmm,' hoping it was enough of a response.

Her eyelids fluttered. 'I worry about you,' she said.

'What?'

'Nothing. Just sometimes I worry about everyone.'

'Well, I'm OK. A bit distracted maybe. You don't have to worry about me. Just worry about yourself.'

A small smile. 'OK.'

On her bed she had a pile of brochures for college courses on childcare. She flicked through them with me. A flash of memory, of poring over university leaflets with my dad, came back to me. A kind of optimism was almost rising out of Megan like sweat on skin. Maybe she was right to be optimistic, it was an exciting time. We occasionally got follow-ups on clients after they finished with us; news of a job, a new home, a graduation. I hoped she would be one of those, that things would turn out OK.

~*~

I had studied law at university. It had been my greatest ambition for a while. Not to be a property lawyer, but a barrister with a black gown trailing behind me like a superhero's cloak. It struck me as a strange coincidence that Nicholas was a lawyer, though not the kind I had wanted to be. The desire was fed by a teenage obsession with a particular legal drama; I loved the glamour of it, the dress-up, the way the rules slotted into each other and made a kind of sense of the world, at least part of it. But my degree slipped out of my fingers. The first year, my marks were good but the course was several diagonal steps away from what I had imagined. Learning the minutiae of the law was at times almost meditative but more often than not I found it burningly tedious.

As an outside course, I took a unit on philosophy. The abstract questions raised in the draughty lecture hall disturbed me. I would sit up in the dark on my narrow single bed in the student hall, wondering what I was and what it meant to be conscious and how did I know time passed and why did anything matter? I could not laugh about these questions in the pub like my classmates. Instead, they seemed to press down on the top of my head, sitting heavily on the crown of it. My study group took to going to the same yellow-windowed student bar near the town centre each week. I remember sitting there one after-noon, listening to the buses whirring by, and one of the lads was laughing and saying, 'Maybe we're not all sitting here after all, if there's no self, no I, then there's no we.' While the others talked, I was folding a piece of paper into smaller and smaller squares, feeling like the space inside my head was getting smaller as I folded. I didn't see Leti for the whole of that first year, except for the Christmas break when we were both home. Her art degree seemed to sweep her up in a way I was not swept up by law.

In my second year I split my time between obsessively reading philosophy and going to protests and parties. I got involved in political activism, particularly around environmental issues. I went on marches, I sat down on roads and blocked traffic and felt silly and important all at once. I didn't spend a lot of time studying law.

I started to have that feeling you get when you've partly broken something; that it might as well be fully broken. I have a memory of a day spent in the library, walking round pulling books off the shelves, carrying them about in the crook of my arm like dolls, putting them carefully back unread. When I opened them, I found I couldn't read them, as if the words were tied to sounds but not meanings.

At the end of my third year, there was a meeting set up about my repeating some courses but I didn't go. Instead I headed out and bought a loaf of bread and walked round a circular, black duck pond, throwing small beads of dough into the water. A letter came about the missed meeting, which I slipped under my narrow mattress. There it ticked, like the tell-tale heart. It was around that time that I started having the strange dreams about extinct animals.

Eventually, I stopped going to classes at all, and not knowing what to do, returned to my parents' house. The mountain watched me, dark and grey, as I arrived back at the village by bus in torrential rain. My parents offered mild concerns but I told them I needed space and they didn't push me. I never actively quit my law degree. Instead I didn't sit my exams or my resits and waited until my letter of unenrolment found its way to my parents' house. In the village, people tilted their heads and asked me what I was doing with myself and I said, 'This and that, you know,' then later, 'I'm on a bit of a break.' I'd eat chocolate cereal dry from the packet, sit on my indent in the couch.

My childhood room became a kind of burrow full of unwashed clothes and unsorted bags.

But on the scale of things, it was a blip. After a few months, I was itching to be elsewhere. I returned to the city where I got a support work job for autistic adults, then moved on to work in a residential place for adults with learning disabilities. I stopped thinking about philosophy. I stopped going on protests and tried to find something that would make a direct difference to an individual's life instead. A few years later, I changed to a job giving benefits advice. I didn't like it; it had the dryness of the law without the glamour. I switched to the housing support role and liked it better and stayed. Gradually, my not having completed my law degree became a joke, something I'd loudly tell people at work when they were fretting about their kids' choices. *Well I never got my degree and look at me.* I found routes I could drive home where I didn't pass the law school, the sheriff court or the high court.

By the time I ended up getting called to do jury service on a case concerning a mugging, I found the whole thing an entertainment. Watching the barristers play their turns was like watching characters in a pantomime, something that I could not believe I'd desperately wanted to do.

The door outside the block of flats was decorated with streamers and silver balloons. A friend of Leti's was having a birthday party and she had suggested we go since we hadn't seen each other in a while. Morna was going to be there and I'd been hoping to see her too, to find a way to ask a little more about Nicholas. I'd sent a follow-up *How are things?* message to Robin but I'd still had no response.

A stranger let me into the small hallway and I squeezed past the clutter of jackets and shoes. The living room was dark, lit by candles and decorated with old-fashioned paper chains made up of bracelet-sized loops. On the tables there were bowls of childhood sweets, fizzy cola bottles and jelly rings and fried eggs made of marshmallow and gelatine. At first a collective shyness floated over the few guests that had arrived so far and I couldn't see the host anywhere. Morna was talking to two women on the other side of the room, waving her arms as if she was already slightly drunk, and I didn't feel bold enough to disturb her.

As I got a drink from the collection of bottles in the kitchen, I saw someone I recognised. A guy I'd known at university. We'd been in a campaign group together, we'd marched in protests and had sometimes ended up sitting on the same patch of road, holding opposite ends of the same banner. He grew up in the east highlands, in a village near Inverness, so we'd always had a small community childhood in common. He recognised me now, raised a hand and smiled. His face was rounder than I remembered, pale and podgy with curly blond hair and a nose with a distinctive dint in it. I felt calmer for seeing him. The woman he'd been talking to said something in his ear, touched his shoulder and then left him alone so I walked over.

I stood awkwardly in front of him. 'No one to talk to?' he said.

'I recognised you, I was trying to be polite,' I said flatly.

He grinned. 'That was meant to be banter. I shouldn't talk to people, really. I always say something stupid.'

'Oh.'

'God, I hate parties,' he said cheerfully.

'Me too, most of the time.'

'People are so awful.'

'People are awful. I thought I would know more folk here.'

'Well, you know me,' he said.

'True. I know you. It's been ages. How are things?'

'Right now, a bit weird.' I thought he was referring to the awkwardness of our conversation but he continued, 'I just saw this girl – well, woman actually – from my village walking down the street.'

'Just now?'

'Just on my way here. It was like I'd gone backwards in time because I probably hadn't seen her in about twelve years and she looked just the same.' I was struck by the coincidence of him seeing someone from his past; the possibility of telling him about the thing with Nicholas occurred to me but I batted it away. He sipped from the dark liquid he was holding in a plastic cup and said, 'Sorry, that's not much of an anecdote but it felt so strange.'

'No, it is, it is strange seeing someone out of context.'

'Like people from one bit of your life shouldn't just be able to slip into another.'

'They should stay in their boxes,' I said.

'Exactly.'

'Did you talk to her?'

'No, she blanked me, I don't think she ever really liked me.' He laughed but the side of his neck reddened slightly.

'Maybe she didn't see you.'

'Maybe. You've escaped from your box too,' he said, 'Last time I saw you we were at a protest. Do you do much of that now?'

'Not really. Just lazy. You?'

'I do now and again, not as much as I should,' he said. 'Remember that time that lad came to the climate protest in a polar bear costume and got the head stuck on?'

I laughed. 'How did he get it off?'

'Maybe he didn't. Could be he's still wearing it.' As he was speaking, I saw Morna laugh behind him. I tried to catch her eye but she didn't see me. At the same time, two guys he clearly knew joined the conversation. They switched into talking about their officemates and I fell silent. I finished my drink quickly and excused myself to pick up another. With my cup fuller than I'd intended, I cut back through the living room to join Morna by the couch, spilling red drips on the carpet as I went.

I sat on an oversized turquoise cushion near her feet. From that angle, I saw Leti was in the opposite corner talking to a couple I didn't know. She gave me a half-wave. Morna was deep in conversation with someone else, so I waited for a lull. The other woman eventually rose to get more crisps and Morna turned to look at me with a glazed, amiable drunkenness. I'd drunk enough to lose a bit of the self-conscious edge by then so

I simply poked her knee and said, 'You work with a guy called Nicholas Blackburn.'

'I do. How did you know?'

'You told me.'

'I did? Oh well.'

'Who is he?'

'What do you mean?' she said.

'I mean where does he come from?'

'Earth.' Neither of us laughed.

'But whereabout?'

'America, I think. From Ohio? Or Connecticut. Yeah, I think so.' She pointed to her head like this was a special act of genius. 'See, even got the state.'

'How long has he been here?' I said.

'Why, are you wanting to ask him out or stalk him or something?'

'Stalk him. Kind of. I think I used to know him.'

'In a good way or a bad way?'

'In a good way.' I didn't want her to think I was accusing him of something. 'He's a nice guy. I don't mean it like that,' I said because she was smiling. 'I mean he's a decent person.'

'Is he?' she said.

'Well, I don't know really. That's the thing. If he is who I think he was then he was a decent guy but that was a long time ago.' I caught myself; I wasn't meaning to suggest he actually was Nicky, but I felt I had to give a reason for searching for him. 'I mean, do you think he's a decent guy?' I let my voice blur, pretending to be a little more drunk than I was.

'From what I know of him.' Her head rolled a bit as she spoke. But maybe she was also pretending to be drunker than she was. There was a clatter and laughter from the kitchen. Morna looked round for a second and then back at me.

'He's not Scottish then? Originally? He didn't grow up here?' I said.

'I don't know. Don't they all have a Scottish relative? When he arrived, I think he did say it was his first time in Scotland.'

'He's never been to Scotland at all before?'

'How would I know? Maybe he's lying. I didn't do a polygraph test. Seriously, are you wanting to ask him out or something?'

'No, nothing like that.'

'Why are you after him then? What did he do?'

'He didn't do anything. He just looks like someone I knew a while back.'

'Someone who's dead?'

'What?' My face grew hot. Behind us, a song I remembered from the high-school common room was blaring from the speakers, something pacey and melancholy at the same time. It brought back an image of the cloudy windows, the scuzzy benches where we ate our lunch.

'He looks like someone you knew in school who died, is that it?'

I gazed up at her. She was studying my expression and she seemed much more sober than she had been before.

'He looks like him, yeah.'

'Why do you want to talk to him just because he looks like someone you knew who died? Do you think he's back from the dead?'

Leti must have told her. I glanced across the room. Leti was in the flow of a conversation, her head bobbing, white wine in one hand. She was wearing a polka dot dress I'd never seen before and she looked beautiful. It must have been Leti, or, I realised, it could have been Nicholas himself. Morna and the girl sitting next to her both started to laugh. I picked at some tassels on the edge of a pillow and tried to rearrange my face. I couldn't quite gather the strength to pretend to laugh. Towards the doorway, someone pulled a party popper, the noise made me flinch and a few pink and blue streamers landed across my knees.

'It's an interesting coincidence.' I took a gulp of my wine and it was suddenly finished. 'It's just I've met him a couple times and he seems like an interesting guy, that's all,' I said. 'Anyway, I'm going to get another drink.'

'Don't take the huff,' she said.

'I'm just getting a drink.'

I stood up and I headed back over to the kitchen. There was a burst of giggling behind me. I wandered into a group conversation around the kitchen table and out of embarrass-ment somehow joined in, nodding along to a story about a bear encounter on a hiking trip. I found myself looking round the room at small details instead of at people's faces. The kitchen was darker than the living room now. Candles in shallow dishes gave it an out-of-kilter festive feeling, the fake vanilla scent of the wax was vaguely like Play-Doh. I didn't speak to Leti all night or strike up a conversation with the man I knew from my student days. After a few more drinks, I left early without anyone seeming to notice.

A few days later, I was walking from the car to a client's house when my phone buzzed in my pocket. The summer air was light on my skin, the gardens along the street were parched or overgrown behind their chain-link fences. I stopped by a gravel garden dotted with plastic animal ornaments and fished out my phone. The new message was from Robin, *Do you want to meet up with Nicholas again? I'm meeting him on Saturday.* I typed an answer quickly – *Yes, where & when?* – without giving space for more deliberation. Putting my phone away, I carried on along the street, telling myself firmly to switch into work mode, but the thought of it buzzed in my head all day.

When the Saturday night came round, I stood looking in the mirror in my flat, trying to smooth out my hair in different ways. It wasn't that I wanted to impress Nicholas, only that I couldn't quite get it to lie in a way that worked. I kept catching my own quizzical expression, as if the face in the mirror wanted to know where I was going and why.

At eight o'clock, I stepped into the same pub where the three of us had met before. Nicholas was already there, sitting at a window table under a jade hanging lamp, his fingers laced together in front of him, smiling up at me like an eager pupil. Robin had not arrived yet.

Nicholas insisted on buying the two of us a bottle of wine. We exchanged a few semi-polite observations about our week, I pulled myself up and said what I wanted to say. 'Are you still pretending to be Nicky then?'

'I'm not pretending.' His face was serious, or mock serious.

'Have you been talking to your colleague Morna about me?'

'Morna? No, why, do you know her?'

'I do.' I didn't want to give him the idea to talk to her about me if he hadn't already so I said, 'Listen. OK, if you're going to keep claiming this, tell me something only Nicky would know.'

'What sort of thing?'

'Doesn't matter. Anything. You're buying time,' I said.

'All right. There was an animal . . .'

'This is going to be vague like a horoscope, isn't it?'

'He rescued an animal.'

'He did?' I said.

'I did. I rescued an animal.'

'What, like from a shelter? He adopted an animal?'

He looked at me narrowly like I was trying to trick him. 'No. I mean a wild animal, I saved it.'

'What kind of animal?'

'What kind? A wild animal . . . in the highlands . . .' He rubbed at his forehead as if encouraging a memory to come to the surface. It seemed that a parade of possibilities were whirring past his eyes. Then he looked at me full-on again. 'A deer.'

'A deer?' An obvious guess but I saw the doe now, tangled on the fence, its wild bucking and pale underside. I felt the mud slipping under my boots. 'What happened to the deer?' I said.

'It was injured . . .'

I had read somewhere that people look up and to the right when they are remembering something, up and to the left when they are imagining things, but his eyes seemed to stay on my face only.

'How?' I said.

'Caught on a wire.' Shadows of people slowed down to talk at the window to the back of our table.

'God,' I said. The obvious thing to guess was hit by a car, wasn't it? There was a cold sensation at my feet as if frost was rising from the ground into me.

Just for a split second I thought he looked afraid. Then he sat back and grinned. 'I told you. It was caught on a wire and I saved it.'

'You're cold reading me or something. I've seen those television psychic shows.'

'Think what you like.' He was back to grinning. 'You know, it was like being under water. In between, I mean. Kind of warm and floating and ocean-like. Or is that too over the top?'

'I wish you'd cut that stuff out.'

He rested his chin on his fist. 'Maybe that's why I'm drawn to water now, why I love diving and wild swimming and baths and hot tubs. Can't get enough of it.'

Robin arrived then, before I could reply, out of breath and slightly flushed. He squeezed through the people queuing at the bar. 'Jesus, sorry, I was working late and then the other staff wanted to go for drinks,' he said.

Nicholas looked at his watch. 'I actually have to get on soon.'

Robin slid onto the other side of the leather seat next to me. He looked a bit more dishevelled than when I had last seen him, his shaved hair was growing out longer around his ears so that it had a tufted appearance. 'What do you think Nicky would be like now?' he said as if Nicholas hadn't spoken. Nicholas looked at him. Robin was obviously slightly drunk already.

'He was smart, wasn't he?' I said, and even as I spoke I almost wondered if I was buying Nicholas time, giving him space to think up an answer. 'Probably doing something with his mind. But something useful. A vet maybe.'

'A property lawyer,' Nicholas said.

'No, not that.'

'But that's what he is doing,' Nicholas said.

'No, it isn't,' I said. Nicholas shrugged and pulled on his coat. I reached out and took hold of the shiny fabric of his sleeve. 'No, wait, are you winding us up? Tell us why you're doing this.'

He paused, frowned. Sat back down. 'It bothers me,' he said.

'What does?'

'That you must remember bits of my life that I don't. Because I don't remember it all, only these little snatches.'

'You're going to keep playing along then?' I said.

'Yes. I'm playing along. When I was alive before, what else do you remember?'

'I'm not playing.' A sentence I hadn't said since I was about eleven. He looked so much the same as the boy I remembered. His creaturely eyes, his pretty face. He picked his almost empty glass of wine up and sucked at a small remaining red circle.

'This is going to mess me up. Here I was thinking I was leading a decent life and now you remind me I was somewhere else, being someone else. Maybe I want to see my old family.'

I sucked in a gulp of air. 'That's kind of sick. Remember, we knew his actual family.'

The pub had quietened a bit so I could pick up individual voices from the tables around us, dislocated words or sharp laughs. Nicholas leant forward on his elbows. 'Sometimes I miss my old life.'

'For fuck sake, would you stop this?' My voice came out jokey again, trying to hide how angry I was getting. Or not even angry, it was more like a kind of tight panic. I glanced over at Robin; he was listening in a kind of daze, his eyes getting that heavy look again.

'Well, I don't seem to have much choice. You're dragging it out of me.'

'Why are you so old then?' I said.

Nicholas blinked. 'I'm not that old.'

'No, I mean, why are you so much older than Nicky? If you were born when he died, you'd be a teenager now.'

'I didn't say anything about being born when he died. I just made my way back.' He made his hands like mole's feet, used a pawing, digging motion.

'Where have you come from? I mean, you're American, right?' I said.

'I come from here and there.'

'Where were you living before you were here?' I asked.

'You wouldn't know it.'

'But you must?'

'Here and there, all over.'

'Your colleague Morna says you're from Ohio. Or Connecti-cut.'

'I may have been to one or other of them. Or maybe she's making things up.'

'You must have grown up somewhere?'

'I must have. My family moved around. I don't remember a lot. I don't really have memories before, oh, sixteen or so. Just a flash of things here and there, I can't really place where they happened.'

'That's not possible.' I could feel my eyes burning.

'I'm telling you it is.' His smile had faded. 'Seriously, that bit's true, I don't remember much of my childhood.'

'OK, I don't know exactly which bits of your life you're making up but I think quite a lot of this you're just pulling out of the air.'

He ran a fingernail along a ridge in the grain of the wooden table. 'I had to wait for the coffin lid to rot.'

'What?'

'Nothing.'

'This is horrible. Don't joke about it like that.' Even in my anger, I could not stop looking at his face. There was this click-ing and clicking.

'Probably time to go,' he said.

'It probably is.'

'Have a good night.' Then he said, in a quiet voice directed at me, 'I was right about the deer on the fence, wasn't I?'

I shook my head but the scene with the doe played through behind my eyes. I saw the animal running away with its open scar, its reddish coat standing out against the grey vegetation. The iron smell of blood. A key turned inside me. It was him, it was him. It is hard now to be clear about this moment, to emphasise its impact, but I felt suddenly sure. He was saying these mad things to push me away but underneath there was something real. He knew about the deer. The belief in my mind had been like a flipped coin that had landed on its edge, that wouldn't tip one way or the other. Now it had toppled face up. Maybe he was not back from the dead, but somehow he was here. Robin was still slouching dazedly as if he'd had a blow to the head.

Just as Nicholas shouldered on his coat, Robin looked up, eyelashes whirring. 'What was it like being dead?' he said.

Without a pause, Nicholas said, 'Not as bad as you might think. Good night.' He turned and, while turning, winked at me in a silly, mock-flirtatious way, and pushed past the queue stretching at the bar, and out of the door into the amber street-light.

'God,' I said.

'Yes,' Robin said, not focusing on me.

'It seemed like he told me something only Nicky would know. About a deer. Only me and him were there. I mean, only me and Nicky were there.'

'That's nice,' Robin said. He was so drunk it was like he'd been drugged. His eyes had small red fans of vessels at their corners. He put his head down again and sat for a while, watching people at the bar.

When Robin seemed a little more sober and he had met someone else he knew, I left him and headed home. The rain came on hard, clattering off shop awnings and bouncing off the pavement. My mind was struggling, looping round the idea that Nicholas was, on some level, telling the truth. I could find no way to make sense of that and yet a picture came into my head of a boy slipping away from the scene of an accident. Then another picture, of hands clawing up through peaty soil, which I instantly blinked away. When I got in and off to bed, I lay awake for a long time, the pillows seeming too solid under me. Robin emailed the next day to ask what had happened. He said he didn't remember any of it.

The next morning back at work, the sun was out but the air had a hint of cold that suggested the change in seasons was not far off. I made a quick visit to the office to type up some notes. It was early and the place was empty. A prickly irritation was sticking to my skin. Everything took too long. The browser was too slow, the printer started chewing up pages. As I was unplugging my laptop, the charger cable became caught up in the mechanism of my swivel chair. Feeling suddenly hot, I untangled it but once I'd got it free, I found that my coat had snagged on the armrest of the chair. As I tugged to unhook it, I banged my elbow on the corner of the desk and let out a low scream, not in pain but in absurd rage. I rubbed my elbow and breathed out into the silent office, suddenly afraid that someone would be there, that I wasn't alone after all and someone had heard me. There was no sound but the mild whirring of the server on the far wall, and a dull clunking from the floor above, which was a residential flat. I worried the people living up there might have heard but I didn't even know anyone on that floor, so what did it matter?

My next client was Tony, the man with the learning disability who liked to wear an eye patch. He was flushed as he opened the door. 'My money's gone,' he said. I followed him inside. His expression was strained with panic though he was still wearing his pirate patch. I chewed on my lip so I wouldn't smile at the incongruence. As I sank into the concave shape of his couch, he sat opposite me and put his head in his hands. After a time I was able to get out a story about how he had given his pin number to someone who had phoned the flat pretending to be from the bank.

It took an hour of phone calls to the bank and the police and then his energy suppliers to start to sort out a plan. During the calls I found it hard to stay tuned in, as if the thread of each conversation was a radio signal I kept losing. When I finally hung up the phone, Tony said, 'Penny's missing and all.' As he spoke, his mouth curved down at the edges.

'How long has she been gone?'

'Three days.'

'That's not so long. Cats do wander,' I said, though I instantly had a bad feeling.

'She's never been gone that long.'

'She'll come back,' I said. 'She'll just be wandering.' I wasn't supposed to give hollow assurances like that, but his expression was so desperate.

'I miss her all the time.'

'I'm sure you do.' Her two pink bowls sat in the corner of the living room, the carpet stained around them with flecks of cat food.

'I thought they were telling the truth,' he said. 'They said they were from the bank.'

'It's not your fault, they're bad people.'

He looked around the room as if looking for an answer and I followed his gaze. His flat had a tendency to gather condensation on the wall facing the outside. It was spotted with black and grey mould now, a dappled pattern like an emperor moth's wing.

'How do I get Penny back?' he said.

I took a breath. 'I don't know, you could try the neighbour's doors, the ones you know anyway. She's maybe wandered into someone else's house or got shut in somewhere,' I said.

He shook his head. 'I've made a mess of things, eh?'

'No, no, no. It's not your fault, neither bit of it is your fault.'

He looked at me with an open curiosity. 'You don't have a pet.'

'No.'

'You'll be lonely without a pet.'

I shook my head, smiling. 'I'm doing OK. I like my own space.'

His look only became more serious. 'You should get a pet. It's lonely without them. You'll be all on your own.'

I laughed. 'I'm perfectly happy the way I am right now. Maybe the right pet will come along one day.' His eyes stayed on my face, as if looking for clues to my loneliness.

When I was walking out the door, he repeated the phrase, 'I thought they were telling the truth.' There was something so desolate about him there without his Penny. He shut the door cautiously, one eye watching me until the gap closed. In the stairwell, as I was leaving, I noticed the loft hatch on the communal ceiling was open. It had never been open before. The square of it was perfectly dark like a cut-out of black cloth. I paused for a moment, wondering if the cat could have got in there somehow but there was no way up. I listened for a sound, in case anyone was up there, but nothing came. I still found myself ducking as I passed under the dark space of it.

~*~

We were in the attic together again, listening to the wind, Nicky and I.

'Why are you here?' I said.

'I like the attic,' Nicky said.

'No, but why are you here? Why are you in our house?'

He scowled faintly for a beat and then smoothed out his expression. 'I don't know. Maybe my parents are bored of me. Or maybe, you know, your parents are bored of you? They wanted someone else around.'

'Ha ha,' I said.

The wind across the roof made the loft space seem like a great boat sailing out at sea. I imagined we could have been on the ark in the bible story. Just the two of us, yet to collect the animals. I imagined the flood waters rising in the bracken-packed valley around us. My parents were visiting a neighbour. It was jarring to me to have someone else in the house all the time. Someone who was not my invited guest for a sleepover or a Saturday afternoon, but someone who lived here. It had vaguely occurred to me if my sister had lived, there would always have been someone else. Next to me now, Nicky pulled a duffle bag towards himself across the boards and started to unzip it. He made faces as he pulled out different items of old clothing.

'What are these?'

He held onto a tweed coat, stiff like someone was still inside it.

'They're clothes from my great-grandparents' house. Put them back.' I stared at the line of fine dark hairs along his forearm in the light of the bare attic bulb. I knew he had a girlfriend, that his girlfriend was Hailey who worked at the hotel. That she had a sharp kind of beauty that I did not. He put the coat on the floor and took out a plum-coloured felt hat.

'Put that back.'

'Why?'

'Because it's my family's.' He didn't put the clothes back, but he pushed them to the side and started looking through a shoebox of photos. I had seen the box before and I knew they were old family photos, the colour leaking out of them, pictures no one had time to sort through. Most were of people I didn't know. Different arrangements of semi-familiar features. I didn't want fingerprints smudging them. 'Why are you here, really? Your dad's still at home.' I knew this because I'd seen him walking the dog.

Nicky shrugged. 'I don't know. Maybe he doesn't want me.' But I was sure he knew why he was here and he wasn't telling me. He put the lid back on the box. 'I'm bored anyway, I think I'll head out.' He stood up as much as he could under the beams and gave the box a small shove with the side of his foot.

'Don't kick it.'

'I didn't kick it. I was just putting it back.'

It was late in the evening. He had been out some nights, perhaps to see his girlfriend, but he hadn't brought Hailey to our house or mentioned her. I would not have been allowed to just walk out of the house at night, down the road, even though the nights were light, the sky still a deepening blue. It annoyed me that he had that freedom. I watched him climb down the ladder. As soon as I couldn't see him any more, I headed down too so I wouldn't be left alone in the dark of the loft.

~*~

On a Tuesday after I got back from work, I found Mr Fletcher had emailed me the information about the other boy who went missing, the one who he believed to be in Nicky's grave. A boy named Mark Allerton, who disappeared near Ullapool. I closed the email and searched for the name online. I found a story about the disappearance. He had gone missing in winter, last seen by someone in a passing car as he was walking over a stone bridge near his house. I remembered now, vaguely talking about it in the school playground. He was found, the article went on to say. He had gone to a friend's house in Glasgow. Some back story of an unhappy home environment, possible domestic abuse, was hinted at. The boy had not died or stayed missing; he was not in Nicky's grave. There was a picture of him with the article, he looked a shade like Nicky, the same wilting dark hair and pointed chin, but that was all.

I decided not to reply to tell Mr Fletcher. He'd only say it was another part of the conspiracy. The fact that he hadn't actually looked it up meant he was not thinking about it in any rational way. Maybe he had even found the article and chosen to dismiss the information.

Later that day a message arrived on my phone from an unknown number.

Hello? was all it said.

Hello? Who is this? I typed.

Guess.

A few names went through my head but I typed: *Nicholas?*

I clicked send. Right away a message came back.

Aye.

I didn't know he had my number. It occurred to me it might not be him because I had given away the name. I sat on my bed cross-legged. Rain pattered against the window.

What do you want? I typed.

I received no reply.

The weekend after the meeting with Nicholas again, Robin and I got together for dinner at a Turkish restaurant in the city centre. Robin said he'd tried to get Nicholas to come, but he had given some excuse about work. I wasn't sure if I was disappointed or relieved. I told Robin about the messages I'd received. 'He was probably drunk,' he said. He confirmed that the number really was Nicholas, though he said he hadn't given him my number. 'Maybe it's online somewhere.'

I nodded, not really sure this could be the case. I watched Robin pick at his rice; a few of his mannerisms were so different that it was as if he had deliberately learned to be a different person. I still felt awkward when I replayed some of our teenage moments together in my mind.

'Sometimes,' I said, 'I look back and think about how I went on about Nicky as a kid, and think you must have thought I was nuts, because I didn't know him like you did . . .'

'But that's teenagers, isn't it?'

'I guess it was an infatuation with me.'

'For me too,' Robin said. 'Well, I don't think I knew that at the time, but looking back. He was my first crush.'

'I guess he was mine too. Could be we've dreamed him back,' I said. 'I saw that happen in a sci-fi film once. I can't remember what it was called. Imagined versions of people's lost loved ones sort of came alive.'

'Solaris.'

'Something like that,' I said.

A couple of weeks went by and I didn't get any more messages from Nicholas. One evening, Leti rang me out of the blue. We didn't tend to speak on the phone much unless there was news. 'Anything wrong?' I said.

'No. Just trying to get hold of you. I've sent you three texts you've not replied to. You're very scatty these days.' I pictured her in her flat, probably in the kitchen stuffed full of pretty, girly things that clashed with her style as an artist; porcelain cups and teapots with chintzy flowers on them.

'Sorry. I've been busy.' I didn't know if that was really true, if I'd been more busy than normal. For a moment, I had that detached, fluey feeling as I listened to her. I had meant to reply to her texts – I had stuck them up on a pinboard somewhere at the back of my mind.

She asked whether I'd seen Nicholas again and so I told her about the pub. I began trying explain why I thought there was something to what he had said. Why I'd found the story about the deer so convincing. But I could tell what I was saying was worrying her. 'Look, the guy does look like him in a creepy way but this is getting too much now,' she said. I made a noise that was not exactly disagreement or assent.

We switched to talking about work. Leti was getting increasingly annoyed with her job. 'It's like another level of being fed up. Before I just thought I was bored but I actually think its wearing away at me and I wonder why I chose an environment like that. I knew going in that school didn't have a good atmosphere, I'd been told that by more than one person, so why did I do that to myself, you know what I mean?'

'Yeah,' I said. I wasn't sure if she was trying to tell me about a deeper pattern that was going on for her and I wondered if there was something better I could have said in response but the moment was gone because she was back to talking about the thing with Nicholas.

'You know, it does remind me of high school, you going around with Robin, this focus on Nicky. Like we've gone back in time.'

A petulant heat came to my face. 'It's been good to see Robin again. I shouldn't have lost touch with him. You can't erase your past.'

'You can't live inside it either,' she said.

I found this annoyingly grandstanding, like she felt we were in a television drama and I was the dippy one, the one that needed warning. 'I'm not trying to,' was all I said.

'There are things you don't see sometimes,' Leti said.

There was a long pause. I swallowed some saliva that had balled up in my mouth. I knew I should say something in response to this but instead I asked about a promotion I remembered she was going for. It had been and gone, she hadn't got it. She hadn't really wanted it anyway. All the way through the call there was a bristliness, a gap between us. My neck muscles felt tight under my chin after I hung up the phone.

Leti and I had begun to drift from each other by the last few years of high school. It was probably a couple of things. I felt left out by her becoming so wrapped up in her art that she often didn't want to leave the house. She had been annoyed by my closeness to Robin. We didn't see much of each other when she was at art college and I was at university. I was faintly intimidated by her new friends, Morna and a few others. I always had a sense that there was some joke about me between them. I knew it was probably a projected insecurity, yet there it was. For a long time, in their presence, I stumbled over words. They took trips up to the highlands together, Morna and Leti and some other classmates, and I wasn't invited. Why would I be? It was a different set. There was a small, petty sadness like a glass bead in my throat, imagining them walking round our old haunts, my old friend with her new friends. Sometimes at parties they'd refer to things I didn't know about from Leti's life in the village, or they'd know things about the two of us I thought no one else would ever know. Morna and I knew each other well enough now to be friends rather than friends of friends but somehow it wasn't like that.

When Leti got the teaching job in Edinburgh, we seemed to gradually slot back into place. To re-stitch our friendship. Now I felt that we were breaking the stitches again – not all at once but in odd places, snapping this one or that one, a single stitch at a time.

The day after the conversation with Leti, I found another of the miniature paintings. It was a pigeon, this time in the bathroom behind the heated towel rail. It was as if someone had painted them in such a way as to make them appear like little surprises, or gifts, for another person to find. The pigeon had a whorl of nest around it, painted simply with two intertwining brush-strokes of yellow and brown. A mother pigeon, or a father. Further along there was another striped cat-like animal. I found these miniature creatures both sinister and comforting. They suggested another world somehow, inside the ordinariness of the flat. As with the other pictures, around this one there was a patch of white as if someone had been painting the bathroom and had chosen not to paint over it. It also struck me for the first time that they were predators and prey. The tigers and the pigeons. Around the skirting boards, the tigers were perhaps hunting the pigeons.

That day, I couldn't stop thinking about Nicholas, thinking of other ways to put things to Leti, and I started to worry that I was going down a version of the same route the chemistry teacher took. That, like him, no one would want to know me. People would keep a polite distance, whisper about me in cafes, not meet my eye. And still that sense of the realness of it stayed with me.

The following Friday, Robin and I went out to a film together. Just the two of us, as his partner was working late. In the over-bright bar after the film, I asked him about the cross he always wore.

'Are you still religious?'

'In my own way.'

'Catholic?'

'Kind of.'

'How does that work?'

He took a sip of his coffee. 'You can make your own sense of it.'

'I thought you couldn't. I thought that was the whole point?'

He laughed. 'Conscience takes priority over church teaching.'

'Do you believe Nicky is still alive in some way? Like in heaven, I mean?'

'On one level, yeah, that's what I hope.'

'But how? In what way?'

He started playing with a sugar packet. 'Conversations like this always get silly.'

I fixed my face into a slightly teasing smile. 'And how does that work if he's also back? If this guy Nicholas is him?'

'Neither of us really believe that, do we?' he said. He nicked the sugar packet with his nail and it began to spill out over the table.

'I think I do believe it a bit sometimes, even if I don't on another level,' I said quietly.

'Yeah, I guess it's a bit like that with me too.'

'Have you heard from him lately?'

He chewed at a piece of skin on his lower lip. 'Actually, yes. He suggested we meet up for a drink again last Wednesday and then he didn't come.'

'You didn't tell me.'

'I suppose I wanted to talk to him by myself, to see if he remembered anything he couldn't have known about.'

'Fair enough,' I said, swallowing a slight sense of being left out, like a child sitting out at a ball game.

'Have you got any more texts from him?'

'No, not lately,' I said.

'Tell me if you do.'

The next day, I visited Tony again. I'd made an extra appointment because of his money problems. When I opened the door he was holding his cat, a bundle of shining black fur, his eyepatch pushed up onto his forehead. I was surprised to see his eye, blinking and blue underneath, as if I had expected it to actually be missing, for there to be only scar tissue. He beckoned me in and the cat leapt from his arms as I reached out a hand to stroke her fur. On the floor, her pink mouth opened and closed silently. She retreated into the belly of the flat. I hadn't been thinking about the cat at all but now relief poured over me unexpectedly, so that I found my eyes stinging.

'Hurray, you found her!' I said loudly to stop myself from becoming tearful. I sat down on his sofa and I took out my folder. 'Where was she?'

'She just walked back one day, just like you said she would.' The cat settled itself in front of the alcove where a fireplace was once. The actual fire had been bricked up and painted over a long time ago but it was as if she could sense a ghost of the heat. As we talked, I found myself stretching my feet towards the non-existent fire.

I made some more phone calls for him about the missing money. I'd put him in touch with a debt relief company to keep up with his tenancy payments while his account was empty. A payment plan had been arranged. 'I don't understand money,' he said happily. He seemed less concerned about it now the cat was back. As I was on the phone to his energy company, she came closer and rolled on the carpet at my feet, a whorl of fur on her belly, but when I reached to tickle her she darted away under a chair.

'Aw, be nice,' he said to her, but she stayed hunkered where she was.

As I was wrapping up, he said, 'I think there's a ghost in the building.'

'What makes you say that?'

'I hear things rolling around, above my flat.'

'Mmm,' I said, hoping this wasn't going to turn out to be some form of psychosis. 'Could be squirrels.'

'It's like a rolling sound, like a rolling pin.'

I didn't like to think what could be going on up there in the attic, if anyone in the neighbourhood had access to it. There could be someone living up there but I didn't want to scare him. 'Well, you just keep me up to date if you do hear anything else, anything that worries you, OK?'

He nodded seriously and the cat watched us both from under the chair. 'Do you believe in ghosts?'

'I would have said no but I've run into one lately,' I said this before I'd thought about whether I should. He looked at me with anxious eyes.

'What do you mean?'

'Oh, not really, I just met a guy who looks like someone from my past. It feels a bit like he's a ghost.'

'You met a real ghost?'

'No, no. I was joking, sorry Tony, ignore me.' He looked at me sceptically but switched back to talking about his cat. When I told him I had to get on, he stood up to see me out. The sky outside the window behind him was armour grey.

On my way home, I dropped by the newsagent to pick up a few things and stopped to stare at a poster on the inside of the shop door. It was a missing poster for Jim attached to the glass by blobs of Blu Tack. I felt a small jarring sensation, seeing his face like that. His eyes looked brightly out of the photo, as if the photographer was someone he liked. Just at the edge of his shoulder was the rim of a pint glass. An unfortunate choice, I worried people would see it and think here was another alcoholic off on a bender. I grabbed bread and a paper and met his gaze again as I was leaving.

The more I thought about disappearances, the more I saw them everywhere. There had been a disappearance in Leti's family once. She'd had a cousin who had vanished. This cousin was her mum's older sister's child. There was a large age gap between the sisters, and the two branches of the family were not in touch very often so the story had the quality of being a tale, a family legend. One day this cousin had walked out on her husband and their three-year-old girl. 'I don't understand how someone could do that to a little kid,' Leti said. She told me about it one night when I was over at her house drinking orange squash and sitting on her bedroom carpet, a cream circle that seemed to transport us to other places, even as we grew too old for imaginary games. Malawi was a country I could barely imagine then. I'd pieced my image of it together from bits of description Leti had given me. I pictured her cousin walking away along a warm, dusty pavement, cars honking beside her. She wore a dress with yellow flowers on it and didn't look back over her shoulder as she walked.

As we got older, we could be more sympathetic to this cousin, imagining tragedies and life circumstances that might have made sense of this disappearance. Perhaps she was ill or her husband was abusive or she had merely gone to buy something for the child and a terrible disaster had befallen her. An accident or a kidnapping or a sudden amnesia.

Our family had a disappearing woman, back in the nineteen twenties. A Catherine, or Cath, who ran away to marry a Catholic priest, but left him once she reached London, for an attempted career on the stage, or something or other. Whenever I asked my dad about it, she became a slightly different person, she was a great-great-aunt or someone's stepchild or a family friend who was like a family member, and the career on the stage became a career in the circus so that I began to wonder if any such person had ever existed.

The trees had begun to gather bright tinges of autumn colour when I ran into Nicholas again. I was out at a late lunch for a colleague's leaving do. On my way home, I walked back using the route that passed Nicholas's office. I told myself I wasn't looking for him, that I just liked that route; the view of the cathedral, the Victorian railings along the building fronts, the diagonal gaps of sky and spires. I walked briskly. I knew I might see him, but I told myself that wasn't what I wanted. I had walked this way numerous times over the last couple of months and not seen him.

And then, there, turning a corner, a familiar laugh among a small group of people. The edge of the laugh came to me before I saw the face. They were all in work clothes, presumably heading home for the day. Nicholas saw me before I could decide whether to speak to him or pretend I had not seen him. He slowed so the others in his group walked ahead. 'I'll catch you up,' I heard him say and then he was stepping right into my path, swaggering, thumbs in his pockets.

'Looking for zombies?' he said.

'I wasn't looking for you.' We were buffeted forward by another group of people leaving another office.

'You were looking for something.'

'I was looking for some fresh air.' That unreal feeling came over me, not quite of being in a dream, but of being slightly unwell, or of everything being behind glass.

'It's a bit of a coincidence, don't you think?' he said.

'What is?'

'That you just happened to be here by my work.'

'It is a coincidence, yeah,' I said. We were swept towards the crossroads by the crowd, I had to step sideways to avoid falling.

'I think you're following me.'

'I'm not,' I said, already scowling. 'And actually, you messaged me. A while back. Didn't you? You got my number.'

'I may have done.'

'Where did you get my number?'

'You gave it to me, or your friend did, or something, when we met.'

'I did not and Robin said he didn't either.'

'Maybe he forgot that he did.'

I opened my mouth to say I didn't believe him but I couldn't be sure Robin wouldn't do this. 'Listen, were you joking about all the things you said?'

'Which things?'

'About the deer, on the fence?' I said.

'What fence?'

'What you said. You know what you said. Don't you?'

'I do,' he replied uncertainly. The lights beeped and we crossed the road, passing a troupe of primary-school-aged children, all linked together in pairs, holding hands.

When we reached the other side, I said, 'Did you just make that up about the deer? Were you just guessing?'

Nicholas tipped his chin up and narrowed his eyes, like a stage-show mystic. 'I remembered a new thing,' he said.

'What?'

'I remember an explosion.'

'You remember an explosion? That's ridiculous.'

'It was kind of ridiculous.'

'An explosion where?'

'In school,' he said. We were part-blocking the pavement; we both had to step aside to let a double pram pass.

'An explosion in our village school? I think you've got the wrong false memory there.'

He wrinkled his nose. 'Not in school but outside.'

'Which is it? Inside or out?' The more I studied his face, the more it seemed to take on a different look, as if he was moulded in a slightly different way. Today his nose appeared sharper, his teeth a little bigger, his chin slightly blunter.

'We were in class but we were outside. We were standing somewhere grassy and the teacher was showing us something.' Small lines of concentration appeared above the top of his nose. 'It was an explosion made of water.'

This did hold me up, even before I could place what it might be. My mind had been searching through images of terrorism, action-film stock footage. Red and yellow fiery blasts in the middle of our small village school. Now a real memory filtered through replacing these, like the graininess suddenly clearing on an old TV set. The smell of damp by the river, the distinct kind of boredom of an early summer afternoon in school, and the chemistry teacher. I hadn't thought of that kind of explosion, with water instead of fire. The burst of water that shot up from the plastic container.

'Do you remember who caused it?' I said.

'Yes, it was the guy who killed me.' His eyes were on me, searching for victory. Then I remembered that he was not there. Or Nicky was not there. It was my class who saw the water trick, the children my own age. But, Mr Fletcher might have shown it to other classes. Probably he did it every year. For all the world, it had been like Nicholas was remembering something difficult to reach, drawing it from the back of his mind. From childhood, or adolescence. Suddenly he looked too pale, a bluish tinge almost to his cheeks.

We started moving again; I realised I was walking sort of sideways along the pavement, trying to keep my eyes on him. There was a dodgem-fairground-ride giddiness to everything. It was getting cold. I took my gloves from my pocket and put them on, and tucked my chin into my coat collar. At the side street where I would usually turn off, Nicholas stopped.

'I'm going this way,' he said, pointing in the direction of my flat.

'So am I,' I said. 'Seriously, is this all a joke? Nicky was a real person who died. It wasn't a joke to us.'

'Who is us?'

I realised I meant me and Robin and Leti but instead I said. 'Everyone, everyone in the village. If this is a joke, I think you should stop it.' I waited for a response but he walked on silently, his eyebrows bunching up like thoughts colliding. A cat crouched on a wall. I recognised it, ginger with its one white paw. It had always hopped down and run before I reached it. Now it stayed, arched up its back and Nicholas ran his hand over its spine. Nicky was good with animals, I thought. No one had been able to pick up the school hamster because it bit and then there he was at the back of the lunchroom one day with it running over his fingers.

'So, what was our school called?' I said.

'I don't remember.'

'You don't remember?'

'Sure, you leave some of your memory behind when you come back.' He was laughing now. I hit the sleeve of his coat with a light sideways flick. It was the sort of thing I'd usually only do with a friend.

'How would you not remember the name of our school?'

'It didn't come back to me. Robin told me the name of the village. If I wanted to cheat I could have gone and looked it up but I wanted to see if I could remember. But I can't. Which is interesting. It must be lost somewhere.'

'Oh please.'

'But then how did I know about the explosion?'

'I'm turning here,' I said. We were near my flat. I didn't really want him to know where I lived, but I was too cold and tired to pretend I was going somewhere else.

'So am I,' he said. 'Go on. How did I know about the explosion?'

'You're just guessing at things.'

'Believe what you want. Anyway, this is me.' I thought he was saying he was being himself, but he stopped in the street and turned towards a door. He meant this was where he lived. We were at a main door on a busy road near my home. This was why I had seen him so often. I had walked past that red door many times. It opened into a converted shop. The front windows looked out onto the pavement. He had probably seen me pass by often enough. He pulled out a key from his pocket, then turned to me. He took a small step closer, his nose was near my nose, his head tilted down. For a second I thought he was going to try to kiss me. I did not think he was attracted to me; it just seemed like it was the next natural movement. Instead he breathed in and took the same small step back.

'You had a sister,' he said.

My mouth opened and closed. I stood still. 'What makes you say that?'

Just for a second I thought I caught the slightest flash of uncertainty, or embarrassment on his face. His voice was quiet. 'You talked about her. I remember that. Am I right?'

'Why are you asking me, if you know?'

'Because the memories are blurry. They swim up to me, and then away again. Sort of like the way the memories of dreams come and go when you lie awake in the morning. She died, didn't she?'

I nodded.

'Very young?' he said. 'Like a baby?'

I nodded again. 'You realise this is a very sick joke. You're joking about someone in my family who died.'

'But you said it never affected you, that you didn't remember her. You used to say that.'

I drew my arms around myself. 'Not to Nicky. We never talked about her.'

'Are you sure?'

I wasn't now. I stepped back from him. His breath smelt faintly of garlic. 'This is a very sick joke. You could have found all that out from records. You could have guessed things.' My mind was clattering, whirring; he only needed to know my second name to find out I had a sister, though it would take some research. I must have told him my last name at some point, or Morna or Robin had.

'It was like being underwater, between the lives, warm and blurry and . . . I sometimes want to go back there.' He smiled weakly. 'I sometimes miss it.'

'Shut up. I don't believe you for a moment,' I said.

'Every time you say that a fairy dies.' He broke into a laugh again.

'Fuck you.'

'Good night,' he said. He turned to the door, his keys jangling, and I turned the other way and walked off, but I couldn't help looking back to watch him put the key in the lock. So much seemed unreal about him, I wanted to be sure that this was where he lived. The door opened in front of him. A slice of light flickered on. Pausing, he turned to look at me, and winked in that mock-flirtatious way before disappearing into the bright space of the flat.

Heading home, two more turns, everything was ordinary. I reached my street. Noises bubbled out from single-glazed windows; an argument, the underwater burble of a television show. A stairwell door slammed. Steam rose from the series of small white boiler flues along the outside walls. It drifted like puffs from the caterpillar's pipe in Alice in Wonderland. I opened my door and stepped in, putting on the lights straight away, as the cloudy afternoon left the flat feeling gloomy.

That night I had another extinct animal dream. A moa bird appeared, ostrich-like and covered in black feathers. It curved its huge frilly neck around my door, moving with a hesitant curiosity towards me, where I lay still in my bed.

At work in the office one morning a few days later, two women came in with a stack of missing person posters. They walked arm in arm, an older woman with her hair pinned back and a younger woman with tired eyes. The posters had the same photo of Jim as the one I had seen in the shop.

The younger of the two women said, 'Will you put them up for us?'

'Of course, no problem,' I said. 'How do you know him?'

Even as I was speaking I realised who one of the women must be. The older woman pointed a thumb at the younger. 'That's his daughter.'

Jim had mentioned an adult child he never saw. 'Oh, I'm sorry,' I said, looking into the daughter's eyes because there was nowhere else to look.

She seemed embarrassed too. 'Och, no, it's not your fault,' she said.

'I can definitely put up some posters.' I reached out, taking a bundle. I'd wondered what had happened between him and his daughter but we'd never gone into it. The rule was to avoid back story, only point clients to the future.

His daughter smiled a shy smile. 'Do I look like him?' she said.

'Yes,' I said, only then realising she did. Something about her cheekbones and the set of her brown eyes. I almost felt like I owed them some kind of explanation or apology but I knew I didn't really.

When they left, I sank back into my office chair with a sudden heaviness, a desire not to move for a bit.

Leaves drifted down in front of the car like snowfall. October already; the year was looping round again. I was the passenger first, Leti the driver. Each of us had arranged a Monday holiday and we were heading up to the highlands for a long weekend together. Leti's parents had moved to a village further north a few years ago so we'd decided to stop at my parents' for one night, then drive on up to hers for two.

We had not talked about Nicholas for a while. We'd not seen much of each other before the trip and there was still a grainy tension between us. I had felt it even as I'd thrown my suitcase into the back of the car while Leti sat stiff in the driver's seat.

We stopped to grab dinner at a roadside cafe, not our usual one. The place was half an hour from closing and no longer serving hot food so we ate limp roast-beef sandwiches with plastic cups of coffee. I ordered a mocha, which always made me feel nauseous; every so often I'd try one again in the hope that it would be nicer and each time I'd end up feeling sick.

I grabbed a newspaper on the way out. A front-page headline stated that the world could be losing up to ten thousand species of wildlife per year. Reading it, there was an old, heavy sensation. The unease I used to experience as a child at the thought of that loss, that eating away. When we reached the car, I threw the paper front-page down onto the back seat. Leti got into the passenger side now and I took over the driving.

We left the lights of the cafe behind, pure blackness rolling out beyond the windows. Though I knew the road well, there were times when I could not imagine what was out there; we might have been driving through the dark of another country. After we'd driven in silence for a while, Leti said, 'Don't tell my parents but I'm leaving the school.'

'What are you going to do?'

'I don't know. I want to do my artwork somehow. Do it properly.'

'Great. I'd be in trouble if I'd suggested that.'

'Well, you didn't.' I glanced at her as we hit a straight part of the road. She was sitting up rigidly, hands on her knees. 'I'm not expecting to live off the art. I'm not delusional. I'll do something else. Just don't say anything yet until I've sorted something out. They'll only fuss.'

We were quiet again for a bit. The dark countryside spun out, cats' eyes flashing in the centre of the road. At this point, I knew there was a river to our left though I couldn't see it. I knew that it would be high and foaming through the trees because there had been heavy rainfall the previous day. I followed the beam of headlights with the sensation that a giant was laying down the tarmac in front of us as we went along.

The hum from the tyres changed pitch as we reached a newly resurfaced area. The car nosed down into a dip and rose again and suddenly there was something large and white flashing across the windscreen. An owl, the white ghosting shape of a barn owl all in a blur right in front of the glass. I hadn't even hit the brakes, my brain not working fast enough, and there was a loud thump and a blur of the pale brown and white across the windscreen.

I braked hard, my head bounced forward, the seatbelt bit into my collarbone.

'Shit, shit,' I said.

'Fuck. What? What was it?' Leti's hands gripped the underside of the glove compartment.

'I hit it.'

'Hit what?'

'It was a bird.'

I slowed. A cleared patch in the woods formed a pull-in
place up ahead. I stopped the car. I had the sensation that I
had slipped into a scene from a film. I looked in the rear-view
mirror. I couldn't see anything. I rubbed at my face. I felt I
should get out of the car and walk back and try to find the bird,
to see if there was anything I could do to save it. I also didn't
want to move.

'What bird are you talking about?' Leti said.

'I hit an owl.' A sickly feeling swelled inside me, partly from
the coffee. The absurd thought spiralled that I was not inside my
real life but instead inside a film, that I had been inside a film
for a while.

'I didn't see anything. There would have been a thump.' Her
hands were still gripping the glove compartment.

'There was a thump.'

'There wasn't.'

'How could you not hear it?' I said. 'It was really loud. And I
saw the owl. It was in front of us, then it just thumped into the
windscreen.'

'I didn't hear anything and definitely didn't see anything.'

I took a deep breath. I could feel the adrenalin coursing.
What a small animal must feel when it is being hunted. 'You
were asleep then,' I said.

'I wasn't asleep. I was looking straight ahead.'

'Maybe you fell asleep for a few seconds and didn't realise.
People don't always know they've fallen asleep,' I said.

The dark pressed at the car windows. Leti was laughing with irritation. 'I was not fucking asleep, I would know.'

'But people don't always,' I said.

'I was wide awake. I was watching the road. I saw you brake. If you hit it, it would have damaged the windscreen.'

I grabbed my torch from the glove compartment and opened the driver door.

'What are you doing?' Leti said.

'I'm just going to check.'

'Check what?'

'If it's injured, we might be able to do something.'

Her eyes were on me like I'd lost my mind. 'Watch you don't get hit by a truck,' was all she said.

'I'll be careful. I'll only be a second.'

'What are you going to do if it's there and it's injured?'

'I don't know. Call the SSPCA. I can't just leave it.' I climbed out of my door. The cold air rippled around me. A lorry full of logs rattled by, straps whistling in the side wind. I ran along the verge and peered into the woods. I could see nothing. I shone the beam of the torch between the trees, the rib-like, ragged pine trunks, and then ran the light over the road. There was nothing. I was sure I had hit something. The thump was clear in my mind and the flash of a highlighted wing sliding across the front of the car. A couple more vehicles whizzed by, their lights pressing into my eyes. I walked back along the verge and looked over the bonnet and windscreen. There was no dint, no scratches, no smear from an oily coat. I had hit a pheasant once and there had been dust and grease on the paintwork. I walked back level with the window and shook my head. I let myself in. 'Well, there's no sign. Maybe it only glanced off.'

Leti put her hand on my arm, scrunched the fabric of my sleeve. 'Maybe it was you that was dozing, maybe you were asleep for a second and you dreamt it.'

'I thought you said people know if they're asleep.'

'Maybe I should drive again. I'm not tired.'

'Neither am I.' I didn't want her to drive, it didn't feel safe. I was sure I had been awake because the image and the sound were both completely clear. She must have been the one who slept. I didn't argue, I just said I'd prefer to do my share. She watched me, though, for the rest of the trip; we talked stiltedly and put some music on, and her eyes kept flickering to my face.

Spending the night at my parents' house, we were like children again, like girls at a sleepover. Something eased between us, perhaps related to the relief of being in from the dark road. The end of the drive had been tiring but once we arrived I was no longer drowsy. We chatted, amassed packets of crisps and sweets, carried my mother's small television into my room so we could watch comedy DVDs. At the window, no moonlight meant the mountain simply wasn't there. I drew the curtains and shut the night out. I no longer felt sick and I ate as if I hadn't seen food for a while, my fingers shining with grease from the crisps. I waited until we had settled, until the giddiness had subsided a bit and the house was quiet around us, before bringing Nicholas up again. I told Leti about meeting him in the street, the things he had known. She sat up straight, legs crossed, listening like her child self to one of my stories. I told her he had known about my sister. It was eerie, thinking of it all together with the shock of the owl on the road, thinking of the way Nicky died. If I wanted to spook myself, I could have imagined I was being haunted, that the disappearing owl was part of it. The first thing Leti said was, 'He's winding you up.'

'But how could he know?'

She crossed and recrossed her legs. 'He gets it out of you somehow. He could guess from the way you were reacting.'

'But it wasn't like that. I know I didn't say anything to him.' I tried to think back to how it had unfurled. The order of the things I'd said. 'Honestly, how about the time in the pub, how would he know about the deer on the fence? How would he guess that? His first guess?'

'Maybe it didn't happen exactly like that. It might have seemed like his first guess but he got it out of you subtly by stages. Anyway, with your sister, you can look that kind of thing up.'

'I know but really it would take some effort. He'd need my second name to find any records and why do that if you don't know what you're looking for?'

'I don't know why he's doing anything. Or why you're getting so caught up in it.'

I was sitting on my bed in my pyjamas, my stubbly ankles poking out of the shooting-star-patterned trousers I kept at my parents. Leti was in a nightdress, her legs tucked into the spare winter sleeping bag on the pull-out mattress that slid on rollers from underneath the main bed. This had been the sleeping arrangements when she had stayed over as a kid. The bedside lamp shone beside us through the lampshade's pattern of blue butterflies.

'Are you sure you aren't letting things slip to him somehow?'

'If I'd given him some clue I wouldn't have been so shocked.'

She looked to the ceiling then back at me. 'So what do you think now? That his death was a hoax or something? It's not like he's old enough to have had life insurance. Where would he even have gone after the accident?'

'I know, I know, I know. But it's just, there is something going on. I don't know.' I wanted to keep uncertainty in my voice to protect myself from the embarrassment of being sure. But the feeling of certainty that had come over me in the bar and on the street was so seductive. Getting rid of it completely would be like pouring a spilt drink back into the bottle. I tried again to find words for it but they weren't there.

We moved on to talking about other things but the conversation faltered. We didn't refer back to the incident with the owl. We hadn't told my parents about that in case it worried them.

After one o'clock we grew properly tired and decided to call it a night. I padded downstairs to get something that wasn't sugary to eat and a cup of water. I picked some blueberries out of the fridge, the bitter-sweet baubles cold on my teeth. A little flash of memory came into my mind, a time with Robin and some wild berries he'd picked. I was finding that happened often now, childhood memories opening up like tiny doors on an old advent calendar. As I headed back upstairs, I passed the front door. I paused there, stepped towards the heavy curtain that covered the side window and looked out. It was something I'd done a lot as a small child. I liked to look through that window by the door at night and imagine I would see something dangerous, a werewolf or bogle, from the safety of the house. Sometimes I would imagine the black road under the streetlamps was a river full of crocodiles.

Now as I looked, I saw a figure and flinched. I had expected the dark space to be tantalisingly empty, as it always had been when I'd looked out as a child. Instead, there was someone out there in the cold. I moved closer to the glass so that I could see my own reflection. Someone was out there, walking while talking on their phone, the blue light of it glinting like a firefly. It would just be somebody from the village, I knew that, someone unable to sleep, but still it spooked me and I left the window before they could see me.

~*~

When we set off in the morning, Leti drove. A number of deer were dotted about the outskirts of the village. A troupe of three young stags raised their heads as we passed the last garden. We made our way in the daylight, the full trip needing about three hours. The autumn had made deep tendrils into the landscape, waterfalls running through the cracks in the mountains, the bracken the same red colour as the deer. We stopped at a viewing point and took photos of each other balancing on the nose of a hill. I was tempted to remind Leti of her childhood trick, but I didn't. We pulled over again at a village on the route and bought unseasonable ice creams from the local shop and ate them from their paper cones, sitting in the car.

Leti's parents' house looked out over the sea. It was part of a hamlet, a scatter of mainly west-highland-style, whitewashed, small-windowed houses set out at the foot of a hill at unexpected angles to protect them from the wind. Leti's parents joked about our old village, their previous home, being *the great metropolis*, their new place tiny and remote in comparison. They were surprised by the pull that isolated, open spaces had over them as they had both grown up in Blantyre, the commercial centre of Malawi.

We arrived in the evening and all ate together as soon as we were settled in. One of Leti's paintings hung on the dining-room wall and Leti sat with her back to it. She'd told me once she didn't like looking at her own artwork, at least not after it was finished. She said it seemed to morph into something else once she was no longer actively working on it, something less alive, and she often almost felt betrayed by it.

We slept through Sunday morning while Leti's parents attended the church service at the windswept kirk on the hill. In the afternoon I stayed in the house while Leti set out walking with her dad. The weather was mild and bright. Sun rippled over the grassy hillside beyond the front windows. It created a sense that the ground was a large animal, stretching and writhing, the grass the rippling fur. I sat in the kitchen and helped Leti's mum snip up pieces of foil she was using to make gift cards. This was how I remembered her, always making some small, exquisite thing.

We talked for a while about the various home improvements they'd been working on, then about the gossip among their neighbours. I got up and brought us each a cup of peppermint tea. I had been shy of Leti's parents as a child. They had seemed strict, having different rules to mine. It was only in the last five or six years that I had come to feel like an adult around them.

When I sat down again, my mind was back to Nicholas. It stung to think of the conversation with Leti. I twisted around the idea of asking her mother about Nicky while we drank our tea and eventually gave in.

'Do you ever think about Nicky Harper?' I said, making a quick snip with the scissors.

She shook her head, meaning yes. 'A sad, sad time.'

'Leti said you knew about the teacher getting into all those conspiracy theories?'

She nodded. 'He's a poor man, really.'

'So he's been saying all that conspiracy stuff for a long time?'

'For years. He started saying those things around the time of his house being flooded. I think it was the last straw.'

'His house was flooded? When was that?'

'Oh, years back, not long after it all happened. Just after he got out of prison.'

'I don't think I remember about that?' Though now that she said it, I dimly recalled something about water, maybe around the time of the charred scarecrow. I guess I would have been focused on school exams around that time.

199

'Someone broke in by the back window while he was away. I think it was while he was visiting his sister. They plugged all the drains, left all the taps running. The downstairs rooms were ruined.'

'But he went on living there . . .'

'Yes, he patched it up and got new furniture.' I thought of the odd collection of things I had seen in the house. 'We gave him a few pieces, so did your mum and dad.' In a way I was touched by this but in another way I didn't like the thought of it. Something from our home ending up in that house.

'Why didn't he leave?'

'Good question. We didn't understand it at the time. With Kristeen being gone and so many people looking down on him.'

'Who did it? The flooding?'

'The question there is did the police try to find out? Maybe they didn't try very hard.' She had switched from cutting the foil to sewing buttons on the cards.

'It wasn't one of Nicky's parents?'

She paused for a long time. 'They weren't petty people.' I couldn't picture them doing it but neither could I think who else would. The children at the school were unsettled and fascinated by the accident, but I don't remember anyone thinking of some kind of revenge against Mr Fletcher.

Her head bent over her stitching. I looked at the sea beyond the window, the deep grey of it. 'Are you in touch with his parents ever?' I asked after a while.

'Not now, no. We sent his mother a Christmas card for a few years.' I felt ashamed, thinking of his mother in real life. Like the thing with Nicholas was a game I'd made up. Here in this quiet room, the certainty shrunk to the size of a pinhead. I realised Leti's mum was looking at me hard, almost the look

Leti had given me in the car – their faces a mirror of each other when concerned.

'What put all this in your head again?'

'Just thinking around it all, I don't know. Getting old, stuff comes back to you.'

I thought she'd laugh about me saying I was getting old but instead she tapped my forearm and said, 'You take care of yourself, that's the main thing. *Forget the former things; do not dwell on the past*. You know where that comes from?'

'I'm guessing the Bible or Shakespeare?'

She laughed and didn't answer. We moved on to talking about Leti's job, whether she was happy in it, and I chose my words carefully and we didn't come back to the topic of Nicky.

I liked watching the sea from Leti's parents' house. This October weekend was not especially wild but I could still see a good number of white horses cantering, breaking on black rocks. Nicholas briefly came into my mind, what he'd said about returning to the water, but I tried to push the thought away. I loved the idea of witnessing a storm this close to the sea, from the safety of the house. I hoped there would be wilder weather that night but instead everything was quiet and still. I slept well and woke remembering a dream of passenger pigeons gathering at the window, cooing and peering mildly at me.

I do sometimes think I have one memory of my sister. She is in a clear plastic cradle and I'm holding onto the rim. I look in and she is sleeping peacefully and I say, 'Wake up, baby.' The sunlight pours gold onto her face, her blankets are white, as if she is a perfect baby in an advertisement. Though a transparent tube leads away from her nose, she is so peach perfect, so golden, not bluish or jaundiced or red, that I wonder if this is a real memory or if it was constructed from something else, something I saw on television or a drawing in a book.

~*~

It was a weekday night back in Edinburgh and I was heading home in the rain after seeing a film by myself. I liked to see films alone sometimes, I liked the slight disorientation of sitting on my own in the dark cinema, surrounded by strangers. This time though, I had partly regretted my solitude. The film had been strange and disjointed, it had gone on a long time and I'd felt as if I'd wandered into a wood I couldn't find my way out of. The ending had been over-the-top bloody in a way that I suppose was meant to make a point, but it had left me feeling chilled and slightly detached from reality.

Walking home, about three streets away from my flat, the rain started to fall hard and heavy like the beginnings of a flood.

My coat didn't have a hood and I hadn't brought my umbrella so I jogged forward with my head down, blinking through the drops that landed in my eyes. The streets were zagged with dark reflections and seemed quieter than usual even for this time. Nothing but the occasional cars and a few shadowy pedestrians up ahead. The coolness kept away the deep scent of the already fallen leaves, but there was still a slight mustiness in the air that I'd catch now and again.

I cut down a side lane and ran along by the tall wall of a city centre graveyard. I found this street eerie not because of the graves but because of the two dark gateways and the way you could not see who might be lurking there. I kept up my pace. I turned a corner at a shuttered-down takeaway and stood absentmindedly waiting for the light to change as a couple of taxis spluttered past in front of me.

A hand grabbed my shoulder. I whipped round to my right, but no one was there. I turned back the other way and grey fabric flashed past my nose. A figure in a grey hood jogged away through the rain. They'd bumped into me, almost knocked me into the road. Now the figure stopped at the far end of the ztreet. I felt I recognised them without being able to think who they were. The outline was short, the shoulders hunched; they wore a hooded top and baggy trousers. They turned around and it was Jim's face looking back at me. He was grinning, showing all his teeth, like he had won a prize. 'Jim, is that you? Where have you been?' I called out.

He didn't answer, only clasped his hands together, and shook them in a kind of victory gesture. Then he was running again, off round the corner. His footfalls slapping the rainy pavement.

I was starting to shiver. The light changed and I hurried on across the road and kept up a sort of half-run until I reached my door with stitches in my side. There were a few seconds, while I was unlocking the door and getting my body through it, where I felt someone was about to push or grab me from behind. The relief after I'd got the door closed and done up the double lock was like slipping into warm water.

Inside the calm solidity of the flat, I questioned what I'd seen. I threw off my wet clothes and bundled them into the laundry basket then changed straight into my pyjamas. I sat on the couch for a long time, wondering what to do. While making myself a cup of sweet tea, I decided I had to call the police, to pass on the information for their missing person file on Jim. If I was wrong, I was wrong. On the phone, a man took down my description of what happened. When he questioned me, asked whether I was certain it was him, I said I couldn't be sure and the voice on the end of the line sounded tired.

~*~

In the attic again, Nicky and I sat together on the rough wooden boards, dust motes drifting about us.

'Let's put the light out,' Nicky said.

'Why?' I said.

'It's a game. See if I can sneak up to you. If you grab me first you win.'

'I'm not playing.' For a moment, his face in the deep shadows looked like someone else's, an older person's maybe.

'Come on, don't be boring.' He was already sliding over to the light switch.

'OK, fine,' I said. He reached the switch by the trapdoor. Snap. Darkness and small islands of orange and purple kaleidoscoping in front of my eyes. I could see the dim glow of the trapdoor at the other end, his torso flashing past it, then he vanished into the dark. I stared at the pure black around me, breathing hard.

I started to feel tiny touches and tickles against my forehead and cheeks, little skin irritations that probably came and went all the time but now it was hard to distinguish them from the light touch of a finger.

My own breathing seemed loud now but I could not hear his. I listened so hard it felt as if the bones of my skull were pushing my ears outwards. I listened for him stepping towards me. The darkness allowed in wilder thoughts; maybe he would cut my throat, maybe he would transform into a demon, maybe he would kiss me. Gradually I could make something out. The slanted loft beam nearest the trapdoor. Then I could see two beams, then three then four. Now a movement, a bulky shape not at Nicky's height but low down, sliding towards me across the boards. I knew I had quite good night vision, I liked to walk in the garden at night sometimes. I saw Nicky stretch an arm out in front of himself. He could not see me, he was feeling his way. Gradually his shape took on more form. He lifted his knees and his palms, placing them carefully.

I raised myself gradually, inch by inch, but I could hear my clothing making a slight shushing noise across the wood. I swept round to the side and saw the edge of something solid, an old trunk maybe, and I sat down on it. Nicky passed near me and it seemed he was going to crawl on by like he hadn't seen me, but at the last moment he lunged for me and in the panic that filled the space of my chest I twisted backwards and fell off the trunk. My back hit against a beam and in an instant I couldn't breathe. I opened and closed my mouth to tell him to stop, to stop playing, but I could not get enough breath to make a sound. I thought that I was about to die, the delicate pink structures of my lungs had collapsed inside me and I would die struggling to breathe, rolling on the floor. Nicky pounced on me.

'Got you,' he said, grabbing handfuls of my top. A deep wheezing, gasping sound came from my throat. There was a terrible emptiness in my lungs. *This is death, I'm dying.* 'Hey, are you all right?' he said.

In the darkness, I shook my head, still gasping. Then the air came back in fits and starts. Still I thought, *I will never get down from this attic.* I rolled onto my side, pain from the blow flashed across my shoulder blades. Gradually everything eased. My breath came back as a slow sifting of the air through my throat.

'You winded yourself, did you?' he said, rocking into a sitting position. I could see his face now, the white moon of it.

'I couldn't breathe,' I said.

'Yeah, you winded yourself.'

'What do you mean?'

'When you fall hard, sometimes you knock the wind out of your lungs.' I had heard the expression before but thought it was only a phrase. He laughed now and hot fury rose in my neck. 'You'll be fine, you just winded yourself.'

'You did it to me.'

'You did it to yourself.'

'Put the light on, put it on.'

'All right, all right.' He slid to the door and light flickered over us. Breathing was still hard and I had to swallow down mucus that had gathered at the back of my throat.

'I'm going back down,' I said.

'All right, fine, don't cry.' I wanted to be away from him, my daydream of a kiss in the dark completely repugnant now. I climbed down the ladder, carefully placing one foot then another. When I was on the landing I looked back up at the dark square of the loft hatch. He had not started to climb down yet; he made no sound as if no one was up there.

~*~

Nicky left my family's house on a rainy Saturday morning with his duffle bag on his shoulder. He'd been with us three weeks. His father came to pick him up, standing at the door, shuffling his feet as if he was kicking snow off his shoes though it was summer. Later that night as we were sitting on the couch before bedtime, my mum told me that Nicky's parents had been going through a 'rough patch' and that's why he'd come to stay with us and I wasn't to tell any tales about it at school.

I did think that we might be, if not friends, then something at a slant to it. That when I started high school in the autumn, he would acknowledge me. But that didn't happen and in the school corridors he paid me no notice at all for the first month.

Much later, my mum told me his parents had been fighting a lot, that she had heard their shouts from the garden one afternoon while she was hanging out laundry. During the time we took Nicky in, his mother had gone south to stay with family, threatening not to come back. Nicky's father had taken him to my parents, saying he needed a break. Why had he chosen my parents? My mum and dad had once been to their house for a party but I wouldn't have said they were friends. 'I don't know, but they knew us enough to know we're decent people, and we're close by.'

I didn't know much about Nicky's parents except that his mother seemed posh and his father owned a gun. I'd seen him with it once. I was dashing along on the main road to the village during a downpour and Nicky's dad walked past me with his rifle on his shoulder. He nodded to me. His expression was perfectly normal. I had never seen a gun in real life until then. As I walked on down the road, my shoulder blades tingled as if he was about to shoot me in the back. At school people said

Nicky's dad had shot an apple off his son's head, like William Tell. I remember kids asking Nicky about it and he would never confirm or deny it, he would just smile. My image of it happening was so clear I could have sworn I was there in the garden behind them, observing the apple shattering into sweet, white shards.

~*~

The night after I thought I saw Jim, I was sitting in my kitchen keeping an eye on a pan of rice when a text pinged on my phone. It made me jump. I thought the phone had been on silent.

Emily let me take you somewhere

I stared at the message. It was from the same number as before. Nicholas. I hadn't saved it onto my phone so it came up without a name. I returned to the pan, which was starting to boil over. Another ping made me flinch and spin round.

Let me take you somewhere.

I felt settled and safe in my kitchen, the water in the pan bubbling. It was one of those nights where I had no intention of going anywhere or seeing anyone. Still, I picked up the phone and typed.

Where?

A message blinked. *Somewhere I want to show you.*

Where?

I always thought you were pretty.

I guessed he was drunk. *No you didn't and no thanks*, I typed. I had closed the blinds but not the curtains. Shadows moved across my window at street level. It felt like he was making fun of me. I didn't believe for a moment that he was attracted to me, I had never got that feeling from him; he was too pretty for me.

It felt more like a taunt, like a high-school boy saying, *I fancy you*, then running away laughing with his friends.

I waited for more, but nothing arrived. After dinner, I sat with my feet up on the couch and phoned Leti. Her voice answered, surprised. I told her Nicholas wanted to take me somewhere.

'Don't go with him,' she said. 'You don't know who the hell he is.'

'Yes, it would be insane, wouldn't it?'

'He could kill you.' In my mind's eye, I saw her in her flat, her expression a look of concern or maybe disgust, one of her delicate china teacups in a saucer sitting next to her.

'He could kill me, that's a good point.' I laughed and Leti didn't. 'You wouldn't meet him with me?'

'No, I'm tired of this. Promise me you won't go.'

'I won't,' I said.

After I put down the phone, I wondered if I'd meant I won't go or I won't promise. I washed up the dishes, then texted Robin to tell him about the messages from Nicholas. *Go!*, he texted back, *find out more!* I did not reply to this. I let the water in the sink drain away. The flat seemed full of creaking and ticking tonight; the water pipes, the ceiling boards, the clock.

On a blustery November morning I stepped into Megan's flat for our last scheduled meeting together. She watched me arrive with thoughtful eyes and flopped back onto her bed as I made my way to a chair.

'I took him back,' she said.

'Who? Your boyfriend from before?'

Her chin rose. 'Yeah, Cam.'

'I thought you were dating someone new and it was going well?'

'It didn't work out. He said I get too clingy. I probably do. We had a big fight about it though. But then Cam messaged and he wanted me back.'

I didn't have a good feeling about that but I didn't say anything. I spent the next thirty minutes helping her finish up her application for the childcare course she'd picked out. A group of smiley toddlers played with alphabet blocks on the page of the brochure she had folded back. I wondered if working with children let her step back into childhood somehow, the childhood she'd largely missed out on. I leant over the laptop screen and read through her answers.

Partway through, when I'd suggested adding a full stop to a line, she peered at my face. 'You don't look well,' she said.

'Do I not?'

'Like, I mean, have you been sick today? You look the way I look when I've puked.'

'No, I haven't. Let's get back to this.'

'Just you look kind of green somehow.'

'I'm sure I don't.'

She didn't want to press send on the application when we finished. She said she wanted to read it over once more.

'You are going to send it though?'

'Of course, I'm not daft.'

We spent a few minutes going over an 'ending' survey I had to complete with all my clients when they finished, ticking a list of boxes that indicated she was happier than when we had started.

As I got ready to leave, I said, 'I hope this Cam guy is good to you. People have to earn your attention.'

I couldn't tell if her smile in response was a little sarcastic. 'I'm sorry I said you look like you've been sick. You don't really,' she said. Somehow that irritated me more than the original comment, as if I looked like I needed the reassurance.

'Good luck, OK, I'll be thinking of you,' I said. And I meant it; I wanted things to go well for her. Often with a client we would shake hands, or occasionally hug when we finished, but neither felt appropriate with her and so I just gave a kind of awkward half-wave as I started down the stairs.

Back on the street, husky brown leaves crept across the pavement in clusters, like dry insect carapaces. I slid into my car and studied my reflection in the visor mirror. I did not look green, but I didn't look well either. There was a puffiness about my eyes, a dough-like quality to my skin, and I wondered if I was finally coming down with the almost-illness that had seemed to be hovering around for months.

Before I could set off again, my phone blinked with a text. I checked the screen. It was from Nicholas and it said, *I remembered more things.* I felt an instant surge of anger at the arrival of another cryptic message. Instead of replying, I pressed the call button. I didn't think he would answer but it rang out three times and then there was his voice, crackly and surprised.

'What?' he said.

'What do you mean *what*? You just texted me. Stop bothering me.'

'You're the one that's been stalking me.'

'That's a load of shit and you know it. I don't want to keep getting these cryptic texts. Go on, what have you remembered?' I wondered if he was at his work or somewhere else. In front of the car the leaves blew along the pavement in a small flock.

'I've remembered a time in the dark.'

'Have you?' My voice was hard.

'You and me were both in the dark.'

I instantly thought of the times in the attic but I kept quiet. I was determined not to give him anything. 'Go on then, what else do you remember?'

'There's not much, it's blurry.'

'Right, I'm going to hang up.'

'Maybe we were playing hide and seek.'

'Is that it?'

'I scared you. I'm scaring you now probably but I'm not trying to. Actually, if anything I'm quite scared by this myself.' His voice on the phone was casual as always.

'I think you are trying to scare me,' I said and pressed the hang-up icon. I put my phone away and placed my hands on the wheel. 'You are not scaring me,' I said out loud to the inside of the car. The memory of playing the game in the attic came back to me so vividly I could smell the dust. I sat still in the car for a while before driving away.

~*~

The extinction dreams started to become regular again. They switched between different types of animals, as if they were cards drawn from a pack and I was dealt a different one each night. Sometimes they were species I didn't recognise that the soup of my unconscious had conjured up. Animals with greyish fur and sharp noses and overly slender legs. I'd wake in my bedroom in my flat over-hot or suffused with cold because I'd kicked off the blanket.

I started to look into where Nicky's parents were now, partly due to an idle curiosity. I also felt like there might be some clue, that I might understand things better if I knew what happened to them, where their lives went after he died. I sent an email to Leti's dad without telling her, asking if he could get in touch with me by phone. I didn't want to write my questions in an email, in case it might be unthinkingly forwarded on to Leti. Her dad and I had sometimes been in touch over the years about one thing or another; Christmas presents for Leti, a big anniversary for my parents. I didn't hear back right away but I didn't expect to; their email use was intermittent.

A week later I was visiting Leti's flat and we were taking turns to eat fruit trifle out of the plastic bowl it came in. Leti had been dating a guy for a month or so and had now broken up with him. She was not especially sad – 'I was never that into him, if I'm honest with myself' – but it was sort of a tradition of ours to get together and complain about the world when one or other of us were disappointed in love or sex or both.

We chatted idly about one thing and another. 'There are only two white rhinos left,' Leti said. 'I read that today. I thought that would bother you.'

'It does bother me. I didn't know that.'

'I thought you'd know. You got kind of obsessive about these things once.'

'I did?'

'You did. You get obsessions.' I noticed now she had blue paint under her fingernails; I guessed she'd been working on her art again.

'I suppose I do.'

'By the way, why are you bothering my dad? Are you going to ask something about Nicky?'

I took a scoop of trifle, getting the most jelly I could on the spoon, and ate it before replying. 'I was wondering about his parents to be honest. Where they ended up, how their lives turned out. Just thought your dad might know.'

'You're not going to contact them?'

'No, no.'

'You're not going to tell them you think Nicky's reappeared?'

'No, God no,' I said. 'You don't think I'd do that? I'm not mental.'

Leti took a small breath and said, 'You know, in that early time after he died, I used to have this daydream that he hadn't really died. That I would meet him sometime, out in my adult life, when I'd left the village. It was just something that ran through my head. It seemed too sad that he had really died, so I had to make it unreal somehow. But that all faded away in a few days, you know, I moved on from it. Because he was gone and, in a sense, he was never really someone in my life.'

'Are you trying to make a point to me now?'

'I'm just saying, you badly wanted him back when you were younger, I think.'

'I don't want him back now though. I'm not a kid any more. This is not something I've concocted. I just want to understand.'

Leti sat back a little. 'You know, I looked at this guy's photo on the website again recently and he really didn't look so much like Nicky. It's strange how your perception of something can change.'

'In person though, in person, he looks so much like him.'

Frowning, she said, 'I remember once he laughed along with this girl who was making fun of my weight. Nicky, I mean. He laughed along and I went home and scratched my leg with a pin. That was the only time I ever did anything like that, by the way. What a bastard, eh? Why did I have a crush on him? Why do girls think that's normal? But he could be kind. Once in CDT I was scared of using those jigsaw machines, and his class were being taught at the other side of the workshop from ours and I couldn't get the fucking thing to work, I was standing there staring at the screeching thing, and he must have noticed I was stuck because he came over and cut the whole thing out for me, all the pieces of wood in about half a minute. Then walked off. I suppose he liked using the machines because he was good at it, but after that I had a crush.' She stopped, looked down, toyed with her spoon, dropping a small blob of cream onto the carpet. 'Remember that time we went to his grave?'

'Yes,' I said.

'I felt so shocked, that it was really him in there. You know? Just that small space. I felt like my sense of reality was sort of crumbling.' I put down the bowl I was eating from. A stillness seemed to take over the air of the flat.

'I was exactly the same,' I said. We had never spoken about that moment before. What she said could have been my own words.

'And we went back to my house and I was so irritated with you being there, I just wanted to be alone.' She dropped her spoon into the bowl at my feet.

'I was pretty freaked out too.'

'You can't contact his family, you know that? It's getting out of hand. It's getting creepy.'

'I'm only trying to find out where they are,' I said, bedding my fingers into my hair.

'Well, why do you need to know?' I took in a breath but where an explanation should be there was a blank, into which she added, 'And, you know, you and Robin. I think you want to watch yourself there. When you were teenagers, you both got so intense.'

'We were just kids and we were grieving.'

'You started being so hostile to me around that time.' She said this quietly.

That wasn't how I saw it. More just that I was embarrassed, feeling like she could shine a light on me that I didn't want at the time. 'I didn't know that I came across as hostile and I'm sorry if I did. That time was a blur. Listen, though, this is not the same. You can see this guy, we've both seen him. He's said some weird things to me, I don't know how he knows them.'

'It seems very similar to me.'

'Robin's met him with me, he thinks there's something going on too.' She made an audible sigh. 'What does that mean? Robin's a good guy.'

'He did go a bit mad over the whole Nicky thing though, didn't he?'

'He struggled with it. We were kids.' I could hear anger coming out in my voice. 'Nicky was his friend, he more or less saw him die.'

'There were other things that people said he did. That thing about flooding Mr Fletcher's house.'

'He did that?'

'Well, everyone said he did. I don't know. Don't tell him I said that. Maybe he didn't. And there was the thing with the scarecrow, I always wondered if that was him.'

'The scarecrow in Mr Fletcher's garden?'

'Yes.'

'How would he get it there?'

'I don't know. He had a quad bike. Don't tell him I said that either.'

'You're making baseless accusations now.'

'God, let's just stop talking about this. You have your view, I have mine.'

Leaving Leti's flat after we finished up in a huffy sort of semi-silence, the air was crisp and smoke scented. The old trees that broke out through the pavement were becoming bare. Just for a second, I thought I saw Nicholas. Someone crossed the road in the dark up ahead. It was his walk, the slope of his shoulders. But before I could see properly, the man had headed up another street between the grey tenements and I hesitated before forcefully telling myself not to follow whoever it was.

At home, when I replayed the conversation with Leti in my mind, being called creepy stuck to me like being called dirty would have. I sat and read a murder mystery book but at some point I fell into ruminating and I didn't see the words. As I tried to defend myself in my head, I found that I was tearing out a page of the book. I whispered 'Oh no,' like a child that had broken a toy during a tantrum. I sat with the page scrunched in my hand like a crumpled paper swan, feeling daft and creepy at the same time. At night, while I was lying on my side in bed trying to sleep, the cover pulled up to my nose, I said, 'I hate you,' out loud and wasn't sure who I was talking to.

~*~

As teenagers, as we got to know each other better, Robin and I began to have longer conversations about what we believed. It was thrilling in a way, I had never had those kind of discussions with anyone, not in detail. One day I found an old yellowed paperback book on my dad's bookshelf that was full of occult topics. It included a chapter on contacting the dead. The front cover was a picture of a woman wearing a kind of toga or shift with a white light emanating from the back of her head. Probably, my dad never read the book. It might have come from a house sale where he'd pick up a whole box of second-hand books to sort through later, keeping the ones that weren't seriously spotted with yellow mould. Alone in my bedroom at night, I flicked through the book and found spells for speaking to the dead through mirrors and candle flames and bowls of water. I assumed because it was an adult book, there must be something to its claim of being highly researched, something to the doctorate the author listed in their bio on the back page. I put it in my school bag to bring round to Robin's farm the next time I was over there.

I was sitting on my couch watching an old black and white thriller, when my phone rang. It flashed green next to me, a ghostly light. Hardly anyone ever actually phoned me except my parents. I peered at the blinking screen and I didn't recognise the number but it was a landline in the UK. I paused the film as a woman ascended a spiral staircase, her heavy eyelashes batting against her cheekbones. I slid my thumb across *answer*.

'Hello, is that Emily?' a cautious voice said. It took me a second, I knew I recognised it. A grey-bearded face emerged in my mind. The image of Leti's dad, always with an air of being serious and jocular at the same time.

'Hi there,' I said.

'Sorry it's taken me so long to call you. Life is busy when you're retired.' I could hear him take a breath of a laugh. 'What is it you wanted to me to help you with?'

'Didn't Leti tell you?'

'Leti has told me nothing. As usual.' Another laugh-breath.

'Well, it might sound weird but I was wondering about Nicky's mum and dad actually.'

'Nicky Harper?' Their phone was by an old green brocade armchair in the living room. He would be sitting solid in the chair, looking out on a metallic expanse of sea. In the picture in my head he put a hand to his chin.

'Yes,' I said. 'Do you know where his parents are? Do you have any contact details for them?'

'They're both long gone from the old village, I expect you know that. I know his mum went south and his dad went north. But what are you wanting to know for?'

'Just, I don't know, I've been thinking about him again.'

'You want to be a bit careful, digging at the past.' I could see my reflection in the laptop screen, stony-faced. He continued, 'Let me think now. We never knew them that well. But I'm trying to place who might have some information. Wouldn't your mum?'

'I don't think so,' I said, knowing I would not ask her.

'You knew his mother remarried?'

'No, I didn't.'

'Yes, she married again. A new start, I suppose.'

Some cog in my mind was turning. 'Do you know if she changed her name?'

'I don't for sure. But the guy's name was Heron. So if she changed her name, that would be it.'

I thanked him, we talked a bit about the garden they were trying to carve out of the wilderness there, their attempts to grow something called walking onions. He told me to be careful twice at the end of the call. I could imagine the conversation he'd have with Leti and a feeling of shame was already sticking to me like sweaty clothing.

After I put down the phone, I minimised the window on my laptop where the film was playing and opened another. Pushing my feet into my slippers, I pulled a blanket round my shoulders and looked up what might be Nicky's mother's new married name. The first search result brought an artist in London, the second was a psychotherapist whose page I clicked on. I could tell straight away from the picture it was not her. The third item was a magazine article headed, 'Circles of Healing'. I opened it. There was a photo of a woman wearing a long blue skirt with tiny polka dots on it, standing under a white blossom tree. I stared. A narrow nose, deep-set eyes. A familiar face in a changed setting. Shoulder-length dark hair. I had that click of recognition. The woman was Nicky's mother.

Outside, a group of girls passed my window laughing, dragging along what looked like a foil birthday balloon. I scrolled down. There were two more pictures of other ponderous-looking women and one photo of a man with a viking beard holding a daffodil, his mouth drawn to a thin straight line. About a third of the way down there was a photograph of Nicky. This caught me up. I stopped and stared at his face. I had not seen a photograph of him in a long time. He was around ten years old in it, grinning under a tyre swing, a white slice of apple held between his teeth as if it was his smile so that I thought of the story about his dad and the gun. Nicholas's face imposed itself in my mind on top of the photo. It seemed to fit into place over the cheekbones, the chin.

The article was about a 'healing circle' created for parents bereaved by road traffic accidents. A fizzing sensation ran along my arms. I pictured Nicholas reading this article. Could he have gleaned something from here? As I read further, there was no mention of Nicky's last name. You would not find this article by searching for him. But it did mention the village.

In her quotes Nicky's mother talked about her marriage breaking up, about being remarried. She said she believed Nicky gave her signs from the beyond; a robin, a white feather, a stag appearing at the end of her garden.

It unsettled me. To be confronted with her real grief next to what was perhaps my pretend grief, a tin copy of it. There she was, his mother, making everything with this Nicholas person seem absurd. And yet . . . and yet.

I closed the browser and put the film back on, letting an image of a shadowy staircase fill the screen, the tremulous string section sifting through the speakers.

Frost was often shimmering on the pavements in the mornings now. One afternoon I was attending a homelessness charity open day. As part of my job, we were expected to go to things like that now and again to share information with other organisations. We were usually just expected to show our faces and drop off leaflets without staying too long. I walked into the large, converted church nave that alternated between a lunch canteen and an art workshop. It was laid out like a school dining hall with picnic-style, plastic-topped tables. I walked round a few stalls and gave out some StartingUp leaflets. Then as I reached the back of the hall, I thought I recognised someone sitting at one of the white benches, his back to me. I gazed at the grey back of his head. He was holding a ceramic teapot, painting a pattern of spots onto it. He didn't notice me, looking down instead at where the brush was going.

I stepped over to him cautiously, as if I might scare him. Or he might scare me. When my shadow fell on the table he turned to look.

'Speak of the devil,' he said.

'Jim.' He had a palette dotted with bright blobs of paint. With a thick, unevenly bristled brush, he was carefully painting red circles onto the clay surface of the teapot.

'Hello. Nice to see you.'

'Good to see you too,' I said. I was aware I was staring at him. 'How are you?'

He grinned. 'You thought I was dead, I bet.'

'I was worried, to be honest.'

He looked over his shoulder. No one was near us. 'Want to sit here for a bit? Join in the play school?' He gestured at the teapot. 'I know I look daft, a grown man, but I find it kinda relaxing. I come here every week now.'

'It looks fun.'

'I know you're lying. I look like a numpty but I don't care,' he said. 'Do you want to know where I've been?'

'I do. And I'm not lying. Genuinely, I like the teapot.'

'Well, you can have it when it's done. I don't take them home. They sell them off in the shop. Where have I been? Things got scary at the flat. The noise and the neighbours and . . . I just wasn't well. I stayed at my cousin's for a while. Then we weren't getting on so I slept rough for a few nights. Then I went to stay with a friend and I was drinking again because he was drinking.'

'I'm sorry.'

'Don't say sorry, doesn't mean anything, not your fault. I had a bloody heart attack, would you believe that?' He looked hard at me and I didn't know how to respond in case he meant this metaphorically or as joke somehow. He continued. 'A minor one, apparently. But it felt like a fucking grizzly bear had sat on my chest. I was in hospital for a while. No more alcohol. I'm on meds for it now.'

'Jesus. I'm sorry to hear you went through all that. I mean, sorry, you know what I mean,' I said. The solid reality of talking to him, the fact that he could just be back now, made the air seem to buzz around me.

'It was what it was. And now I'm here. I sort of died and came back.'

He laughed and I tried to smile but half grimaced instead. I did feel like I was talking to a corporeal ghost. I thought of the strange night with the man in the grey hood. 'I saw you, in the street. A few weeks back. It was at night. You were by the graveyard. Do you remember?'

'I don't think that was me.'

'It looked just like you.'

'A few weeks back? No, I wouldn't have been out at night then, I still felt like shit.'

'I was sure it was you.'

'I'd remember seeing you, I've not lost my memory.' I thought maybe it was drink or something, he could have been off his face the night I saw him. To think I'd been wrong, that it was just someone who looked like him, grabbing my shoulder like that, created a new seed of anxiety inside me.

His eyes brightened. 'You know my daughter was looking for me?'

I knew to be cautious here. 'Was she?'

'She was. It's led to us getting back in touch. I don't know. Seeing her standing there and she's in her forties but she's a wee girl too. When she was born, I was so young, I fucked things up, I fucked things up, you know?'

'I do.'

'Of course you don't, you never fucked anything up in your life. I bet the worst thing that ever happened to you is spilling a pint of milk.' He grinned at me and I smiled tightly. 'But I have a chance.'

'That's wonderful.'

We moved on to talking a bit about his new temporary accommodation, the people he'd met through the homelessness charity.

'Well,' I said at last, 'I should let you get on.' I was glad he was alive, but I found it unsettling being in his presence. I pushed my chair back with my feet, started to stand.

'Escaping the bampot?' Jim said.

'Yes, that's right,' I said. He laughed.

'The bampot painting a teapot, eh?'

'That's about it,' I said.

He looked around as if distracted by the visitors milling about behind us, then back at me. 'I know you can't stay in touch but I'm sure I'll see you around. You always bump into people in the end.'

'True.'

'You can't escape people even if you want to.'

'You can't,' I said.

I walked over towards the exit. By the large glass sliding door, I glanced back. Jim was not looking at me, he had recommenced painting the circles on his teapot. I headed down the wheelchair ramp and away. Outside I breathed in deep lungfuls of cold air. Everything looked over-precise, more real than it had when I'd stepped into the building. Then an old memory was playing through my mind, prompted by the school-hall style of the tables and chairs in the church.

~*~

He kissed me once, Nicky. He did it after I started high school. I was sitting in the school lunch hall, one table away from him. He was with a few other boys from his year. There was all this raucous laughter at the boys' table then Nicky suddenly got up, dashed over, and grabbed the back of my head. He clasped my hair, entwining his fingers in it tightly and kissed me on the lips, pushing his face into mine. He forced his tongue between my lips. His mouth was wet and tasted of the school lasagne and peppermint mingled together. The girls around me screamed with laughter. One of them swiped at his legs, telling him to *fuck off* as he ran back over to his table. My scalp stung where the hair had been pulled. The boys were cheering around him, round balls of echoing sound. 'You're a paedo, she's only twelve,' one of them said. I caught a flash of his laughing face as my gaze flicked about the canteen. I couldn't steadily look at anyone. I understood he had chosen me for a joke; I guessed that the boys had decided I was less attractive than the other girls and that would make it funnier. I felt that he had taken a layer of clothing away from me so that everyone could see me, not naked exactly but partially exposed. No one except me knew that he had used his tongue. I didn't know why he had done that; I didn't think he fancied me, it was more just to show that he could. As I sat there, the room seemed to buzz and ripple around me. The noise of the place ballooned. Cutlery clattered into bins, plates clanked onto plastic dining trays. I suppose that was my first kiss.

~*~

Leti sent me a message after I spoke to her dad.

Jesus Christ I can't believe you did that, it said.

I thought about phoning her. Then about writing out a long explanation by text. In the end I simply wrote a short text with an apology. I pressed send. I waited for the tick to turn blue to show she'd opened the message but it never did over the next few hours, then days.

A week later, I ran into Morna in the supermarket a few streets from my flat. I was buying satsumas and she reached across me for bananas with her manicured hand, with its one silver skull ring. 'Hey,' I said.

'Hello.' Her expression was like a closed door.

'How are you?' I said, blinking, almost trying to draw back the words because she was still looking at me unsmilingly.

'Fine, fine.' Now a tiny glint of amusement flickered on her face. 'How are you?'

'I'm well,' I said, 'Busy, you know how it is.'

'Not still stalking Nicholas?'

'What do you mean?' I took a step back, shifting with the weight of my basket.

'You know.'

'No, I don't.'

'Well, you should leave him alone.'

'I've no idea what you mean. We've run into each other a few times, that's all.'

'You've been pestering him.' She said this like it was something we both knew.

'No, I haven't. Actually, if anything he's pestered me.' I wondered what conversations they'd had about me.

'You know he's not well.'

'Do I? Not well how?' I stepped further back from her. The harsh aisle lights made everything too clear, the rows of identical fruit in plastic wrapping gleamed at us.

She shook her head. 'You know.'

'He does seem troubled,' I said.

'Well, he doesn't need any help from you anyway.' She turned around with her pack of bananas and disappeared towards the dairy section. I found myself wanting to giggle, but also a long slow wave of heat was washing over me and breaking.

I received a package at work. A cardboard box, wrapped round and round with brown tape. I cut into it and dug through layers of kitchen towel. Nestled inside like a large egg was the ceramic teapot Jim had been painting. I put it on my desk as if it was an ornament. I was filling it up with spare pens when my phone buzzed in my pocket. I took it out and read the text.

I'll take you somewhere, let's meet up.

From Nicholas, the same as before. I turned the screen off but as I tried to work on a spreadsheet, I could feel the phone sitting in my pocket, waiting for an answer. I switched it off and moved it to the bottom of my bag.

When I arrived home that night I took out a plastic box from under my bed. A fluffy layer of dust had settled on the top. Inside was a collection of objects from my old bedroom in my parents' house, and other things that had travelled with me as a student, and on into various flats, little totems that couldn't be parted with. Removing the lid let out an odour of mouldy paper. There were various high school certificates, some old CDs, a drawing of a magpie Leti had done on a scrap of paper, some gift soaps and candles I hadn't got round to using. Underneath all this was a curling newspaper clipping with a tribute to Nicky on the anniversary of his death. As I looked at the picture of his boyish face, an emotion stirred, that old melody again. The picture snapped together in my mind with the image of Nicholas.

The face clicked and whirred. I wanted to know. I got out my phone and reread the message.

I'll take you somewhere, let's meet up

I typed, *You're not taking me anywhere but I'll meet you somewhere.*

Immediately, another line of text appeared. *It's somewhere out of town, I can give you a lift*

I don't need a lift, I typed.

I'll take you

No I'll drive myself. Where?

I'd been joking when I spoke to Leti, saying he might be a murderer, but I didn't really believe he was dangerous. I believed I could read people well enough. There was no edge of violence to our conversations. I was annoyed about Morna telling me to step back. I was also intrigued at the fragility she'd hinted at. I wanted to hear more of his story at least. I picked up the phone and stared at my message against the white background. It occurred to me I could be doing something stupid but there was also that same sense of certainty, like being bathed in light. I knew this person well enough. I felt as if I knew him from childhood. I didn't trust him exactly but I didn't fear him.

A new message flashed up. A map to a pub that I didn't know, outside of town, and a suggestion we meet there at the weekend. I wondered if I should really go. I tried calling Leti but it rang through and then cut off. I realised maybe she wasn't speaking to me. Had she actually seen my number and hung up? I texted Robin and he replied a minute later, *Great, find out what he's up to!* I felt spiteful towards Leti. It was childish to ignore my calls, if indeed she was ignoring my calls.

I sent a message in response to the map, saying I would be there.

Later that night, an unexpected email arrived. It was a note from the guy I'd met at the party months back, the guy I'd known at university with the curly blond hair. It read:

Is this still your email address? Just wondered if you'd like to get coffee on Saturday?

I couldn't quite tell if he was asking me on a date or if he was just being friendly, or wanting to talk about something from the past. I was too nervous about seeing Nicholas to fit anything else into my head and so I messaged him back to say thanks for asking, but I wasn't free.

~*~

There was a time, when we were teenagers, when Robin and I started to think Nicky would come back somehow, or at least that he'd find a way to contact us. As Robin and I became better friends, I started to go round to his farm as well as meeting him at the den. We would base ourselves in his plain white shoebox of a bedroom at the back of the farmhouse and play card games, blackjack or rummy. Sometimes we'd lounge on the pristine, cream carpet and listen to music. Though the farmyard was always full of mud, everything in the house was spotless. We did not meet at my home because it was more central and more noticeable and we still didn't want anyone to think we were going out.

One afternoon, when I walked into Robin's bedroom, there was a cardboard box sitting on his bed. It was thin and black and it looked like the kind of box that might contain a board game but there was no writing on it. 'Hailey gave it to me,' Robin said. He took the lid off the box. Inside was a square, unvarnished wooden board with letters and numbers written by hand in black ink down the sides. I realised what it was.

'Is it from the hotel bar?'

'I think she kept it after they left the séance thing,' Robin said.

'How do you know her?'

'From school. Everyone knows her.' His mouth twitched and I saw he was making fun of me.

'Obviously. But I didn't know you knew her enough to hang about together.'

'I see her about sometimes.' I had an image of them at the back of the hotel where the bins were, sitting on the wall in the evenings, the square light from the hotel windows on them. This picture was not romantic but they were talking about Nicky, all the little things that no one else knew, and I wanted to lean in and hear what they were saying.

'Why did she give it to you?'

'She wanted to throw it away. She said it grossed her out so I asked for it.'

'Can we use it? How does it work?'

He sank back. 'I don't totally know. I think you just put your hands on the pointer bit and see what happens.'

We hung a blanket over the bedroom window, tucking it round the curtain rail, to shut out the mid-afternoon sun, then we sat with our legs folded under us like primary-school children sitting on a story carpet. We placed our fingertips on the hard plastic of the pointer. It felt cool and smooth.

'What do we ask?'

'Ask if anyone's there,' Robin said.

'You ask.'

'We'll both say it.'

He nodded to me. Our voices came out in unison. 'Is anyone there?' Straight away, the pointer moved over to the word *no*. We pulled our hands back.

'You did that,' Robin said.

'Shut up, it was you.' I had felt it move, the lifeless plastic for a moment becoming a determined little animal under my fingers.

'It doesn't even make sense. Why not move the pointer to yes if I was going to pretend?' he said. 'What should we do now?'

'Ask for a name?'

'OK.' Gingerly, we returned our fingers to the pointer.

'What's your name?' I said.

The pointer shot to *no* with the same speed, and then the number 1.

'No one?' I said. The pointer moved to *yes*.

We took our hands off the board again. 'I don't like this,' Robin said.

'Are you doing it though?'

'No.'

'Let's try it again.' We put our hands back on the pointer. This time it spelt out I – L – L.

'Ill,' I said. 'Who's ill?'

'I think you're doing this,' Robin said.

'I think you are. Someone's ill?'

'You're doing this,' Robin said, his face starting to blaze coral.

'I'm not,' I said. 'You're doing it.'

I realised we had kept our hands on the pointer but nothing had happened while we spoke, while we focused on each other. As we looked at the board again, it moved towards the letters. B – B – A – C – K.

'Bee back?' Robin said.

'*I'll be back*?' I said. 'Like fucking terminator?' I slapped at Robin's hand. 'That wasn't funny.'

'It wasn't me.'

'You arsehole. Why did you do that?' There was acid reflux in my throat now, I swallowed and swallowed.

'Why would I mess around? He was my friend, he was my fucking friend.' Robin shook his head. His eyes were focused on the pointer, his nostrils flared. 'Let's stop. Let's not do this again,' he said.

'You did it, I know you did it,' I said. I shoved the board over towards him and he stood up like it might singe him. 'I'm going home,' I said. 'I'll see you when you're not being an idiot.'

~*~

The day after agreeing to meet Nicholas, I received another set of conspiracy theory links from Mr Fletcher. The same sort of thing as before. Black helicopters and secret international governments. I spoke to my mum that evening on the phone and I found myself telling her about them; it just spilled out of me somehow. 'Why would he email you?' she said.

'I spoke to him, when I was up.'

'When you were with us?'

'Yes. I bumped into him a few times actually.' There was a small crackle on the line. 'We got talking. He sent me some websites.'

'What kind of websites?' I imagined her in the kitchen with the phone cord twirled around her fingers even though they'd had a cordless phone for years.

'Weird, conspiracy stuff.' I paused, switched ears with the handset. 'He said Nicky didn't die. He doesn't believe he died, he thinks it's some kind of conspiracy. Did you know that?'

'Yes. He's been saying that for years. The whole thing has driven him crazy. He can't accept it so he's made up a story to comfort himself,' my mum said.

'Why didn't you mention it?' I began drawing on a notepad, marking out a little spider's web.

'I never thought to. It all seems so sad.'

'Yes it is. Poor guy.'

'He's a poor soul. Don't take any of it seriously.'

'I'm not an idiot.'

'No you're not. You're absolutely not. Just watch you don't get too involved with him. He's not well.'

'I know. It's just a weird coincidence.'

'Coincidence with what?' my mum said.

I leant forward on the couch, doubling my knees up to my stomach. I felt over-full from dinner. 'A couple of times, around here, I've bumped into someone who looks like Nicky.'

She was silent for a beat. I heard her breathe in, then there was another beat of silence. Then she said, 'Oh love, I hope you're not starting all that again.'

'I'm not, I'm not,' I said. 'It just struck me as a weird co-incidence.'

We changed the subject, talked about what we were reading, where I might travel next year, I was thinking about a trip to Scandinavia. We hung up after she had told me to take care a few times. I went back to my computer and read more about the conspiracy theories until I became vaguely dizzy from staring at the screen too much and turned the computer off altogether.

Later that night, I found a new picture in my flat. It was behind a small set of drawers where I used to keep old socks and underwear and belts and bits of things I didn't use but didn't want to throw out. I'd accidentally knocked a bracelet behind the drawers and when I moved them forward to reach down, I saw a couple of blotches. I shone a torch in there and moved the drawers further away and I could just make out a tiger and a pigeon. The tiger was above the pigeon, paws raised to strike or so it seemed. Life and death, life and death; it was hard not to feel they were saying something to me. The pigeon was in full flight, its wings angled sharply. Again, it had a black circle eye, the tiger's iris was a yellow ring. The simplicity gave a kind of daft cuteness to the picture. It bothered me that their chase had progressed. I had liked the pigeons and tigers to be separate.

~*~

Robin and I didn't fall out over the Ouija board incident. We just acted as if it hadn't happened the next time we saw each other. We were still curious. We started to pore over that musty old book of spells I'd found, with its mixture of folk belief and pseudoscience, its claims that you could talk to the dead. One day we decided to try a spell that involved burying a rabbit's foot and something belonging to the dead under an old yew tree. Rabbits' feet were easy to get hold of on the farm and Robin had kept a pair of Nicky's old gloves that he'd left behind at the house one day. The spell said the dead would contact us in unexpected ways. Three days later the light appeared. Our village sat on an inlet of a large sea loch and within the body of the water was a rugged island about the size of the school gym hall. This was where the light came from, a blink like a signal that we could see flashing from Robin's bedroom. From far away it looked like a penlight, the kind of light a doctor shines in a patient's eyes. We began to tell each other that it could be Nicky, over on that other shore, signalling to us somehow. As always we were half joking with each other, half playing with the idea that something supernatural might be happening. Neither of us fully admitted to believing any one thing, though one night Robin said to me, 'It seemed like he went away through the water, you know? Like he drowned. I know he didn't but I remember the water most.'

'What do you mean?' I said. He shook his head. But I guessed that he meant that because Nicky died in the loch, or seemed to when he was beside him, it held a slanted kind of logic that he would come back from water if he did return.

On the third evening after the light appeared, we made a decision to find a way to get across to the island to see what the light was. Robin knew a boy whose family owned a rowing boat and he managed to scrape permission to borrow it. The next day, I asked Leti to come with us. I wanted to involve her. I told Leti about seeing a mysterious light, but I did not say anything about Nicky. She'd started to become even more absorbed in her painting, setting up an old easel in her family's garage and disappearing for hours at a time. We'd been seeing less and less of each other. I didn't understand her paintings, what they meant, but I knew she was good at it from the things the art teacher said. Most days when I met her she'd have paint under her nails. At the same time, she had started to drop sarcastic hints about the amount of time I was spending with Robin; I guessed she was trying to imply I fancied him. I wanted to bring her to the island, hoping we'd see something together, hoping I'd impress her in some way.

We borrowed the small wooden boat with its peeling tongues of paint on a Monday night after dark, when the village was quiet. I'd told my parents I was at Leti's house; she had said she was at mine. I don't know what Robin told his parents.

We struggled to untie the boat between the three of us, and, when it was finally loose, we pushed it out from the muddy bank. Jogging along beside it, we slipped and splashed through the cold water and jumped in as it began to bob. We didn't know how to row. We took turns over the oars, going round in half-circles for a while in the tar-black water and arguing with each other.

When we finally reached the shore, we managed to haul the boat up a short way onto a gravelly bank. We began searching around the scrub of the island using handheld torches. It occurred to me that for anyone looking from the village, we were now the ones creating the ghostly lights. We poked through the undergrowth for signs that someone had been living there, splitting up to search further.

Eventually, on my own at the far side of the island, I caught a tiny glint of metal like a silver tooth shining in an open mouth. A crushed beer can, tucked into a clump of bracken. I wanted to hold it up, triumphant proof that someone was out here, but as I reached my fingers towards it, I felt a sense of disgust. I couldn't touch it and I left it where it was. Someone was wild camping on the island; it didn't mean a thing. When I walked back to the boat, Leti and Robin were exchanging angry words. Leti was saying Robin had let a branch snap back to hit her in the face. Robin claimed she had walked into a branch. I imagined some invisible hand playing a trick on them, flicking the twig between them. Without much discussion, we gave up there. The air was becoming frigid. We sailed back together, fighting over the oars again, almost tipping ourselves up. Robin and I didn't see the island light again after that.

~*~

On the Sunday afternoon, I set out for the country pub where Nicholas had asked to meet. It was cold inside the car and November ice marked the windows where I'd done a bad job of scraping it away. I wondered why he'd insisted on such an out-of-the-way place, if it was somewhere that had some special significance to him – if it was connected to what he wanted me to know. From the map, I could see it was isolated but I wasn't worried about Nicholas's intentions in choosing it. The pub itself would be public and, more and more, my perception of him was not as a threat but as someone slightly vulnerable.

I left the greying city behind and made my way onto the bypass, then cut off it to a series of smaller country roads. I followed the instructions spoken by the voice in my phone until I slowed down on the road where the pub should be. It was a single track, lined with high hedges. When I turned a corner and saw the pub's signboard through trees I felt relief. I realised I'd started to imagine that the building would be boarded up or that it wouldn't be there at all.

Gravel crunched under the car tyres as I drove into the car park. The pub was in a building that must have been converted from an old farmhouse, the façade made up of pale-grey stone. When I stepped out of the car the air had that winter country smell, of frost and old leaves and open space.

As I headed in through the entrance, a wave of unnatural heat hit me from a fan above the door. Scanning for Nicholas but not seeing him, I made my way to a small table for two. The carpet was a yellowish tartan and the atmosphere smelt musty, as if the windows had been jammed shut for a long while. A group of older men at the bar looked round at me as I sat down. I did not want their attention on me so I got out my phone and pretended to read something on it. Across from me two white-haired women leant together in talk that was punctuated with loud bursts of laughter. Despite the fan heater, they were still wearing their padded winter jackets, which made them look like birds puffing up their feathers to keep warm. The two groups, the men and the women, were the only other customers.

I waited. The signal on my phone was patchy and I wished I'd brought a book. Ten minutes, fifteen minutes passed. No one arrived. I got up and ordered an orange juice. The bartender was friendly, a young guy with crucifix earrings and a fashionable beard. Behind the bar were mounted sets of horns from goats or sheep. They weren't attached to a head or skull but just a small plate of bone. Somehow that made them more sinister than if there had been whole skulls. I headed back to my seat, and spent another ten minutes looking through pictures on my phone. I thought over what I knew about Nicholas as I sipped the fruit juice. I told myself again that whoever Nicholas was he was not Nicky, and yet it did not feel that way. That is the only way I can describe it; he felt like Nicky. The atmosphere of him and that clicking and whirring in my mind when I looked at him. I texted the number I had for Nicholas, asking him where he was. Another five then ten minutes passed. There was no response. The message had not been read so I decided to leave. I sent a single line saying, *I don't know what's happening but I'm going home.* As I walked out, the women carried on chatting and laughing but the men watched me go in silence.

In the car park, the old trees groaned in the wind above the gravel. I shut myself back inside the car. Just for a moment, until I could get the engine started, I had the twitchy sensation that someone was going to grab the door and pull it open or press themselves against the window.

I drove back out into the lane and on between the hedges. Soon, I was relieved to get off the single-track road. I came to a long, straight stretch with browning hedges on either side. The next part unfolded quickly and slowly at the same time. Two cars were approaching on the tarmac ahead. As I was drawing near, the one at the back pulled out as if to overtake the one in front. But there clearly wasn't enough time. It was rapidly approaching on my side of the road. A red car, speeding towards me. Behind the windscreen, the face of the other driver became the face of Nicholas. For a second, his face and expression were so clear. A sensation of perfect terror expanded inside me, I looked to the verge, a blur of grey hedge and grasses and dips. There was not enough room for the whole car to get onto it.

But there was no sign of the red car braking and so in a surge of adrenaline I pulled to the left anyway. The bank rumbled under the wheels, my car part off the road, part on, as the body of it shook underneath me. Ahead I could just see a gap opening up between the two cars and yet the red car was still on the wrong side of the road. It swerved just as it was about to hit me but not by enough. I heard a screech of metal and a crunching sound as my wing mirror flew off. The verge widened and I instinctively pulled further off the road and braked hard. My car jerked and slowed and came to a halt, the bonnet pushed against a hedge, branches reaching up at the windscreen.

I sat for a good time with my hands shaking on the wheel, breathing and not really thinking. Beyond the hedge, through an iron gate and up a further bank, I could see something like a farm. Dull-green industrial-sized sheds with floodlights already on, looking alien and unsettling. I opened the door a slice and breathed in the cold. I wasn't sure what to do. My mind was a whirring blank. The air smelt of frost and of the undergrowth. Eventually I closed the door again and drove until I could see the calm scatter of city streetlights beginning to come on.

A few months after Nicky died, I was messing about in the hall-way on a rainy day, searching through old newspaper clippings and bits and pieces my parents kept in the drawers under the hall telephone. I reached my hand into the back of the bottom drawer, and my fingers touched something knobbly and wooden. I pulled out a small, carved manger scene intended as a Christmas decoration. It showed the nativity complete with a tiny donkey and cow and 'baby's first Christmas' was printed along the base. I took it out, thinking it was mine. There had always been a manger scene, one I'd been given on my first Christmas, that we put on the mantelpiece every year in mid-December. I thought someone had forgotten to put it back in the Christmas box. But, as I held it up, I saw that it was subtly different. Mary wore blue and Joseph's cloak was painted white whereas my ornament had a pink Mary and a blue Joseph. I guessed then it must have been bought for my sister, and that my parents had hidden it away. I put it carefully back, under the notepad, as I had found it. I don't remember being sad or shocked but thinking, *this is the sort of thing that would be sad if I had known my sister*. Instead, it was a small surprise.

I don't remember ever feeling like I grieved for that baby as a child, but maybe I was left with a watchfulness, an expectancy. I remember sometimes looking out on winter nights and feeling like the dark bulk of the mountain might choose to eat me if it wanted to. Whenever the phone rang, I had a feeling it was bad news and I would wait silently until I heard the calm in my mum or dad's voice as they spoke to a friend or relative. I cannot think where this came from except some general awareness that the world was unpredictable, because my sister had died.

~*~

After I arrived home from that drive in the dark, I curled up in a blanket on the couch and watched episodes of MASH one after the other so I didn't have to think. Eventually I moved through to the bedroom, took my socks off and got under the duvet, pushing my feet down into the coolness of the sheets. The face in the car coming towards me had seemed determined, like he wanted me to die, and yet I questioned whether I could really have seen such detail in that short blink of time. I had been sure that it was Nicholas's face, but I questioned whether I could have picked him out in that blur of speed. I had thought about calling the police but I didn't know what I would tell them. I did not know what kind of car Nicholas drove. The strangeness of the things he'd said came back to me in single lines; the things about wanting to return to water like he wanted to die, and the comment about the coffin lid, and, really, how disturbing every-thing he'd said was if he had just been pretending. I could have died in that moment in the car. Throughout the next few days I checked my phone and each time no new messages arrived from Nicholas. I promised myself I would not contact him again, that it was time to let it all go. Robin texted me asking how the meet-up went and I did not text him back. Suddenly I did not want to see Robin. I decided it was time to stop. That I could just snap it shut like a padlock, case closed.

~*~

Robin and I returned to the book of spells after the incident with the island and the light. We did not give up. One of the rituals in the book involved taking intoxicants to induce a state in which you could hear the voices of the departed. I sat on Robin's bed and stared at the list of herbs and unknown substances.

'Belladonna. Isn't that deadly nightshade?'

'I don't know,' Robin said.

'I think it is.'

'If it is, that grows in Scotland,' he said. 'It grows in the wild patch behind my cousin's house down south.'

'You could get us some. Next time you're there.'

He gave me a look. 'Isn't it deadly? Isn't that the point?' he said.

'I don't know. You'd think it wouldn't be in the book if it just killed you.'

We looked it up on one of the school computers, in the quiet corner at the back of the library. The processor whirred and sputtered as the search engine results appeared in slow pixelated strips. We found a website about alternative medicines that said small doses of belladonna could be fatal. Tiny doses could cause hallucinations, visions. We found a chat forum in which people described trying the berries of the plant. One person said they had no effect, another said they'd thrown up for half a day and nothing else had happened. A third person claimed they'd seen the shadowy figure of their dead father beside their bed.

A month or so later, one Monday afternoon, Robin led me up to his bedroom after school, tugging on my sleeve without seeming to notice he was doing it. When we reached his room, he shut the door behind us, panting slightly. From the top of a bookshelf, he pulled out a knotted-up cotton handkerchief, slightly damp. Inside it lay a handful of small black berries, beady orbs like the button eyes on a stuffed animal.

'You got them.'

'I got them.'

'We're not going to eat them though,' I said.

'No, no. But it's quite cool, eh?' he said. 'If we wanted to, we could poison someone.'

I could imagine the taste of them, sweet like ripe blackcurrants. I was afraid to touch the berries and a small part of me ached to try one to see what would happen. I imagined that the cool feel of them on my tongue would be like rolling a black marble around my mouth. I imagined the tiny dark spheres as portals to some other part of reality.

The next day, I saw Leti at the ruined house and I told her about the berries. Not why we had them, just that Robin had found them. The berries seemed powerful somehow and I guess I was showing off, but she didn't seem impressed at all.

In the week after the car incident, I kept running through what I wanted to say to Nicholas Blackburn if I saw him again. I had decided I wouldn't speak to him and still I'd ruminate on it, mouthing words while I was washing my hair in the shower, or rushing to put breakfast together on a weekday morning.

I continued to use his street as a cut-through. I had decided I would not avoid his flat, the street was on was a convenient route and why should I be the one to be inconvenienced? The flat had once been a shop so it had two large street-level windows covered in a stick-on film that made it look from a distance as if the place was permanently full of steam. I didn't see any sign of him over the next weeks and there was no car parked outside that fitted with the red car I had seen. I had heard nothing from Robin and the thought of a message arriving from him now came with a vague unease, almost a fear, as if he had been the one I thought I'd seen driving the red car.

December spun round again, with its grey spindles and damp mornings. In the middle of the first week, I was out with a few colleagues for our early Christmas dinner. We were squashed into a small Italian restaurant near the docks. Everything was cheerful enough but I was tired, drained even after what I thought had been a good night's sleep, as if I had been awake all night and forgotten it in the morning.

As I was leaving, it was still early, a mild night. I spent too long making my goodbyes and missed the bus I had intended to catch. I decided to go for a wander by the water's edge before the next one was due. It was the middle of the week but there were people milling about in ones and twos so I didn't feel anxious walking on my own. Voices shimmered through from other streets and the ground was free of frost.

I approached the sharp edge of the quay and I looked out over the water. It gave me small chills, the way the darkness was so deep and undefined. My eye searched for something and reached nothing until the lights from the flats on the other side. There was that slight tang to the air, that faint sea smell mixed with a murky, underfloor scent of something abandoned.

I'd been walking around the cobbles for a minute or so when I noticed someone in the distance by the water. They stood beyond the line of the old tenements, before the blocks of new flats, a good few metres away from the tethered boats that acted as floating cafes and bars during the day. A figure, like a little Lowry stickman, stood past the ornamental trees, behind the parked cars. I squinted. That click of recognition. I thought it was Nicholas. I walked closer and he turned to look at me and, still at a distance, I felt sure it was him. It was his figure, his face shape, his coat, his manner. I looked around behind me. No one was near me now. We were on the other side of town to my flat, to his flat. It was possible it was a coincidence and yet I thought he must have followed me, that he had perhaps even been waiting in a bar near the restaurant. He moved forward a few steps by the edge of the dock and stopped. For a moment, there was something that seemed almost ghoul-like about the figure. It was too thin, or the wrong proportions somehow.

I froze. Partly I wanted to step forward, to show myself it was only this man again, to confront him, and partly I wanted to get away, to run. Before I could make a movement either way, another thing occurred to me – he was going to jump into the water. This thought appeared and was clear as a new coin. Maybe it was to do with the sense I'd got that Nicholas was reckless with his life. Maybe it was something in his stance. And then suddenly the figure was stepping forward again.

'Stop,' I screamed, my voice changing pitch as the word came out, the sound seeming to bend. I ran towards him. I don't know what I thought I would do.

The figure took another stride, stepped over the safety chain and then feet together, leapt forward, like a diver taking a plunge. He was over the edge into the depth of the water. An explosive white splash rose up and he had vanished.

I dashed towards the place where he had been, it seemed to take an age, my lungs burned. When I reached what I thought was the spot, I clasped my knees, gasping for breath. The water had glossed over him like wet paint. I stood looking down, not too close to the edge because I had the feeling now that someone might push me from behind. He was not there, the dark surface was rocking crazily with the reflected streetlight splintered across it.

There was nowhere for him to go. A few bubbles rose to the surface. A little further back from the space where he had vanished, a boat with a cafe menu painted on the side rocked, a single light in one of the windows. I stared at it as if it held some clue, as if he would jump up from the deck in a moment, laughing. But the night around me was quiet, just the babble of voices and laughter from nearby pubs and restaurants. The murky scent of the dock.

I had seen someone go into the water, I was sure I had. I looked around me. No one was nearby. I knew I had to phone the police, that if I didn't call, it would be my fault if he was dead. I could feel the ice-burn of the water even as I stood there on the bank. I took my phone out and dialled 999.

The voice on the other end was calm, a woman's. I asked for the police. She put me through to another calm woman's voice, older this time. 'I thought I saw a man fall in the water at the docks.'

'OK, so you thought you saw a man fall into the water?'

'Yes.' I could hear the sound of her typing. She established the address, and her tone was absolutely level. I knew they were trained to repeat things in a neutral way but it was helpful, as if what I was saying was not outlandish but also not very serious.

'Is the man someone you know?'

'Yes, no. Sorry, I know him but not well, if it was who I think.'

I gave Nicholas's name, a guess at his age. After a time, I heard sirens in the distance and it took me a few seconds to understand that they were for me. The fire brigade arrived, lights flashing, the truck an oversized toy. The police were there minutes later, a female and male officer stepping towards me. They must have known from my dumb, stationary expression that I was at the centre of it. I felt self-conscious in a way I wouldn't have expected to find space for. I wanted to blink my eyes and wake up under my duvet. I talked to the female officer while something metal was set up near the water's edge. I turned away deliberately and the thought came to me again of the things Nicholas had said about wanting to return to the water. The officer wrote on an electronic pad. Her face was round and young, her hair smoothed back under her cap. She must have been younger than me. I could hear my dad saying, *you know you're old when the police look young*. The officer asked how I knew Nicholas and I garbled something again about not being sure it was him and about having got to know him because I'd mistaken him for someone else. She showed no scepticism, writing this down. She asked if I knew if he'd been having suicidal thoughts and I said no, wondering if I should mention about the car but not saying anything. The odd person walking by stared at me. They might have guessed that I had been mugged, or had stolen something. I was too numb and cold to blush. I was also afraid that I would be charged with something at any moment, making a hoax call, or wasting police time. But the officer was only quietly attentive.

I took a taxi home. When I arrived back into the warm burrow of my flat, I dropped my clothes on the floor and pulled on my pyjamas and curled up in a ball under my duvet. I gripped my cold toes with my palms. My eyes were sore as if there was grit in them. I fell asleep almost instantly.

I'd left the heating on by mistake so the flat was overwarm when I woke in the dark. I felt afraid, and sick; all that I'd eaten from the three-course meal the night before was churning inside me. I put my hand over my belly. My stomach bulged out as if I was carrying an early pregnancy. The food had been rich and I'd had plenty of red wine and then some kind of elaborate ice-cream sundae for a dessert. I got out of bed and turned the heating off. I thought I was going to vomit but once I was through to the living room and sitting on the couch with my bare feet on the wood floor the nausea faded. A sensation of panic remained somewhere inside me like a rodent nibbling behind a skirting board. I hadn't put the living-room lamp on, and the light from the hall fell through the doorway in a cone shape. My flat seemed foreign, as if I wasn't in my own home but someone else's. As if I'd opened the wrong door when I got back from the water.

Out of nowhere, someone banged on the window. I jumped, dug my nails into my arm and sat frozen. My ears straining for another sound. The dark ticked onwards. Minute by minute, my heart was beating in my throat. Nothing happened. People did bang on the windows from time to time. Drunk people coming back from the pub. That was all it would be, I told myself. At the same time a picture unfurled of Nicholas outside dripping wet, hitting the glass with his fist. But it would be nothing, nothing, just drunk people who wanted to briefly intrude on the life of another living soul. I didn't look outside but instead sat still until my breathing slowed again. There were no more bangs. My heart thrummed in my ears. I couldn't think over what I had seen at the water's edge or decide what it was that had happened. The idea of checking the local news made me feel sick again so I just sat on the couch until my head grew too heavy to hold up and I returned to bed.

The next day I phoned in to work sick with flu. I was exhausted in an even deeper way than before, so that it seemed my bones themselves were heavy. I drifted back to sleep and was woken by a knock at the door. I rose from the covers with a feeling of dread, pulling myself up felt like I was trying to drag myself out of a bog. I had a sense there was something disturbing behind the door. I staggered to the window first, opened the blinds to let some light into the room, then pulled on my dressing gown and stepped into my slippers. I crept to the door and looked through the spyhole. It was only the postman, I could see the orange dayglow jacket well enough, but I still found myself not wanting to open the door. A sense it was a trick. The man stayed where he was, shifting on his feet; he must have heard my steps. He knocked again and I undid the chain. He smiled, asked if I'd take in a parcel of wine for my neighbours. I signed for it and shut the door. A dream filtered back to me as I carried the heavy crate into the kitchen. I'd dreamt about Nicholas again, that we'd had sex. The dream came back in flashes; I had worn blue lace underwear, we were in my own bedroom, he ran his tongue up the back of my neck. The dream was not sexy, instead there was a suffocating sense of threat left over from it. I let more light into the kitchen and gulped down cold water and blinked the dream away.

Later that day there was another knock on the door while I was eating dinner and I jumped with the fork partway to my mouth. I put the cutlery down and walked to the spyhole, pulse flipping over in my wrists. It was the neighbour, to collect her package of wine. I opened the door. 'Thank you,' she said when I brought it to her, eyeing me like I had answered the door naked. I realised there must be something off about my appearance but I couldn't figure out what. After closing the door, I walked to the hall mirror. My hair lay flat, my eyes were bloodshot. I wondered if I had begun a process of turning mad that would take some time but might already have reached an irreversible point.

I sat and looked through the text messages I'd had from Nicholas, up until the day with the car. I decided I had to try phoning him. I would not speak to him. I had perhaps not seen what I had thought I had seen and if so he would answer the phone and I would hang up instantly but I would have an answer.

My fingers shook as I pressed dial. Before I could really think, a recorded voice was curtly saying, *This number is no longer available*. I looked at the phone in in my hand for a while. The next thing it occurred to me to do was to call my mum. I'd made a resolution not to talk to her about Nicholas since the first time I'd mentioned him, but I couldn't have this question only in my own thoughts, rolling over and over like debris caught by a wave.

The phone rang for a while before she answered. We started with our usual chat about how each of us were and I just said I was fine and then I said, 'You know how I said I started running into someone who looks like Nicky?'

'I do remember that.'

'And you know how I said I thought it was only a coincidence?'

'Yes.'

'Well I think I said that not to worry you. This will sound weird but it was so like him I almost think it was him and now this person is maybe gone, they might have died, actually, and I don't know what to think.' I was sitting near the window, watching people go by. I was still feverish and I put my hand up to the cool of the glass.

'Oh,' she said.

'Well, oh, what?'

'Died how?'

'An accident . . . I think, I heard about something happening, someone might have drowned, it might have been them . . .' I felt explaining the docks and what I thought I'd seen was too much to begin with.

'But you know it can't be Nicky?' My mother's usually calm voice was wavering.

'I know. But I mean, he looked so much like him.'

'I worry this is starting to sound like before.'

'It's just it was exactly like him. And then some weird things happened.'

'Like what?' Beyond the glass, a man with a small dog walked by, a dachshund on a red harness. They were battling against the breeze, both the owner and the dog, the animal's ears flapping back in the wind.

'He knew about things,' I said, feeling very young suddenly.

'What things?'

'Just little moments between us, things only I saw.' There was a pause. A long pause. As if my mother was watching something happen outside her window, the kitchen window where the phone was in their house. Dachshunds walking by, perhaps.

'What sort of little moment?' she said.

'There was a time when a deer got stuck in a fence and he freed it. An experiment we did at school, how our house is two

253

doors down from his. And he knew about my sister dying.' The feverishness of the flu came full force into my forehead then, making me reel a little.

My mum made a tiny noise in her throat. 'Don't you think he could have guessed at things, if you were primed to expect them?'

'Maybe,' I said.

The receiver went quiet. A thin crackle. I imagined a line of animals were parading past her window and she had paused to watch them all. At last she said, 'Are you feeling well?'

'No. No, I'm not feeling well. I feel fluey. My head feels like it's on fire.' I was about to say that's got nothing to do with it but then I thought well, possibly it does. I said, 'Also, I think I might be going mad.' A bubble seemed to burst inside my head releasing pressure. I waited through another pause. I felt comfortable in that silence like it was a little hammock I could fall asleep in. Then my mother began speaking again.

'I don't think you're going mad but I think you are getting too caught up in all this again. You know, I didn't tell you this at the time because I didn't want to upset you but I saw him at the hospital.' For a brief moment I thought she was telling me she saw Nicholas Blackburn, the same man I was seeing, at the hospital up north, that she was talking about a recent meeting. I pictured him walking past her in the corridor in his black coat, giving her a sly smile, and her shock, and her not wanting to tell me. But then she said, 'I saw him at the hospital after he died. His dad was there and he didn't want to go into the mortuary on his own so I went and stood beside him. Poor wee lad. He looked so untouched. There were no injuries on his face except scratches and that was the only part we could see because he was covered by the sheet. He was dead though. Absolutely dead, there's no mistaking it. Pale like marble. I want to say he looked peaceful but they never do, they just look unalive. The eyes sink down. Even when you're used to it, it's awful to see a kid, never mind one you knew. I never mentioned it because I thought it would be disturbing for you. It broke his parents. They adored him, you know. It broke both of them. I thought it would trouble you, to think of his body like that, and me being near the body.'

I was silent. I stood up holding the phone. From that vantage point I could see pigeons gathering on the pavement. I watched them shuffling about.

'Now, maybe I shouldn't have said all that,' my mum said.

'No, no, you should.' My voice was tiny. A child's voice.

'But he was there and he was dead so you see why it doesn't make sense to say he's not dead.'

'I do see that.'

'I only say it because it's important to face the truth of things. And that is the truth. The poor lad was dead and he still is.' Another pause. 'I've shocked you, haven't I?'

'No. Yes.'

'His poor, poor mother and father. A child is the love of any parent's life, you know.'

'I know, I know that. Though I thought their relationship with him was a bit patchy.'

'Emily, they adored him. They fell out sometimes like any parents with any teenager.'

'I thought you didn't know them that well.'

'We knew them well enough to know they were decent people. God, I was heartbroken when I heard about Nicky. Your dad too. You know I really think it took us years to get over the shock of it.'

'It did?'

'Yes, a loss like that, a boy we knew. Who'd even stayed with us, poor thing. We'd got to know him. Your dad had taught him some crafts, taught him to mould clay.' I didn't remember this. She carried on, 'We were fond of him. It doesn't just go away. And of course it reminded us of losing your sister. That might be why you struggled so much too.'

'Maybe it was,' I said quietly.

'Well I hope I've not said the wrong thing.'

'You haven't. It's . . . helpful to know. But it's getting late, I'd better go.'

We said good night and she asked me to phone back if I was upset and I said I would and we ended the conversation there. I realised that *sorry for your loss* was not a thing that I ever said to my parents. Their child had died too and I had never said that to them. Because it was our collective loss, it had never occurred to me to say something about their independent grief. And I thought of him, that boy I'd known, lying in a mortuary. The adult Nicholas faded and I saw the boy, his face utterly pale above a sheet. It did disturb me to think my mother had seen his body like that, she was right.

The next Monday a police officer rang my doorbell. I was still off work sick with flu, my nose red and swollen.

'I'm here to update you on the report you made.' A lone man stood at the door, thin and tall even for a police officer. He stepped into my flat and politely declined the invitation to sit down.

'Nothing was found in the water.' He read from one of those handheld devices, the same electronic kind the woman had used. He scrolled over it with graceful fingers and bitten nails. 'No one else phoned the police about any incident on the water that night. No one else has come forward about witnessing anything. No one fitting the description has been reported missing. We contacted the person you mentioned and were satisfied that they were not at risk.' It took me a moment to figure out what this meant. The police had been in touch with Nicholas; he was alive.

'Is he still living in the same place?'

'I can't tell you that sort of information.'

'No, I suppose you can't.'

'Is there anything else you'd like to ask, or tell us?'

'Most things I'd like to ask, I guess you can't tell me.'

He nodded. 'But anything else you'd like to say or add to your account?' I shook my head. He kept a steady, poker-faced gaze but I realised he was waiting to see if I'd admit to making the story up.

'Nothing else,' I said.

Once the officer was gone, I picked up my phone to ring Leti but I saw that she still hadn't opened the last message I'd sent her weeks back and so put my phone away. It seemed that we weren't speaking and it seemed that she had decided to let me figure that out.

That night I dreamt of Nicholas again. In the dream I followed him over the edge of the quay; I jumped too, but this time there was no water. We landed on a soft pile of bedding inside a hotel corridor. The walls were papered with a gaudy gold pattern, and people in uniform carried trays with those domed silver covers. I was searching for Nicholas but I couldn't find him among the many doors, and in the end I forgot what I was doing and wandered off to sit down in the hotel dining room, where I ate a large meal with some friends and acquaintances who had suddenly appeared all around me; Leti and Robin and people from work and even schooldays, who I had not seen or thought of in years.

In the morning when I woke, before having breakfast, I rang Nicholas's work. I wanted an answer to where he was. As the dial toned, I sat with my feet up on the chair in front of me. I felt dizzy – I guessed it must be a hangover from the flu, or just low blood sugar from not having eaten yet. I didn't plan to have a conversation with Nicholas, I just wanted to confirm for myself that he was alive and I had not seen what I thought I'd seen.

'I need to speak to Nicholas Blackburn please.' I had planned to say it involved an urgent, confidential matter.

'He doesn't work here any more.' The Scottish female voice was clipped, as if I had asked something offensive and I wondered if it was Morna, but it didn't sound quite like her.

'Do you know where he went?'

'I can't tell you that I'm afraid.'

'Can you forward an email to him?'

'I'm afraid I can't do that, no.'

'OK, thanks for your help.' I hung up and headed into the kitchen to find some sugary food. I watched a mother with a pram go by the window. She could not see me through the blinds. She was looking down into the blue fabric hood. I found myself thinking of my sister. The thought came to me with a sadness it hadn't held in years. Of the baby girl who also vanished in a sense, all that time ago.

I phoned Leti to apologise in the end. It was the next weekend and frost was etching patterns on the pavement outside my window. She picked up after five rings, her voice on the phone suddenly near my ear. I apologised for contacting her dad, for acting strangely, for not being in touch enough. She didn't say anything directly in response to the apology.

'Are you still seeing Robin?' she asked after we'd talked around a bit. I was sitting on my bed with my back hard against the wall.

'We haven't caught up for a few weeks actually.' I did not say that the idea of talking to him now made me uncomfortable.

'You be careful with him. Things went too far with Robin before.'

'What do you mean?' I said, though I knew what she must have meant.

'When we were teenagers, when you got ill.'

I was silent. With one hand I smoothed over the bedsheets. Then I said, 'That wasn't Robin's fault.'

~*~

Robin and I ate the dark, round berries, sitting on the floor of the ruined house. We had dared each other, joked, cajoled, refused, and finally given in. The berries tasted sweet and, underneath that, strangely savoury, like garden herbs. The skins burst, the flesh softly came apart. After we ate them, we both acted normally for a while, continued talking, sitting up, but gradually a dazed, seasick feeling came over me. I lay on my side, breathing through my mouth, listening to the steady thrum of the rain, the resounding drip from the blocked guttering behind the living room. I don't remember when but I fell asleep there on the floor. I recall waking to see Robin sitting up, looking at something. My head felt full and spinning. Two feet with black shoes had appeared in front of me. A figure was walking towards us. Though I didn't look all the way up to the figure's face, somehow I recognised him. It was him. Nicky had come back. There was an internal sense of the atmosphere I associated with him. The figure walked across the living room with dry, scuffing steps on the concrete, and didn't walk back. There was no door on that side of the room. I waited for him to return but he didn't. In my hazy state, I assumed the figure had walked on through the wall and I fell back asleep.

A few days later I woke up in that hospital bed, my mum sitting beside me, reading. Only later did I find out that I had nearly died. It was Leti who'd discovered me unconscious on the floor of our den. Oscar the cat was crouched near me, watching with his green eyes. He slunk away when Leti approached. She was the one who went for help. When she found me, I was alone.

After that time I didn't really speak to Robin. He didn't get ill from the berries, or not ill enough that anyone heard about it. I felt angry at being abandoned but also understood he probably didn't know what he was doing, he was probably as spaced out as I was.

When I was well enough to answer questions, I said I'd eaten some berries not knowing what they were, that Robin had picked them thinking they were blaeberries. My parents had several meetings with his parents but didn't tell me what came of them. Because Leti knew about the nightshade, I told her that Robin must have put some of the juice from the berries into my cup. I told her it was probably a joke gone wrong and not to tell anyone. I don't know why I lied. I felt stupid and embarrassed and she was asking me about it again and again and there was an answer.

I don't think Robin knew that I had lied about him. We did not have any kind of angry falling-out. In school we would walk past each other in the wide corridor, nod and move on. We would work together calmly if we were put into the same group for a maths or English exercise, though usually without speaking to each other directly. There was just a gulf between us that meant we could not approach each other or talk things through. Probably, we were not old enough to have the tools to try to address what had happened.

~*~

I picked up one of my pillows and wedged it between my stomach and my knees. 'To be honest, I ate the berries, we both did, on purpose. It was probably more my idea if anything.'

'You said Robin put the juice in your cola.'

'Yeah, I made that up. I was a kid. I was embarrassed. I thought you'd judge me.'

'I'm judging you right now. You've never told me it wasn't him.'

'Well, I guess it never came up again. We never spoke about it again, did we? So it didn't seem relevant. I'm telling you now. We just wanted to see what would happen.' I thought of the berries, like little black ball bearings, I could almost feel them in the palm of my hand. 'It was a sort of game,' I said at last.

'You knew they were dangerous.'

'Come on, teenagers experiment. They're not exactly hard drugs.'

'You could have been killed.'

'I know but I wasn't. Look, I'm really tired, I just wanted to apologise. I'm sorry for not telling you about Robin and the berries. That's another thing I'm sorry for.'

There was a small exhalation of breath on the end of the line. 'I'm going to go to bed now. Just, you know, take care of yourself.'

We ended the call there. I didn't tell her yet about the man disappearing into the water. Partly I was embarrassed, partly I wasn't sure that we were quite back to being friends again.

I searched for Nicholas Blackburn's name on the internet and came back to the page belonging to the law firm where I had first seen his photo. His headshot was still on there, they had not got round to taking it down. It was the same photo, as far I could tell, the background was the same pale blue, he was wearing the same greenish tie. But he looked significantly different and much less like Nicky. When I had first seen the photo, the resemblance was less marked than in person. But now it just looked like someone else, both someone different to Nicky but also different to the Nicholas I'd met. There were dark smudges under his eyes that I didn't remember noticing before and his smile seemed less intelligent. After a while I stopped staring at it and clicked back to the search engine. I thought about sending it to Robin, or even Leti, to get another opinion but I decided not to.

~*~

Early in my first year of high school I started taking flute lessons on a Thursday, second period. I was terrible at it, I could hardly get a high-pitched squeak out of the instrument for the first few weeks and forming the notes hurt the pads of my fingers, leaving round blisters like little moons. Last thing, after the school day was over, I'd go to the girls' changing rooms to lock the flute up, so I didn't have to carry it home. The flute belonged to the school and I wasn't allowed to take it away, not that I'd have practised if I was. One day, I was in the changing rooms alone, turning the small plastic key in the locker door, when I heard three light taps coming from the other side of the far wall.

I stood completely still, waiting a long time. No further noise arrived. I thought it must be the pipes making strange sounds. Still, I said in a loud voice, 'Is anyone there?'

There was no response and the noise did not repeat. I left hurriedly, shoving my bag onto my shoulders. On my way out, I looked to see what was next door to the girls' changing room. It was a languages classroom I'd never been in. The room was empty, a corkboard was pinned with Gaelic words in speech bubbles, the chairs put away on top of the desks. I tried the door but it was locked and there was nothing against the wall that lined up with the changing rooms, nowhere a person could hide.

The next time I was locking away the flute, I heard the same three little taps again. I wondered if it could be water dripping inside the wall but it sounded like something with agency. I checked each of the stalls of the changing room, shoving the peeling doors back so that they banged. One, two, three, four. No one was there.

'Who is that?' I shouted. No one answered.

The third time it happened, I tried tapping back on the wall, making my own little knocks. There was silence and then the three taps were repeated. I tried tapping again. Nothing, no sound. 'Who's there?' I said loudly to the wall. I waited. A bird sang somewhere outside the high, frosted window and my pulse came again at my wrist. There was no further noise. On my way out, I glanced through the glass panel of the door to the languages classroom. It was empty, the chalkboard wiped clean, the bins cleared and upside down, the desks in their calm rows.

The next week, it happened again. Three little taps. I tapped back and stood completely still, waiting. Three more short raps replied. I tapped again and stood in the tingling, sweaty locker-room air as another three solid taps followed. I muttered to myself, 'Who are you?' Then I heard a noise that made me flinch. Snorting, gasping. I paused. Another muffled rasp like a sharp intake of breath.

Suddenly, three boys jumped out of the nearest stall howling with laughter and I screamed even as I recognised them and wished to bite back the noise. The tapping on the wall became thumping, a drumming like two fists. Laughter came too now from behind the wall.

I ran out of the room and down the corridor. When I turned the next corner heading towards the assembly hall, I ran right into Nicky. Almost a headbutt into his chest, into the fabric of his jumper, the subtle sweat and blue shower gel scent of him. He grabbed me by the shoulders. 'Did you like your ghost?' he said grinning, his fingers digging into me.

To my embarrassment, tears filled my eyes as I pushed my way out of his grip. He wouldn't stop grinning, seeing my tears. 'Don't cry,' he said in a sing-song tone as his face blurred and doubled in front of me. I felt how he enjoyed it, seeing my embarrassment and rage.

I learned later that there was a crawl space between the changing room and the languages classroom, but you couldn't access it from the same side as the changing-room door. Instead you had to cut down the narrow corridor on the other side and slip behind the back of the stage in the assembly hall. He had run out and round as I had run from the changing rooms. I had hated Nicky in that moment, and moments like it. This was the kind of memory of Nicky that I smoothed away when he died.

~*~

A few days after I apologised to Leti, I tried ringing Robin. I decided I had to speak to him, to find out if he knew anything more about what had happened with Nicholas. It was a weekday evening and I was back at work again by then. When I got through, I apologised for not being in touch and he suggested I come round to his place for a drink.

I'd never been to Robin's flat before and when I arrived at the door I had a feeling almost as if I was there to give him bad news, or as if he was going to give me bad news. Robin showed me in, his demeanour slightly flat somehow. I hung up my coat on the iron pegs behind the door. He told me his partner was away in London for a week. 'I'm all abandoned.' The flat was tidy and painted in rich colours; a dark-green hall led into a powder-blue living room. The living room was full of thriving pot plants; ferns lurched from cabinets and spider plants dangled off book shelves.

'I'm impressed. I always kill them.'

'I don't do much with them, they just seem to like me.'

I decided not to immediately say anything about the dock, or the driving incident. I sat on his couch with a bottle of berry cider in one hand. 'So, have you seen Nicholas lately?' I asked.

'He's gone back to America.'

'He has?'

'Yeah, gone.'

'How do you know?' I made myself sit steady.

'He told me.'

'Oh. When did you see him last?'

'A couple weeks or so ago. We met up for a drink. He said he's fed up and he's going back home. His contract was up anyway.'

'A couple weeks ago?' I tried to level out my voice. 'Did he mention anything about water? About falling or diving or being in an accident?'

'I don't know. He does go swimming or diving or something, doesn't he? I don't think he mentioned anything specific, though. Why?'

'Oh, I don't know. I just, no. Wait. I'll tell you. I saw someone I thought was him fall in the water at the docks.'

'Jesus, were they all right?'

'I don't know. I called the police. It's hard to explain. The police didn't find anything. I guess they didn't think anyone had fallen in. I'm not exactly sure what I saw. Maybe the person swam away, it's just about possible, though it's hard to see how. It was night-time and ice cold. Maybe it was some kind of trick.'

'That's quite a thing to see. Nicholas didn't mention anything like that.' He was looking at me almost with suspicion, as if I was lying to him.

'What else did he say to you?' I asked.

'This and that. The same as always.'

'The same as always?'

'Yeah.'

'Robin, how often have you been meeting him?'

'Not that much.' His voice had a slowness to it.

'But more than you did with me? How many times have you met him?'

'Let me think, there was the time with you, then another time, then we both met him in the pub, then he invited me out for a drink. I don't know, I've seen him a few times.'

'Do you talk about the past?'

'Well, yeah, just, you know, the past, life stuff, this and that.'

'Have you been feeding him things?'

'Like food?' Robin laughed a little. I realised once again he was a bit drunk already.

'No, like information about the past?'

'No, no. Not deliberately.'

Something was winding up and winding down in me at the same time. The wind-up toy again. 'He could have picked up things from you. You saw him before that second meeting with me?'

'Yes, maybe, I don't know. I think everything he's said about memories and things has come from him, though.'

'When we met that first time, what did you say to him exactly, to get him to come?'

'This and that. I don't remember.'

'You just texted him and he agreed to come?'

'Well, no, I texted him and he rang me. We spoke on the phone.'

'You didn't say that at the time.'

'You didn't ask.'

'So what did you say? You didn't mention about the past?' All the little things Nicholas had known, Robin had known them too; I knew that, I'd always known that. As teenagers, Robin and I had talked about my sister some nights when we were alone together, in that slightly inarticulate way of ours. I had told him my memories of Nicky. This was so obvious and yet the fact stared boldly at me now in a way it hadn't before.

'Well, I had to mention something to give him some context.'

'What exactly did you say?'

'I don't remember exactly. I might have said we thought he was someone from our village.'

'And you met him between the two pub visits, the first and second time I met him?'

'We had a drink. Was that before or after? I don't remember the exact order of events. I think he was genuine about being lonely. He always seemed genuine to me, maybe a bit troubled, maybe a bit strange. I think he's a decent guy, whatever was going on.'

'I think he's been playing a game with us.' I put my cider on the floor. My voice was rising. 'Look, something weird happened when I went to drive out to that country pub. He didn't show up and then someone tried to run me off the road on the way back and I was sure I saw him in the driver's seat, I was sure he tried to run me off the road.'

He was silent for a bit. 'You didn't tell me that. Why didn't you go to the police?'

'Well, I couldn't have been certain it was him.'

'You just said you were sure.'

'Well, not absolutely. It's hard to explain. It felt that way in the moment. I thought I saw him.'

'Look, you can't accuse him of things like that based on nothing. The things Nicholas said, I think they came from him. Nicky was my friend, I'm not going to deliberately let someone make things up about him.' He picked up an ornament, a small jade elephant, from the coffee table, and toyed with it. I thought of him in his room at the farm, sitting on the bedroom carpet, his face as we played with the Ouija board.

'You were so obsessed with Nicky when you were younger,' I said quietly. 'Do you think you wanted this guy to be him?'

His fingers tensed around the ornament. 'I was obsessed with him? What about you? Nicky was my friend. You hardly knew him. You were only interested in him after he died.'

I could feel my face flushing. 'I don't think that's exactly right.'

'You told me, I always remembered, that thing with the deer, that was when you first started to think about him differently,

269

that you were impressed by that, but you only really started to feel connected to him after he died. You said that to me. Like a thread had been drawn between you, that's what you said. To be honest, I found it a bit creepy at the time. You took things too far, with all the spells and fucking crazy things.'

'That was as much coming from you as it was from me.'

'You said your own sister dying hadn't affected you like Nicky dying.'

'When did I ever say that?' Though as I spoke, I realised I might well have said it.

'You told me one night when we were playing cards or something, I can't remember when,' he said.

'Wait, the thing about the deer. Did you tell Nicholas the thing about the deer?'

'I don't think so.'

'About my sister?'

'Why would I bring that up?'

'I don't know, did you?'

'I don't think so.'

'You're sure?'

'I don't remember every word we've said to each other. I wasn't recording our conversations like some kind of nutter, for fuck's sake. By the way, why were you talking to Mr Fletcher?'

'How do you know that?'

'People saw you talking to him.'

'Well I was. I suppose I was just curious. To see how he remembered things.'

'He killed Nicky.' There was a pinched kind of rage in his expression now.

'Not on purpose,' I said, though I found it hard to look at Robin directly.

'It's bad enough having to see him round the village without people acting like he's just a normal person.'

'He was devastated by the whole thing too.'

'It was entirely his fucking fault.' His voice rose now. 'You weren't there. It happened in front of me. He was my friend.'

We sat together dumbly for a few seconds. I had nothing to say in response to this. I reached for and drank the last of my cider just to have a reason to look away. 'I think I'm going to go home,' I said at last.

'I think that's a good idea.' Robin got up to let me out the door and I stepped out into the night without us saying anything more.

Over the winter holidays, I holed up at my parents' house. I didn't talk a lot about what had happened except to reassure my mum I had no intention of getting in touch with the person who looked like Nicky.

In the new year, on a day when the mountain was bright with frost, I went walking along the farm track by the graveyard. In the old farmyard, a new extension was being built and a tractor sat lazily on the verge. The pigs were gone, or not outside today. I didn't go through the first gate that led into the graveyard but instead carried on further down the hill to where I saw what I had known but not remembered on that day in the storm. That there was a second newer section to the graveyard beyond the first. The slope and the wall hid the graves from the viewpoint of the first section.

I entered the newer part of the graveyard by the small iron gate and walked to the far end. There it was, in the third row, along the line of dimpled turf. A bare rowan tree stood frail and grey nearby. The black marble headstone was carved with silver letters. *Nicholas Harper, beloved only son.* That boy who never got to live a life, lying still under such a small span of grass. I had known it was there, really. It still gave me a jolt to see it but the skin of the earth felt like a barrier, I didn't feel like I would tip down into it.

After a time, I stepped away and cut back out to the village.

A few days later I was back in Edinburgh. One morning, while I was leaving the bathroom after brushing my teeth, the shutters still closed against the dark, an envelope came fluttering down from the letter box. I picked it up from where it had slid under the doormat. The envelope had prepaid postage on the outside and a New York postmark on it. Inside was a greeting card with a picture of a stag on a dark background, its antlers tangled up in vegetation. The card contained a short note in scrawling blue handwriting. It read:

> Emily,
> I'm sorry if I scared you. But I was telling the truth. I can't explain it but I do have these memories.
> N.

I don't know how he found my address, though no doubt it was findable. Or, of course, he could have seen me walking to my flat since he'd lived so nearby. Belief is a strange thing. I think people can believe different and contradictory things at the same time. I couldn't in that instant have said what I believed. Still, I had no intention of contacting him or doing anything at all to follow up the message.

Two women set out for the mountain. Leti and I headed off walking together. We were back up in the highlands for a weekend. We followed the path by the road first, the one the boys used on the day Nicky died. It was late summer, birds were singing around us. Thickets of blackfly lazed in our path now and again so that we had to duck or step round them. The bracken was green and waxy, the heather on the further slope was almost glowing purple.

'I did love him, you know,' Leti said out of the blue.

'Who?' I said, thinking she meant the last guy she was dating.

'Nicky.'

I looked at her. 'You had a teenage crush on him. I suppose.'

'Yeah, I suppose,' she said, 'but at that age it's the same thing. What I'm saying is you felt something so intense for him as a teenager too, maybe you needed him to come back.'

I nodded while not wanting to nod, thinking that didn't seem to be all of it. We'd begun to make small steps towards getting back to normal with each other, though there was still a lingering tension between us. I sometimes sensed a hidden sharpness behind something Leti said, or feared it was there behind something I said. We followed the route Robin had told me about as a boy. I'd been drawn to do it after everything with Nicholas, though I was surprised when Leti agreed to go with me. We skipped the rock climb, taking a sheep path that skirted

273

round and above the cliff face instead. When we were teenagers, I had gotten Robin to repeat the route over and over so I could picture it clearly. Now, walking the ridge, there was that godlike sensation that I had imagined the boys must have experienced on their trek. Looking over the world and feeling that you could just step on outwards off the mountain and stride across the fields and rivers. A curlew was crying its way diagonally from us. I felt an unexpected peacefulness, like the world was offering its unanswerability and that was all I needed in that moment.

We stopped high up on the ridge. We sat on our waterproof coats on the deer-compacted grass, avoiding the sheep shit, and ate a picnic of things we had bought in the local shop. Crisps and ham and apples and yogurt drinks, which had grown warm and lumpy in our backpacks. I could say it was like we were teenagers again but that is not quite right, really we settled there as our adult selves, stretching out our feet. A trio of buzzards were calling, circling, somewhere in the clouds, perhaps a pair and this year's fledgling. We tilted back our heads and squinted at the sun to watch them and didn't say much for the rest of the journey.

Later that year, Leti had an art exhibition, her dark square canvases filling two small rooms. Against the white walls, they looked like windows to other places. I didn't say that, in case she thought it sounded naive. The scraped-away figures on some of the canvases had started to look like familiar forms, particularly a recurring, boyish figure on what looked like a road bordered by pine trees. I didn't comment on that either in case the figure wasn't meant to be who I thought. She sold some of the paintings, something she'd never chosen to do before. Little pink circle stickers appeared in the corners to indicate a sale. When we spoke at the end, gripping our over-tall flutes of sparkling wine, she was quietly elated. Leti had left her job at the school. She was doing a mix of tutoring and running adult education classes and selling her paintings. She had moved out of town and bought a small double upper in the country with a little garden and a separate room she could use as a studio. She said she was in love with the small town life, in love with her garden patch.

We went on out for a drink in a nearby pub and she got onto talking about old times, about the village. She told me she'd heard from her parents, who'd heard from my parents, that the chemistry teacher had finally left the village. He had moved further north to an island in the Outer Hebrides. He left early one morning, his car stuffed with suitcases and cardboard boxes. A small van arrived a week later to collect the rest of his things. His house was emptied of furniture and put on sale.

I had the bizarre idea that the teacher had been trapped in the village, like he was under a spell. I imagined that Nicholas dying, drowning at the docks, was the event that had let him go. But then, Nicholas Blackburn didn't die so that was absurd. I didn't say any of this to Leti.

From the exhibition onwards, Leti began a partnership with the gallery and then with another one across town. She said to me once in passing that the whole thing with Nicholas, the eeriness of it, had fed into her art and been useful.

The next time I visited the village, I passed by the teacher's house. Someone else was living there. I could see a man hanging out laundry in the back garden, a woman digging small bedding plants into an ornamental barrel. A girl's BMX bike lay sideways on the lawn.

When I returned to Edinburgh I found a new pigeon and tiger behind the microwave, while cleaning. The tigers and the pigeons seemed less sinister now, appearing in the bright light of day. It almost felt like they represented the naturalness of life and death. The natural rhythm of it.

I stopped meeting up with Robin. We let things slide after the incident at the docks and our subsequent conversation; I never felt the urge to call him and he seemed to feel the same about me. I heard from other people who had seen him that he was doing well at work, that he had married his partner, but I never saw him myself, and I wasn't invited to the wedding.

The sense of needing answers was gradually replaced with a sense of needing to do things, to carry out small acts. I joined a campaign group for a wildlife conservation charity, I signed petitions, I occasionally attended protests again. I couldn't be sure any of that had a real effect but that uncertainty troubled me less than it might have in the past. The extinct animal dreams faded away again.

All this happened years ago. I have a partner now, and a child. My partner was there in the background but hidden. The man I met at the party, the one I'd known at university. It turned out that when he asked me if I wanted to meet for coffee he had meant it as a date and he took my *no thanks* as a rejection so he didn't get in touch again. One afternoon, about a year and a half later, I bumped into him in a park. We were both queueing at the same kiosk under our umbrellas, and I saw him differently, like a lamp had been turned on in a shady room. The growing puddles reflected an elephant-grey sky, music clashed around us from two competing buskers. Instead of getting the cup of coffee I'd planned to order, we both bought ice-cream cones and ate them in the rain walking round in circles. And off we went together. We got on so easily as if we had been friends all our lives. Our daughter turned up a couple of years later, an unexpected arrival. All energy and curiosity, an imp and a wrecking ball.

In the years that followed the incident at the dock, I received several more cards from Nicholas. They contained similar, short protestations that he was telling the truth. I gathered them into a carved wooden box I'd bought as a teenager when I'd been taken by the romantic idea that I might have secret letters to hide one day. On a hazy afternoon, when I was home and off work sick with some bug, I went as far as writing a long, detailed letter explaining why I thought he was lying, even though I had no address to send it to. I put it in the recycling bag the next day.

I left my job around that time and took a sideways step, working in a community centre out of town, running groups and events for older people. I found I no longer wanted the intimacy or the pressure of turning up alone in people's homes, one to one.

When the baby was on the way, another card from Nicholas arrived. I put it in a ceramic breakfast bowl and set fire to it. The smell of the smoke reminded me of childhood birthday celebrations. I watched the letter crumple away into a black butterfly. Then I searched out the others and burned them too, one by one.

I craved soil while I was pregnant. One of my favourite things to do was to take up handfuls of compost and breathe in the scent of it. I know it was probably to do with an iron deficiency but it occurred to me that having a child is like taking someone out of the earth. You make a life out of inanimate matter, the things you eat, the food that comes out of the ground. I thought about this, but I didn't let it take up too much space in my head.

I asked my parents for a photograph of my sister as a baby. We talked about her in a way that we hadn't before. I put the picture on a pinboard in the kitchen, along with other photos of family and friends. When I meet new people now and they ask if I have siblings, instead of saying *no*, I say *yes*, I did once, and I tell them about her.

My partner and I moved out of town just before the baby arrived. We settled into a house with a garden overlooked by woodlands. A couple of years later, a stripy stray cat moved in with us, to add to our family. The letters from Nicholas did not follow me.

Until a few months ago, when there was a flutter at the door as I was sitting sorting toys into their different plastic boxes on a Saturday morning. I got up to see what had arrived, and there on the doormat was the familiar handwriting. Somehow he has found me again, though so far I have had no desire to open the envelope.

Acknowledgements

A huge thank you to my mum and dad, Jane McDonagh and Mike McDonagh, for their boundless love and support. Thank you to all my family and friends, including Steven McDonagh, Aoife Skeffington, Fiona McBryde, Catriona Twigg, Betsy Andrews, Mel Grenfell, Elizabeth Welsh, Sharon Boateng, Hollie Ruddick, Alison Martin, and Bill & Margaret Galloway. Thank you to the many writers who have given support, encouragement and feedback over the years, especially Devika Ponnambalam, Emily Prince, Zenon Bankowski, Catriona Windle and Fiona Robertson.

Thank you so much to the team at Trapeze and Orion, in particular to my editor Serena Arthur, for all her patience, hard work and enthusiasm for this novel. Many thanks to Jess Hart for a beautiful cover.

Thank you to all at PFD, especially my agent Kate Evans, for championing the book from an early stage and providing so much encouragement and support along the way.

Much love and thanks to my husband, Ross Galloway, to whom this book is dedicated, for all his kindness, encouragement, thoughtfulness and love.

Finally, my love and gratitude to my son Arran, for bringing so much joy and wonder to our lives.

About the Author

Rose McDonagh was born and grew up in Edinburgh. She has a degree in English literature and history and a masters in creative writing. She has worked in a number of charity roles including twelve years as a trauma counsellor for a mental health charity. She lives in Midlothian with her husband, their son and two cats. Her writing has been shortlisted for the Bridport Prize, the London Magazine Short Story Competition, the Dinesh Allirajah Prize and the Bristol Prize. Her first short story collection, *The Dog Husband*, was published in 2022 by Reflex Press and was longlisted for the Edgehill Short Story Prize.

One Came Back – which was longlisted for the Caledonia First Novel Award and the Lucy Cavendish Fiction Prize – is Rose's debut novel.

Orion Credits

Trapeze would like to thank everyone at Orion who worked on the publication of *One Came Back*.

Agent
Kate Evans

Editor
Serena Arthur
Sareeta Domingo

Copy-editor
Donna Hillyer

Proofreader
Kim Bishop

Editorial Management
Clarissa Sutherland
Carina Bryan
Jane Hughes
Charlie Panayiotou
Lucy Bilton
Bartley Shaw

Audio
Paul Stark
Louise Richardson
Georgina Cutler

Contracts
Dan Herron
Ellie Bowker

Design
Jessica Hart
Nick Shah
Joanna Ridley
Helen Ewing

Picture Research
Natalie Dawkins

Finance
Nick Gibson
Jasdip Nandra
Sue Baker
Tom Costello

Inventory
Jo Jacobs
Dan Stevens

Production
Claire Keep
Katie Horrocks

Marketing
Yadira Da Trindade

Publicity
Aoife Datta

Sales
Catherine Worsley
Victoria Laws
Esther Waters
Tolu Ayo-Ajala
Group Sales teams across
    Digital, Field Sales, Inter-
    national and Non-Trade

Operations
Group Sales Operations team

Rights
Rebecca Folland
Tara Hiatt
Ben Fowler
Alice Cottrell
Ruth Blakemore
Marie Henckel